P9-CRG-491

BOOKS BY STEVE ALLEN

Bop Fables
Fourteen for Tonight
The Funny Men
Wry on the Rocks
The Girls on the Tenth Floor
The Question Man
Mark It and Strike It
Not All of Your Laughter, Not All of Your Tears
Letter to a Conservative
The Ground Is Our Table
Bigger Than a Breadbox
A Flash of Swallows
The Wake
Princess Snip-Snip and the Puppykittens
Curses!
What to Say When it Rains
Schmock!-Schmock!
Meeting of Minds
Chopped-Up Chinese
Ripoff: The Corruption that Plagues America
Meeting of Minds (Second Series)
Explaining China
Funny People
The Talk Show Murders
Beloved Son: A Story of the Jesus Cults
More Funny People
How to Make a Speech
How to Be Funny
Murder on the Glitter Box
The Passionate Nonsmoker's Bill of Rights (with Bill Adler, Jr.)
Dumbth, and 81 Ways to Make Americans Smarter
Meeting of Minds, Seasons I–IV in Four-Volume Set
The Public Hating: A Collection of Short Stories
Murder in Manhattan
Steve Allen on the Bible, Religion & Morality
Murder in Vegas
Hi-Ho, Steverino!
The Murder Game
More Steve Allen on the Bible, Religion & Morality
Make 'Em Laugh
Reflections
Murder on the Atlantic
The Man Who Turned Back the Clock and Other Short Stories

MURDER ON THE ATLANTIC

Steve Allen

KENSINGTON BOOKS
KENSINGTON PUBLISHING CORP.

chapter 1

"Can I be alone in thinking that *The Atlantis* is not the hippest possible name for an ocean liner?" I asked my wife Jayne, who was standing next to me on the sidewalk in front of New York's Plaza Hotel.

Because she was giving me only about one-third of her attention, Jayne said, "Yes, dear, you can be alone any time you want."

"I am not Greta Garbo," I said. "Remember me? Tall fellow, with glasses?"

Although I've never been sure what Jayne's IQ is, I would not be surprised to learn that it is considerably higher than my own. But her very intelligence sometimes works against her, in that her mind vibrates so quickly she frequently leaves out details in spoken narratives. These omissions render some of her accounts indecipherable. There are times, for example, when she will start a conversation in the middle—or at least in what appears to me to be the middle.

"I should have told her I wouldn't dream of doing that," she had said to me about three weeks earlier, as I was coming into the house at the end of a long, hectic day at the office.

"Told who you wouldn't do what?" I asked.

I was, naturally, immediately blamed for my lack of understanding.

"Don't you remember a word I said to you this morning?"

"I'm sure I do. I distinctly remember hearing the word *lino-leum*, the word *ibuprofen*, and there was one word that sounded like *Islamic, balsamic,* or something of the sort." The employment of such digressions is my habitual way of suggesting to my wife that no one on earth could have fully understood such opening statements, in the absence of other clues. But sometimes a more direct approach works better. "Who are we talking about?" I said.

"Dortha, my dressmaker, for God's sake."

"I doubt if God would so perceive it," I said. "But since we've established that Dortha is to play a major role in your account, what about her?"

"I should have told her I wouldn't take the suit back. I gave it to her, and I wouldn't want to be an Indian giver."

"It's not necessary to malign the entire race of Native Americans to establish your point," I said. "But if you did give her a suit, of course you should not ask for it back."

"Oh," she said, "I didn't mean permanently—just for this trip."

Well, she had asked, and dear Dortha had obviously loaned the suit back on a short-term basis—Jayne was wearing it at this very moment, three weeks later. The jacket and trousers were the same color as her lipstick and the large, red, filmy handkerchief tied around the bun at the back of her head; she was attracting a great deal of attention.

There have been times, in public, when I have seemed relatively invisible to passersby, until suddenly Jayne—at my side—has been recognized and my cover has been blown. This time a puzzled-looking fellow in a seersucker suit smiled at me shyly and said, in all seriousness, "Mr. Martin, I love your work."

People who recognize celebrities often say peculiar things, possibly because they are nervous. A man came up to me outside a TV studio one night years ago, handed me an envelope and pen, and said—I swear—"Mr. Allen, would you please sign this for the back of my wife?"

Since Jayne and I are not in the habit of loitering on sidewalks outside internationally famous hotels, even on lovely April evenings such as this, I should explain the reason for our being rooted to the cement at that moment: Our luggage was being loaded into a limousine, which although of the stretch variety, evidently had not been stretched enough to accommodate such massive impedimenta.

The limo driver was a polite man, who appeared to be of Middle-Eastern background. He told us his name but, because of my longstanding Western cultural bias—no worse, I suppose, than a Northern, Eastern, or Southern cultural bias, though leading to a different form of ignorance—the name sounded to me like Listerine Okefenokee. I'm quite aware that would make his first name a mouthwash and his second name a swamp, but I can only work with what I'm given. I've always had a bit of a problem remembering people's names anyway, and the growing shortage of Charlies, Bobs, and Bills in our country is making my predilection worse. I had been in a New York cab two days earlier, and I swear the printed name of the driver looked to me like Dyslexia Jones.

In any event, Listerine—or whatever his name was—and Jimmy Cassidy, our all-around Man Monday, as he likes to describe himself, stowed our excess luggage in the passenger compartment of the limousine, and we were finally crushed inside with it. So much so that when the vehicle pulled out onto the busy New York street, the suitcase on my right shifted and fell onto my right leg. "Ouch!"

As we drove along Fifty-seventh Street, riverward, Jayne suddenly shouted, "Kris Kristofferson will star in *The Kenny Rogers Story.*"

"Very good," I commented. For several days, including that part of the time spent on the plane coming East, we had been playing a little game I invented, just to pass the time. Called the

Interchangeable Casting Game, it's based on the premise that in the 1930s and '40s film stars tended to be one of a kind, whereas today they seem to come in matched pairs. For example, as we look back, we can clearly see that there was only one Mae West, one W. C. Fields, one Clark Gable, one Charlie Chaplin, one Jimmy Cagney. But now the situation is so different it should be a relatively easy task to cast the lead in any motion picture that details the life of a prominent performer.

"Susan Anton will star in *The Lynda Carter Story*," Cass called from his up-front perch.

"And Susan Sullivan," I said, "will star in *The Marriette Hartley Story*."

"Wait a minute," Jayne said, fumbling in her purse. "I wrote down some good ones on the plane. Oh, here's the list."

She proceeded to read, "Ron Liebman will star in *The Judd Hirsch Story*, Sally Kellerman will star in *The Loretta Swit Story*, and Ned Beatty will star in *The Charles Durning Story*."

Cass chuckled. "That's a funny one! How about Slappy White will star in *The Nipsey Russell Story?*"

Jayne, after a few minutes' silence, topped us both by shouting, "Stefanie Powers will star in *The Jill St. John Story*."

"Hey, they have horse racing on board. I read it in the brochure," Cass said from up front, changing the subject. "How do you think they manage that?"

"They're little wooden horses on sticks, Cass," Jayne said. "Someone rolls the dice and moves them around a table track."

"But there's betting, huh?"

"And a casino, too," I mentioned. "So watch yourself. Remember when you had to pawn your car in Las Vegas?"

"This time I'm going to put myself on a strict budget, Steve—twenty dollars a day to gamble. That way I can't get into too much trouble, I figure."

"Good idea," I told him. "Just remember to stick to it."

Cass is one of the great innocents of the world, a natural optimist, and I worry about him when he collides with such things as casinos, big cities, and real life. I first met him soon after he left Wyoming to come to Hollywood to be a cowboy actor: Westerns went out of style at just about the moment Cass arrived, so he ended up being my Man Monday instead.

And he took his fate in stride. Now that Hollywood was making a few Westerns again, I sometimes asked him if he didn't want to audition for a part. But he always said he was probably too old now, and anyway Jayne and I would not be able to survive long without him. He was probably right. Cass had become part of our family, a tough, wiry elf of a man, with dark hair that was beginning to gray, bushy eyebrows, and blue eyes that had gazed into many Western sunsets. At the moment he was dressed in a white linen suit, a gaudy multicolored sports shirt, and brown cowboy boots.

"Look, there she is!" Jayne said, pointing out the window.

"Wow!" Cass peered out to get a good look as we drove alongside the huge new glass-and-steel terminal that had been built on the old midtown pier. The ship was enormous, white and sleek, with two great smokestacks slanting back, as graceful as any vessel ever set down upon the water. I could see what all the fuss was about. *The Atlantis* was the most expensive ocean liner ever built, and Jayne, Cass, and I were about to head off on her maiden voyage—though we might have backed out if we'd known what fearful times lay ahead.

chapter 2

"Hot damn, if it isn't Steve and Jayne! How the hell are you guys?"

Rusty O'Conner, a large, gaudy woman and one of the wealthiest inhabitants of Beverly Hills, more or less mowed us down as we waited in line. I considered a variety of clever replies but did not want to encourage her, so I settled for, "Fairly well, thank you," as she made little pecking sounds near my cheek, then did the same to Jayne. When she turned to Cass, he quickly busied himself with our luggage.

Rusty had been married—about three marriages earlier, to a friend of mine, a famous actor of the fifties—so we chatted about where he was now, while Rusty scanned the room, presumably on the lookout for husband number six or seven. Then she caught sight of some Hollywood friends, said we'd have to play gin rummy some afternoon, and left us, followed by half a dozen porters and a safari-load of luggage. Jayne, Cass, and I edged our way forward, toward a man in a white uniform who was checking passports. The huge terminal was filled with a mostly elegant crowd in various stages of boarding. I caught sight of a number of people we knew—studio executive Brandon Tartikoff, director Martin Scorsese and his lovely lady Ilyana, best-selling author Sidney Sheldon and his wife Alexandra, actor Michael Douglas, three columnists, and a famous clothes designer (they all look alike to me). The long-awaited maiden voyage of *The Atlantis* was clearly the social event of the season. The newspapers had been full of the trip for weeks, discussing the sumptuousness of the vessel and the tantalizing question of whether it would indeed usher in a new age of transatlantic travel. Jayne, of course, was keeping an eye peeled for Princess Mudgie, who was rumored to be making the voyage, but there was no sign yet of her much-photographed face.

Meanwhile everything was as merry as could be. A small orchestra was playing "Everything's Coming Up Roses" in a frolicking cha-cha tempo. Colored streamers rained down, balloons galore floated in the air, and I had already declined two glasses of champagne, a beverage neither Jayne nor I enjoy, or ever ask for.

In fact, for the last few months I'd been doing some work on a manuscript with the title *Big Nothings*. This title refers to various artifacts, customs, and comestibles that are, in my opinion at least, actually unworthy of their formidable reputations. Since I would not want my argument to be buttressed only by my own opinion, I solicited the views of many others, asking them, "Millions really enjoy that first good hot cup of coffee in the morning, or an ice-cold glass of freshly squeezed orange juice, or a cold beer on a hot day—do you derive that same sort of zesty enjoyment from drinking champagne?" I haven't yet encountered anyone who answered yes.

Suddenly a young, East Coast Brahmin voice coming from behind me caught my attention. "Look, that man's carrying a gun!"

"A gun? Don't be silly, Chelsea," said a second voice, female as well, but older. "Which man?" the older woman added nervously.

"The one near the desk."

I glanced casually toward the man checking passports but didn't see the bulge of a gun anywhere on his person. Chelsea, I thought, had an overactive imagination.

"Not *that* man," Chelsea said to her companion. "The one next to him."

My gaze shifted to the right, where a second man was standing. He appeared to be forty or so and had closely cropped, blond hair and a rugged, deeply tanned face. His dark gray suit somehow appeared even more official than the other man's uniform. He stood quietly watching the room, and surely enough, I could detect the small bulge of a shoulder holster beneath his left arm. It was a very slight bulge, and I would not have noticed it except for the young woman's observation.

"I'll bet he's killed people. He has that cold, hard look," she now whispered.

"Chelsea!" the older voice reprimanded. "If you don't stop imagining things, I'm going to send you right back to Vassar!"

"Oh, Grandmother, you will not. I'll get that man to protect me." Her voice was teasing, and I heard the old woman chuckle as I studied the fellow with the gun. In the dark gray suit, he *did* have a certain cold and killerlike look.

The women behind me continued their banter, and I smiled, becoming curious to get a look at them. Contriving to glance at a large clock on the wall to my left, I kept turning as though I were looking about vaguely for a friend. When I had turned all the way, I found myself staring directly into two brightly challenging, greenish eyes only inches away. I had to refocus to see Chelsea in her entirety. She was perhaps twenty years old, with short brown hair cut in a feathery way and with freckles on her nose. I had a feeling that when she was younger she'd been a great tomboy, climbing trees and raising hell. She had become quite pretty, but the tomboy lingered. She was dressed in baggy clothes that made her look like a shapeless sack. The greenish eyes, her most appealing feature, continued to measure me openly. The girl's grandmother was a tall, gray-haired woman. She wore sensible clothes and shoes, and had a slightly distracted aristocratic smile.

"Well, Mr. Allen," the girl said. "Do you always listen in on other people's conversations?"

"Only when I can't help it," I said. "And when they mention guns."

"*I* eavesdrop all the time," she confided seriously. "I think it's a perfectly valid way to learn about the world. No one will ever tell you anything, of course, if you just come out and ask them."

"Perhaps you're not asking in the right way."

"All right, let's try an experiment," she said eagerly. "How old are you?"

"None of your business."

"You see what I mean?"

She really was a brat. "Incidentally," I told her, "the gentleman you were discussing is security. That's why he has a gun."

"I knew that."

I smiled and turned away because we had arrived at the desk. Jayne handed over our passports. The man with the gun, now wearing dark glasses, studied us intently. "These bags all yours?"

"Alas," I nodded.

"How long will you be abroad?"

"Three weeks. We're staying in Sussex with some friends."

"Did you pack everything yourselves?"

"Everything," Jayne said.

"No one has given you any packages at the last moment?"

"No."

"Are you carrying any explosives? Live ammunition? Weapons of any sort?"

At that, Cass, a very honest citizen, showed his Swiss Army knife. The man actually cracked a smile—but quickly hid it as he watched our luggage being tagged and wheeled away.

"If anyone *attempts* to give you a package of any sort before you go on board, would you please notify me immediately?" We promised, like good children, and were allowed to pass on through to the next desk, where we had to show our tickets. Ev-

eryone was full of smiles, but I could see that, beneath the surface geniality, security for our voyage was exceptionally tight.
No one was getting anywhere close to *The Atlantis* without being
thoroughly vetted and checked off against the master passenger
list. Farther along we had to pass through a second security
checkpoint, where they sent our carry-on bags through a scanning machine. Cass, Jayne, and I were patient throughout the
procedure, happy to be safe rather than sorry. These days, terrorism is unfortunately a possibility during international travel.

At last we were free to step up the gangplank onto the ship. It
was exciting to be going on the maiden voyage of a great ocean-
liner, but halfway up the ramp I had vague misgivings. The distance from ship to shore momentarily became immense, a
separation of two worlds—the solid land I knew, and this floating city, with its own laws and customs, that would be our home
for the next four days. A shiver rippled up my spine. Undoubtedly my imagination had been set into motion by young Chelsea.

"Look out!" someone cried from the wharf.

I heard the sharp *pop* of a small gun and instinctively ducked,
but it was just a fly-away champagne cork, not a pistol, and I felt
a little foolish.

"Are you all right?" Jayne asked.

"Just saying goodbye to dry land," I told her. Shrugging off
the odd feeling, I strode confidently onto *The Atlantis*.

chapter 3

My first impression of the ship was one of spaciousness, almost endless vistas of clean, modern lines. A famous Italian had designed the vessel, and I heard that the old man, Marcus Wilmington, had had a few Hollywood set designers work on the accommodations because they were the only people he could find with imaginations big enough to carry out what he envisioned. Creamy white was the predominant color, but pastels—yellow, amber, and rose—worked off the white to give everything a cheery, early morning glow. And there was a great deal of glass and marble; huge crystal chandeliers lit the public spaces. The decor managed to be striking yet intimate and comfortable. Occasionally you would turn a corner and find a Picasso on the wall, or an Henri Rousseau or a Braque—not reproductions. There were many such touches: vases arranged with beautiful flowers, intriguing nooks and crannies where you could curl up with a good book, gaze into your lover's eyes, or just watch the waves go rolling by.

Every now and then human beings get it just right and come up with a really soaring achievement. *The Atlantis* was one. More than beautiful, she verged on the magnificent.

Jayne, Cass, and I found ourselves in a spacious reception room at the top of the gangplank, where another crisp-uniformed officer greeted us, examined our tickets, and handed us over to an attractive young woman.

"Welcome aboard *The Atlantis!*" she beamed. "My name is Cheryl, and I'll be giving you a brief orientation to the ship." She was cute but a little too bubbly, like the young things who give away refrigerators on daytime-TV game shows.

"We're on E Deck now," she explained. "First, I'm going to take you to the Purser's Office on C Deck so you can pick up your Atlanticards. They work just like a credit card; you'll use them for everything you buy shipboard."

"Say I want to get a haircut," Cass proposed, always one for specifics, "I just show my credit card?"

"Your *Atlanti*card!" Cheryl corrected gently. "No one on *The Atlantis* accepts cash. It keeps things nice and easy."

"Almost *too* easy," I agreed. "And yet there comes a day of reckoning."

She giggled and turned to Jayne, "If you get the urge to shop, the Galleria on D Deck has Neiman Marcus, Saks, Van Cleef & Arpels . . . Everything is duty free, of course."

Jayne's interest was perking up. "Isn't that lovely, Steve?"

"Yes, dear, but remember, our bags are full already."

Cheryl escorted us into an elevator paneled in black ebony. The cubicle lifted noiselessly upward to C deck, the door hissed open, and our young guide led the way down a long, rose-colored Oriental carpet toward the Purser's Office. Here I handed over my American Express and Visa cards, and a few other pieces of financial liability so that Jayne might have the illusion that everything on *The Atlantis* was free.

"I noticed on the schedule that you're performing in the Grand Ballroom on Tuesday night, Mr. Allen," Cheryl mentioned.

I said I was indeed doing two separate shows that night, and Cheryl then told us about the other performers who were set to entertain during the four-day crossing. There was Candy L'Amour, the big pop star; a troupe from the Kirov Ballet; a singer who headlined in Las Vegas, although only there; and among the other celebrities was our friend Michael Feinstein, who deserves the Congressional Medal of Honor for keeping the flame of Golden Age music alive in culturally barbarous times. Inevitably he enjoyed great success with his concerts on Broadway because the musical-theater audience still prefers "All the Things You Are" and "If Ever I Should Leave You" to "Switchblade Baby, I'm Gonna Stab You Tonight" and "Let's Hip-Hop All Over A Cop."

Atlanticards in hand, Cheryl led us along a different corridor toward an elevator at the bow of the ship. She tried to explain where we were in relationship to everything else, but at such times one feels like a mouse lost in a maze. The vessel was so large, just getting oriented would probably take two or three days. For the moment I concentrated on essentials. Our accommodations were on the Upper Promenade Deck, where we were now headed.

Jayne and I had The Virginia Suite, a bedroom, sitting room, and bath with large outside windows. The color scheme was again cream-white with pastels; the post-modern sofas and chairs made me think of a 1930s Hollywood set. A bottle of champagne, in an ice bucket, waited us, compliments of the captain. It was Tatinger, several notches up from the usual complimentary brands, though I would have preferred Snapple's fruit-flavored iced tea. Cheryl pointed out the brochures and maps on the writing desk, saying they would explain all about *The Atlantis* and adding that a bon voyage party was just getting underway in the Cafe Cabaña one deck above. She then ushered Cass off to his stateroom down the hall.

"You gonna need me tonight, boss?" he asked as she led him away. "I thought I might do some exploring."

"Explore away," I told him. "I think Jayne and I'll go to the party for a little while and then turn in early."

Our trunks and bags arrived, courtesy of a small convoy of porters, and Jayne and I spent the next half-hour unpacking.

Finally I dragged the empty bags out into the hall for the porters to put in storage during the voyage, and a little weary, we sank down facing each other on plum-colored easy chairs in the sitting room.

"Champagne, dear?" I asked.

"No, I think I'll wait and have one of those drinks with an umbrella in it when we go to that thing upstairs."

Jayne, despite her brilliance, is often a little vague. "The bon voyage party," I said. "In the Cafe Cabaña."

"Right," she said. "So what do you think so far of *Wilmington's Folly?*"

"She's a beautiful ship."

"But will she float financially . . . or sink a global empire?"

That was the question of the moment, of course. *Wilmington's Folly* was the name some news-media people had given *The Atlantis*. Though a very grand vessel, she had taken years to build, and at a cost of over thirty million dollars. It was a staggering amount to spend, even for someone like Marcus Wilmington, so a lot of people were nervous. The aged entrepreneur was betting the farm that there was a new market for old-fashioned, luxury sea travel between America and Europe, a nostalgia for the days before jumbo jets and the Concorde. The craft was booked solid, of course, for its maiden voyage to England, but the big question in all the financial journals was what business would be like a year or two down the line. Even the cheapest stateroom on *The Atlantis* was several times the cost of a first-class plane ticket to Europe. Unfortunately, if *The Atlantis* went down, so to speak, it could take the entire Wilmington empire—an international consortium of banks, newspapers, book publishing companies, hotels, and even a Hollywood film studio—with it.

"I think, dear, old Marcus fell in love with the idea of building the most beautiful ship ever," I said. "So it's not very practical—so what? It's a child's dream, a work of art, Wilmington's great toy. And why shouldn't he have it?"

"Because even a tycoon can go broke buying toys this expensive."

"Well, he's never lost money on anything yet, and personally I root for the dreamers of the world. Besides, even if he loses his shirt on this, the poor fellow will probably have a few billion left, with which he can buy some new shirts for his old age."

"He must be eighty already," Jayne remarked. "I heard a woman at Elizabeth Arden say he went to some secret place on a Greek island recently and spent two million dollars to have his entire body remade."

It's fun to speculate about someone as rich as Marcus Wilmington. No one had seen him in public for years. Everything about the man was shrouded in mystery. He did have two grown sons who sometimes spoke on his behalf, but even they never said much.

We decided to take a turn around the deck before wandering up to the "thing," as Jayne called it. She took my arm as we made a slow circumference, taking possession of our new home. A steady stream of passengers continued their ant-like progression up the gangplank. People were waving at each other from ship to shore, and there were bright flashes as cameras clicked away. The night air was full of music, distant laughter, voices, and excitement. We stopped for a moment at the bow of the ship and looked across the Hudson to the Palisades of New Jersey. The distant buildings, all lit up, gave the night an enchanted glow. Jayne suddenly kissed me on the cheek in a shy, schoolgirlish sort of way.

"Boats are very romantic," she said.

"And so are you," I assured her.

We continued in our slow circle around to the Manhattan side and then found a flight of stairs to take us up one deck.

The Cafe Cabaña was a large, glassed-in sunroom, with a long wiggly-shaped bar, subdued lighting, and a jungle of potted palms and ferns. A jazz quartet was playing a spirited samba near a dance floor that wasn't much larger than a weighing scale. Only one person was dancing, a fortysomething man whose bowtie was hanging loose around his neck. He was doing a very meditative samba, alone, apparently already fully into the bon voyage spirit. All in all, the cafe made one think of Rio de Janeiro. I almost expected to hear parrots chattering in the potted trees.

We sat down in some low curvy chairs at a small marble-topped table, and two waiters hurried over with trays of canapes. I took a smoked salmon something and Jayne a deviled egg. Then another waiter came by with glasses of champagne, which we declined, requesting "two island drinks with umbrellas." This entailed a conversation about whether we wanted our cocktails with rum, tequila, or gin. I said very light on the rum, mostly fruit juice please, and maybe an extra umbrella. It seemed to go with the jungle atmosphere of the room.

Meanwhile, people strolled about and smiled at each other. A few of them we knew.

"Steve," Jayne said suddenly, her face lighting up, "there's Tony Newley!"

Turning, I was pleased to see Anthony Newley, long a good friend and one of my favorite entertainers. I hurried across the room to greet him.

"Steve," he cried when he saw me, his formidable eyebrows lifting. "Did you get my fax?"

"Yes, I did. And I've already written a thank-you for it, but I guess my letter will not have reached you yet."

A few days earlier, out of the blue, I had gotten the warmest, loveliest message from Tony, saying that he had had an odd dream about me the night before and was reacting by sharing his sentiments with me now, rather than waiting, as is all too common a custom, until after I had departed this earth.

"If you're alone at the moment," I said, "come sit with us."

"Delighted," he replied.

"How's your darling daughter?" I asked.

"More darling than ever," he said.

One lovely night, years ago, Tony's daughter, then eleven, had been my dinner date on an evening when Jayne had been indisposed. She was a charming creature and struck me as more poised at that tender age than I had been at thirty.

Jayne, after kissing Tony fervently on the cheek, said, suddenly lowering her tone, "Tony, dear, is Princess Mudgie aboard?"

"No, she's not a *board*, though I've seen her *stiff* as one. Actually, she's a princess."

"I'm serious," Jayne said.

"So am I," Tony said.

"I think," I ventured, "Jayne is more impressed by English royalty than most of the English are."

"Steve, you're *supposed* to be impressed," Jayne said.

"If she were a nuclear physicist I'd be impressed. Or if she wrote a good novel or came up with a cure for AIDS. But you have to do something besides get your name in the tabloids and go to a lot of charity balls to impress—"

"Look! There she is!" Jayne whispered, jabbing me slightly in the ribs.

A few tables away, the Princess was settling into a chair. Two nice-looking young men with scrubbed English faces sat down as well, one on either side of her. She looked . . . ordinary, neither too pretty nor too plain. No one had seen her much in public since her separation from the Prince, so her presence on *The Atlantis* was quite a publicity coup, just the thing to make ocean travel appear indispensable to sophisticated people.

"Tony," Jayne whispered, "is it true that the Princess is in love with the young man on her left?"

"No," Tony said, in mock seriousness. "The one on her left is in love with *me*."

"Oh, stop," Jayne chided.

Our umbrellas arrived, and Tony declined to order a drink. I made a toast to beautiful ships and beautiful women. Jayne clinked her glass with mine and then gazed over my shoulder.

"Do you know anyone with thick eyeglasses who looks a little like a frog?" she asked.

"Maybe it's a prince who's in need of a good kissing," Tony said.

"Well, he's coming this way."

I turned and saw the frog Jayne had in mind. He was a balding, middle-aged man in a dark pin-striped suit—the sort you probably wouldn't look at twice if you didn't know he was Marcus Wilmington's oldest son, Richard, CEO of Wilmex Corporation, second in command after his father. I had met him briefly in Los Angeles when he came to talk to me about doing the Tuesday-night show on the ship. I had been surprised that so important an individual was personally attending to such a relatively minor matter until it occurred to me that, despite the younger man's grand title, Richard was only his father's glorified errand boy. Tony excused himself as Wilmington approached and greeted us.

"Well, are you both settling in?" Mr. Wilmington asked. "Do you like *The Atlantis* so far?"

"Yes on both counts, Mr. Wilmington," said Jayne.

"Call me Dicky," the man said. "All my friends do." He was a pale, sunless person with a bead of sweat gathering on his upper lip. His palm had not been entirely dry when we shook hands, and his glasses were excessively thick.

"Well, Dicky, you and your father must be very pleased to see *The Atlantis* finally in the water," said Jayne.

Dicky attempted a mirthless smile. "It's been stressful, Jayne, getting everything ready. Yesterday it looked as if the waiters' union was going to strike. Can you believe it? God, it's just one thing after another! They scalped us for another forty-five cents an hour. It will probably bankrupt us. Then this morning the main generator went out for about fifteen minutes. The generator! For a while it looked like we weren't going to have electricity for the maiden voyage!"

"You poor thing!" Jayne said.

"It's been murder," he complained. "A week ago no sane person would have believed we'd be sailing out of New York harbor tonight."

Poor Wilmington really did look stressed out. He turned to me and lowered his voice. "But look, I don't want to bore you with my problems. It's Father I want . . ." Dicky scowled as Rusty O'Conner and two busty women we knew slightly from Beverly Hills sat down loudly at the table beside us and drew Jayne into their conversation; when he continued, his voice was even softer, "I just got word through Stewart that Father wants to see you."

"Great," I said. "Why don't we invite him to join us?"

"Uh, well, he's eccentric about crowds."

"Then I had better go to him. Just set a time."

"I suggest right now, Steve. The old man hates to be kept waiting."

"All right, I'll bring Jayne and—"

"Oh, no, you're to come alone." Dicky obviously believed a summons from the old man was like a command from God.

Personally I'm not inclined to humor autocratic billionaires, but I was curious. Jayne was listening avidly to the latest gossip about Princess Mudgie, so I leaned over and spoke into her ear, "Sweetheart, I have to go. Someone wants to see me."

She patted my arm distractedly, her attention captured by Rusty's story about what someone had overheard Captain David Dodsworth-Ellis of the Horse Guards—Doodie—say on the telephone to Mudgie.

I glanced back as I followed Richard Wilmington from the room, but Jayne wasn't even aware I was leaving. A while later, I thought it was the last glimpse of her I'd ever have.

chapter 4

Dicky Wilmington, sad, middle-aged rich boy, led the way out of the Cafe Cabaña to a bank of elevators at the end of a long, pink corridor. I tried to make small talk about falling bond prices, thinking this might interest him, but he appeared too preoccupied to respond.

As we approached the elevators, a man in a dark suit joined us, seeming to step out of nowhere. I recognized the closely cropped blond hair, dark suntan, and cold, killer eyes of the armed man at our first checkpoint when boarding. An elevator arrived, and the three of us stepped in together. An older couple tried to join us at the last minute, but our friend with the gun said in a soft but firm voice: "Would you mind taking the next car?"

Then the door closed, and the man with the gun pressed the stop button. I looked at Dicky for some kind of clue. He smiled nervously.

"I always feel bad about things like this," he apologized. "But you know how my father is."

"No, I don't, Dicky. Perhaps you'd better tell me."

"Well, he's a bit of a nut for privacy. But don't worry. Your safety is my first concern."

I snorted to indicate ironic contempt for his first concern and any other concerns the Wilmington clan might have.

"Do you have a cold?" asked the man with the gun.

"No."

"When was the last time you had a shower?"

"I beg your pardon?"

"The old man's a stickler for cleanliness."

"I hope he keeps stickling," I said. "I had a shower this morning, if it's anybody's business."

"Good," the blond man said, suddenly slipping a black hood over my head, putting me in the darkest world I'd ever seen.

"Listen—"

"Relax, Mr. Allen," said the cold voice. "My name is Stewart Hoffman, and I'm head of security on *The Atlantis*. You have nothing to fear. You're simply required to humor an eccentric old man who wishes to meet with you but doesn't want you to know his precise location."

"What if I say no?" I asked from beneath my hood.

"As you wish, sir. You *may* return to the Cafe Cabaña. Take a moment to decide."

I took the moment. The problem was, I am curious by nature—and this was about as curious a situation as I had ever encountered. So I said, perhaps unwisely, "Well, okay then."

The elevator began to move, but it ran so smoothly I didn't know for certain whether we were going up or down. Then the door hissed open, and I was guided forward. I tried to memorize my way, noting there was carpet underfoot as we marched forward thirty-eight paces. I presumed we were in one of the ship's many long corridors. But then we stepped outside—I could tell by the sudden smell of New York City in the air and the distant sounds of cars and sirens. I could hear two orchestras playing not far away, one on the dock and the other in the Cafe Cabaña. I wondered what Jayne would think if she could see me now, a hood over my head like a prisoner being led to the gallows. It wasn't quite the carefree image the ship conveyed in its brochure.

We walked thirteen paces over a hard deck.

"Careful now, we're about to go up some steps, Mr. Allen. Six of them. The first is directly in front of your left foot . . . Don't worry, I'll guide you."

"This is turning into somewhat of a hassle just to see your damned father," I said, letting off a bit of steam.

"Young Mr. Wilmington is no longer with us, sir," came the quiet voice.

"Where did he go?"

"Back to the party. Where does he ever go?"

I was not particularly pleased to be alone with Stewart Hoffman, but in certain situations, believe it or not, celebrity confers a certain amount of protection. It doesn't mean a damn, of course, to professional holdup men, muggers, or social monsters of other sorts, but there are contexts in which killing or assaulting a well-known individual is more trouble than it's worth. I clung to the fact that this was surely one of them. In any event, at the moment there was nothing to do about it but climb the steps. I had lost my orientation and had no idea where we were. Going up the steps I thought perhaps we were climbing to the captain's bridge, but I entered a small, cramped room that did not fit with anything I could imagine on board *The Atlantis*. Hoffman guided me into a padded bucket chair and then, to my surprise, buckled a seat belt around my waist. I was starting to feel claustrophobic with the hood on my head and told him so.

"Not much longer now," he said soothingly.

I heard a metal door close, and then a strange whirring began, softly at first, but getting louder by the moment. It was a familiar sound, but I could not quite place where I had heard it before. The room began to vibrate.

"I think I'll go back to the Cafe Cabaña after all," I said nervously. But there was no answer from Hoffman. It was too late to change my mind.

I felt the ground fall away, and that's when I realized I was in a helicopter, heading God only knew where. I had flown in helicopters on two earlier occasions and had actually enjoyed the experience. On your first flight, the only scary moment comes when you feel you're going to slide out of your seat as the craft takes off nose low and tail high.

I was getting a bit angry now; no one had mentioned a helicopter. The claustrophobia was getting to me. I reached toward my hood with the definite idea of liberation.

"Please don't," Hoffman said, his voice sounding close to my left ear. "I'd like to make this trip as pleasant as possible for you, under the circumstances, but please do not remove your hood."

I tried to keep track of where we were going by counting the minutes we were in the air. It wasn't easy, but it gave me something to do. I counted the seconds by saying, "One thousand, two thousand, three thousand, four thousand . . ." under my breath. At sixty thousand, I bent a finger to mark a minute of my life gone by that I would not wish to live again.

When you can't see and haven't the foggiest notion where you're going, time slows to a dull tedium. Hours might have gone by before the helicopter set down on hard ground and the rotor blade wheezed to a stop. Hoffman guided me down the steps to the ground. I was happy to find myself once more on Mother Earth.

Wherever we were, there were no city noises to be heard. I smelled pine in the air and heard insects whirring; an owl hooted nearby. It was a lonely sound. Heavy tree branches sighed restlessly in the cool night breeze.

"For an ocean voyage, I could almost swear we were in woods," I mentioned, so Hoffman wouldn't think I was a dummy.

"Don't let your imagination run away with you," said my guardian. "We're almost there now."

We drove in a car—a limousine, I supposed—one that smelled of very good leather. It seemed to be old, English, and expensive. The drive was short, and then I was up again, led forward into a big house and down a long corridor. I knew the place was large from the way our footsteps reverberated. A country estate in Connecticut, I wondered? But for all I knew, we were in Pennsylvania or Vermont.

Then a door closed behind me, and my guardian said I could remove my hood.

I found myself in a huge baronial room paneled with dark wood. At one end there was a great stone fireplace where enormous logs blazed, although a glass shield prevented the heat from emanating into the room. The room, in fact, was air conditioned. To have a fire going and air conditioning at the same time struck me as a waste of energy. There was not a single window in sight, and this seemed peculiar as well. I noticed a few armchairs, what appeared to be a Rembrandt on the wall, and a wooden desk so large it took me a moment to perceive the little man seated behind it, watching me get my bearings with an amused smile.

"Good evening, Mr. Allen," the man said. "I apologize for bringing you here so dramatically. You've been very kind to indulge me."

"Think nothing of it," I said breezily. "I've always loved Connecticut." Wilmington smiled at my feeble attempt to draw him out.

He was the strangest-looking human I had ever seen—a gnome, really, with a wizened, ancient face. His head was bald and slightly wrinkled, his ears large and a bit hairy. He looked rather like an alien creature from *Star Wars*.

"Excuse me for not getting up," he said. "The legs don't quite work as they used too. You see, I share your tendency to sciatica. Please have a seat by the fire. Would you care for some carrot juice?"

I was impressed that he knew of my habit of drinking cold carrot juice, something that, as far as I know, had never been publicized, nor mentioned during any of my television appearances. If he knew so trivial a fact, he undoubtedly knew a good deal else as well.

I sat in one of the enormous chairs by the huge, heatless fire.

Stewart Hoffman came in with two large glasses of carrot juice with ice. I hadn't noticed the old man buzz or make any gesture to summon the security man with our drinks, but I was prepared for almost any sort of miracle here.

"*À votre santé*, Mr. Allen," the old man toasted, raising his glass after Hoffman had withdrawn.

It was the best carrot juice I had ever tasted, and I told him so. He said he raised the carrots himself and they were a special kind. I was curious to know more, and we could have gone on about carrots all night, but he interrupted and got to the subject at hand.

"Do you know what they're saying about me, Mr. Allen? They're saying I've lost my mind. *Wilmington's Folly*—that's what they're calling my little craft! What do you think of her?"

"I think it's very impressive. But it does look expensive."

"Little minds!" he scoffed. I wasn't sure if I was included in the statement. "Fifty years from now *The Atlantis* will still be sailing the ocean, making money with every trip. Very few people take the long view anymore—they want their money back all at once. It's what's ruining America."

"One of the things certainly," I conceded.

"But that's neither here nor there," Wilmington continued. "The reason I've brought you here is that I'd like to hire your services."

"You already have," I told him. "I'm doing two shows in the Grand Ballroom on Tuesday night. I'd be happy to arrange a ringside table for you," I said, aware of my impudence.

He smiled. "You're funny. But I'm more interested in your other talents."

"You want me to play the piano?"

"Entertain as you wish, but as it happens you're ideally placed to render me a more important service. I want to hire you as a private investigator."

I laughed and shook my head.

"Why not?"

"Because that's one field in which I am strictly an amateur."

"And yet I hear that you have certain gifts. You've dealt quite effectively with at least a few police matters in the past."

"What I'm trying to tell you, Mr. Wilmington, is I am not for hire, except as a performer. If I've done a little sleuthing here and there, it's been for my own amusement, or to get myself or a friend out of a jam. It wouldn't appeal to me to do it for money."

Wilmington nodded, then got deadly serious. "I propose," he said, "to pay you one hundred thousand dollars for four days of your time."

"You win," I conceded.

"Good," he said. "And the nice thing is you're *not* being asked to do anything against your principles. I assume you're as willing as the next decent fellow to unmask skullduggery."

I smiled and nodded. Despite his peculiar appearance, Wilmington was turning out to be an entertaining fellow.

"Mr. Allen, our time is limited, so let me lay this out for you," he continued. "There are a number of people who would very much like to see my ship go down—people who hate me personally and/or professionally—and I find myself rather vulnerable at this time. I can't afford to have anything go wrong on this maiden voyage. You see, the business reports you may have read are accurate. It has become known that *The Atlantis* cost me nearly three times what I planned; consequently I'm stretched rather thin. If anything happens on this first voyage—bad weather, negative publicity, anything at all . . . Well, all I'm asking is that you keep an eye out for anything suspicious the next four days at sea. You will receive your one hundred thousand dollars when the ship arrives safely in Southampton."

He was looking hard into my eyes, and I looked back just as hard. I won't say I wasn't interested, or even flattered, still it seemed a strange offer and just a little too vague. "Mr. Wilmington, from what I see, you have a very capable staff. Stewart

Hoffman does not strike me as an amateur. Why do you think I would do better?"

"Oh, not better, Mr. Allen. You will simply be an additional pair of eyes. Besides, everyone thinks of you as an entertainer, and you have no connection to me at all. You see how advantageous that is, don't you? People will talk to you freely. You will mingle easily with the guests. You will have access where Mr. Hoffman will not."

"What would I be looking for exactly?"

He shrugged. "How am I to know? The main thing is you will be on board, watching and listening. It will make me feel better."

"Aren't you coming on your own maiden voyage?"

"Mr. Allen, a crowded ship would make me very ill. And besides, I've already enjoyed the *real* maiden voyage. I rode on *The Atlantis* as its only passenger when it left dry dock in San Diego and passed through the Panama Canal to New York."

I had a nagging feeling there were things he wasn't telling me. "Mr. Wilmington, if I am to do an effective job for you, I will have to know more. Like who specifically you want me to keep an eye on."

"Well," he said, "there's Peter Moon, for one. Wall Street fellow. Do you know him?"

"Only by reputation. He's the king of leveraged takeovers I understand."

"He's the king of slime. He's made some nibbles in my direction in the past, but I've always been able to hold him off. If my shipping venture fails, however, there would be pieces of my company up for grabs. A man like Moon could make a killing."

"So what's he going to do? Drill a hole in the boat and let it sink? With him on it?"

"All he needs to do is start a rumor. These things can be very subtle. Or maybe, with a little help, there will be a case of food poisoning on board and no one will ever want to travel *The Atlantis* again."

"You think Moon would go that far?"

"Oh, he would go much farther! Believe me, the man is a piranha. He's been jealous of my success for years."

"Why don't you just kick him off the boat?"

"No, I think it is better to have him on board where we can watch him . . . where *you* can watch him, sir. Then again, he may try nothing destructive at all, and you'll earn the easiest hundred grand of your life."

"And what if I do see something suspicious, like Peter Moon sneaking into the kitchen with a box of rat poison or something? Who do I report to? Your man Hoffman?"

He shook his head. "No, you will report directly to me. Before you leave, Stewart will give you a small electronic device, like a beeper but more sophisticated. If you need to talk with me, press the little button and I'll get back to you. It's as simple as that."

"Frankly, Mr. Wilmington, none of this sounds very simple at all."

"But you will do it?"

"I'll tell you what. I'll take your little beeper, and I'll keep my eyes open. But I'll decide when we reach Southampton whether to bill you for my services or not."

"Fair enough," he said. "All you're agreeing to do is keep your eyes open and be curious, as long as it interests you. From what I've heard about you, you would probably do that anyway. But now you must be getting back on board before your wife misses you and the ship sails. Oh, Mr. Hoffman has instructions to give you a gun, if you wish."

"No guns," I said. "Guns kill people, despite what the bumper stickers say."

"Very well, but you may change your mind. One more thing . . ."

"Yes?"

"I would suggest you keep a special eye on my children,

Dicky and Alexis. They like money a little too much for their own good."

I smiled. "You don't trust anyone, do you?"

"As I mentioned, news of my financial situation has leaked rather too freely from my closed boardrooms to the press."

I nodded that I understood and turned to leave. His voice stopped me.

"There's one other person I want you to watch."

"Who's that, Mr. Wilmington?"

"My wife, sir. Gertrude. She will be on board—enjoying herself immensely, I'm sure. Keep a close eye on her, Mr. Allen. A *very* close eye."

chapter 5

My paper umbrella was soggy, but other than that nothing had changed in my absence. Rusty O'Conner, her two cronies and Jayne were still discussing the broken royal marriage. I threw my own two cents into the conversation. "Why not let them mate and unmate in private?"

The women stared at me as if I were mad.

"Did you have a nice chat?" Jayne asked. "You weren't gone long."

"Oh, it was loads of fun. They put a hood over my head and flew me in a helicopter to Connecticut or Vermont or Wyoming, I'm not sure where."

"Yes, darling," said Jayne. The other women gave her sympathetic looks, knowing it could not be easy to be married to a comedian.

Just then Candy L'Amour came into the room, followed by a good-looking young fellow in a white dinner jacket.

"That's Alexis Wilmington," Rusty said. "Alex is the handsome son who was going out with What's-her-name until just a few weeks ago."

I perked up when I heard the name. The youngest Wilmington was perhaps thirty years old and about six feet tall. He was built like an athlete and had wavy dark hair and an easy smile.

Fortune had obviously smiled on Alexis while passing over his older brother.

Then there was Candy L'Amour, who was doing her usual best to look like Marilyn Monroe. Miss L'Amour, the rock star with the voice like Minnie Mouse, had a hit a few years back with the song, "I Wanna, Wanna, Wanna." We have it on the authority of *Time* magazine that the early pubescent crowd would just about die for her.

Candy and Alexis Wilmington were greeted at the far side of the dance floor by an elegant, gray-haired woman whom Alexis kissed on the cheek.

"Who's that?" I asked, hoping to put my gossipmongers to good use.

"Gertrude Wilmington," Rusty said. "The matriarch herself."

"She's originally a Van Gelder of the Albany Van Gelders," another of the Beverly Hills ladies added. "Her mother was a Philadelphia McEagle."

"Isn't that a football team?" I asked.

"*Steve!*" Rusty cried. "The Philadelphia McEagles are related to the Baltimore Donahues, only they're richer. They make paper products."

"They say that Marcus Wilmington married her for her money," said one of the Beverly Hills ladies. "Iris, I believe her name was. Or perhaps Rose. A flower of some sort."

"Gertrude was a Van Gelder, and they own—"

"The First Empire Bank of Albany," I said, glad to be able to contribute some information. When the woman looked at me in an admiring way, I added: "There was a Lawrence Van Gelder in the news recently for absconding with funds. I think he ran off to Uruguay with an eighteen-year-old girl. Or maybe he ran off with Uruguay to Argentina."

Rusty chuckled briefly, then continued imparting information with a true gossiper's air. "Anyway, Gertrude Van Gelder was the one with the money. It's hard to believe now, but at the time everyone thought Marcus was a ne'er-do-well. He used her money to make his first investment—a shopping mall, I believe. The rest, as they say, is history."

I gazed across the room at Gertrude Wilmington, wondering what she was saying to her youngest son. She had managed to separate him from Candy L'Amour and had engaged him in an earnest conversation by the bar.

"I'm going for a glass of mineral water," I told Jayne.

"Why don't you just ask the waiter to bring one?"

"No, I need the exercise. I was sitting all the way to Connecticut, or wherever the hell we were."

Jayne gave me a worried look. "Steve," she said, "have you taken too much vitamin C?"

I wiggled my eyebrows at her and headed across the room, managing to find a spot at the bar near a potted palm, a few feet from mother and son. Nonchalantly positioning myself with my back to them, I strained to hear their conversation. At first I heard nothing, then the young man's voice rose angrily above the cocktail din.

"It's that damned Dicky!"

"Alex, keep your voice down," said Gertrude.

"Mother, you *know* what he's been doing. Meanwhile I don't have a cent to get married with. It's embarrassing—I hardly had enough to pay for that Porsche I got Candy for Christmas. I'm going to lose her if I don't have a bigger allowance."

The woman sighed wearily. "How much do you need, Alex?"

The bartender was staring at me, and I realized he was waiting for my order. "A pineapple juice," I said.

"Anything in it?"

"Yes. Pineapple." He did not smile.

I missed hearing how much money Wilmington needed to keep Candy L'Amour at his side. Life is very hard for the young and the restless, not to mention the bold and the beautiful and the big and the fat. The mother and son were conferring once again in low voices. It was very inconsiderate of them; I couldn't hear a thing. Then, to make my job even harder, a well-modulated voice came over the public address system, telling visitors to depart the vessel unless they wished to take an unexpected trip to England. *The Atlantis* would sail in half an hour.

I picked up my pineapple juice and sidled closer to my subjects. I guess I was getting a little gung-ho because I stood with my back almost touching Mrs. Wilmington's, gazing off across the room as if looking for . . . oh, my wife.

"I'm going to kill him, I really am," the young man erupted angrily.

"Alexis, you have to be patient. How many times do I have to tell you that?"

"Mother, I'm thirty-five years old, for God's sake! How much more patient do you want me to be?"

I had snuggled too closely into the conversation, and Mrs. Wilmington bumped against me. We turned to look at each other.

"Oh, sorry," I said.

She had suspicious gray eyes and the most autocratic face I had ever seen on any woman who was not Queen Victoria. One could tell she had once been pretty, but her face had gone a bit wide with the years.

"I'm Steve Allen," I said with a smile. "I'll bet you're Gertrude Wilmington."

"Yes," she said, friendly but not encouraging. "I've seen you on television. 'What's My Line?' . . . isn't it?"

I pumped her proffered hand. "That was forty years ago," I said.

"Well, I don't watch much anymore."

Her son was so caught up with his own problems he barely acknowledged my presence.

"Well, this certainly is exciting," I said. "The maiden voyage. I'll bet you two have been waiting for this a long time."

"Fifteen goddamn years!" the young man exploded. He appeared ready to say more, but his mama shot him a look that sealed his mouth. Then she turned toward me with her best chairwoman-of-the-opera manner, a smiling demeanor impenetrable as steel plating.

"What a pleasure to meet you, Mr. Allen," she said.

We nodded at each other, and she guided her son safely out of earshot. I sighed; my task was not going to be easy. I was momentarily tempted to do something James Bondish, like search their staterooms—but I didn't know where their staterooms were or how to pick a lock.

I hadn't learned much for my trouble. My blood had pulsed just a bit when I heard the young man say he was going to kill *him*—whoever "him" was—but on calmer reflection this seemed only the sort of thing rash young men occasionally say, with no blood being spilled.

Such investigative experience as I'd had in the past had all been ex post facto, trying to figure out who had committed a particular crime. In the present situation there had not yet been a crime, at least as far as I knew. No crime and two thousand suspects. I was glad I hadn't agreed to take old Marcus Wilmington's money. I could still walk away from this assignment whenever I chose.

At least that's what I thought.

chapter 6

There's nothing quite like sailing out of New York harbor at night on a big, white ocean liner. Jayne and I stood, breeze-swept, on the highest deck we could climb to, alongside the forward smokestack, and looked out upon the tall, steel-and-concrete monoliths of Manhattan. The city sparkled like a jewel in a silver shroud.

"Look at that moon! How lovely," Jayne said, pointing to the monstrous orb that hovered over the Empire State Building. Soon, in another direction, we saw the Statue of Liberty, all aglow with spotlights, behind which I could see a chunk of Staten Island. When we turned away from the city we saw the most intriguing reality of all— the empty, black vastness of the ocean. Then, without warning, the ship's great horn sounded, a shocking, thunderous blast, coming up from the smokestack.

Jayne patted my hand and gave me a sympathetic look during the few seconds the ship's whistle continued its maddening blast, silently reminding me that with the racket over we could once again enjoy the sights and the increasing saltiness of the night air as the ship moved smoothly forward.

"Well, this is nice," she finally said. "Happy ocean, darling."

"And a happy ocean to you," I told her.

"Now, tell me all about Marcus Wilmington. You went to his stateroom?"

I smiled mysteriously. "In a sense."

"You should feel honored to have seen him. Rusty says Wilmington hasn't even been photographed for twenty years."

"He's not very photogenic."

"You'd probably prefer to look at Candy L'Amour." She was kidding because she knows I would not touch Miss L'Amour if God temporarily suspended all moral rules and personally pleaded with me to approach her. Everything about that woman seems calculated. Obviously unsatisfied with her own persona, she has contrived to affect some vague approximation of Marilyn Monroe. But Marilyn was truly beautiful and had a sweet, vulnerable quality that made you want to pat her shoulder in encouragement—after which one could, no doubt, think of further developments. But there is nothing sweet, vulnerable, or appealing about Miss L'Amour. Jayne says I shouldn't get so emotionally concerned about things of this sort, but if Miss L'Amour's being the current role model for America's teenaged girls doesn't tell us how depraved our society has become, then I don't know what will.

Anyway, I ended up telling Jayne all about the conversation I had with Marcus Wilmington, his offer of one hundred thousand dollars, the beeper gadget, the works. Only the tops of the twin towers of the Trade Center still peeked over the horizon by the time I had finished my story.

"So are you going to do it?" Jayne asked.

"Well, who couldn't use an extra hundred grand?" I said. "Although I'm not sure what I'm supposed to *do*, exactly. Lurk behind potted palms?"

"He only asked you to report *if* you see anything suspicious. That's not much to do, darling."

"But what's suspicious?" I asked. "How will I even know?"

"Well, how about that down there?"

"What? Where?"

"Lifeboat number nine. Look."

My eye followed where she was pointing to a deck directly

beneath us. A handsome young man, dressed well for a stow-away, in one of those shapeless double-breasted sports coats the young people wear these days, was crawling out from under the canvas cover of lifeboat number nine. He swung a leather duf-flebag from his shoulder and rummaged quickly through it. After a moment he pulled out a hairbrush, which he ran through his longish, dark brown hair—a cute touch, under the circumstances. Jayne and I shrank back as the young man looked nervously up and down the deserted deck. He appar-ently hadn't spotted us because he left his bag where it was, grabbed hold of the rope and pulley by which the lifeboat was attached, pulled the canvas cover back into place, and swung lithely onto the ship's deck. With a quick look around, he disap-peared through the doors, into the ship.

"Well, that *is* suspicious!" I said. "Should I alert Wilming-ton?"

"I shouldn't think so," said Jayne. "I thought he was cute."

"Maybe he's a cute terrorist."

"He didn't look the type," said my wife.

"What type would you say stows aboard a ship?"

"Someone who can't afford a ticket. Or somebody in love. Maybe there's a girl on board who's sailing off with someone else. Maybe he wants to stop her before she makes a tragic mis-take."

"Then again," I said, "he doesn't look much over twenty. Perhaps he's just looking for adventure."

"Maybe," Jayne said. "That's why we have to keep an eye on things."

"We?" I said with a raised eyebrow.

"Of course. I found something suspicious, now it's your turn. After all, I'm not going to do *every*thing for you. Not if we're going to split the one hundred thousand dollars!"

chapter 7

"Look at the woman over there," I whispered to Jayne. *"What* is she doing with that baby?"

You can be suspicious of everything if you look hard enough. The most common occurrences may hint at some dark meaning.

"Steve, she's carrying a perfectly ordinary baby across the dining room."

"Yes, but this is the second time in ten minutes she's carried the little guy out of the room."

"Maybe she's going to change his diaper."

"Maybe," I said.

We were having breakfast in the main dining room, surrounded by hovering waiters in pink jackets who kept offering fresh juice, pastries, and more coffee. So far, my conflict of the day had been an epic struggle between eggs benedict and waffles smothered with fresh blueberries. I won the war—and had a bran muffin instead. On board a ship, it's always a good idea to start the day modestly and build gradually toward midnight excesses.

Sun was streaming in the large window by our table; there was no land in sight, just blue water as far as the eye could see.

"Listen to this, you guys," said Cass. "You can learn to tango in the Flamingo Lounge at ten A.M., or sign up for the Ping-

Pong tournament at ten-thirty. Or how about this? . . . 'Winning at Blackjack,' a lecture and demonstration at two-thirty. . . . I took a little peek at the casino last night. Won five bucks on the quarter slots!" He was stuffing his mouth with pancakes and reading aloud to us from the ship's daily newspaper. *The Atlantis* offered aerobics, lectures, movies, bingo, horse racing, shuffleboard, a get-acquainted tea, a cocktail dance, a singles mixer, and three different bands in three different lounges starting in the late afternoon—entertainment galore. The library opened at nine A.M. You could sign up for skeet shooting off the stern beginning at eleven o'clock. Lunch was at noon or one-thirty, depending on whether you were first or second seating. (We were first seating.) Dinner was at six-thirty or eight o'clock. Tonight Candy L'Amour would perform in the Grand Ballroom at eight o'clock and ten o'clock. The casino, for the convenience of the guests, was open twenty-four hours a day. There was a teen disco, a wine-and-cheese tasting, a lecture on shopping hints for London, and other events as well—including a compulsory lifeboat drill at four P.M. The day's news ended with a reminder to set our clocks one hour ahead, to keep up with the time zones as we moved eastward across the Atlantic.

So much for life aboard a large luxury liner—more food than you can eat and more fun than you can have, with two swimming pools and a gymnasium for working off the calories. After breakfast, Jayne, Cass, and I explored the ship; then each of us went off to a chosen pleasure, having made plans to meet for lunch. Cass thought he'd learn how to tango and then wander into the casino. Jayne was headed to the beauty parlor and the Galleria with its expensive shops. I planned to find a deck chair in the sun, dictate a few notes, read a bit, and watch for suspicious events.

I parked myself on the Sun Deck, shielded by a glass windbreaker to keep me warm and cozy. It was a beautiful day, not a cloud in the sky, and quite balmy for April, though you needed a jacket when you stepped into the rush of ocean wind. I was on deck above the outdoor swimming pool and cafe, so I gazed down upon the crowd gathered below. The adults seemed to be drinking Bloody and Virgin Marys and island concoctions; a few young children splashed about in the water, squealing. I spent a few moments getting my deck chair angled into the sun just right and finding the proper notch in the chair. Getting comfortable in a deck chair is an art, of course; usually you have to stand up a few times and experiment with different possibilities. But finally I got settled; if I had been a cat I would have been purring.

I had brought along a few books and a pad for letter-writing, so I'd have everything within easy reach, depending on my mood. Writing a letter seemed like too much work at the moment, so I studied my reading material: *Cats of Any Color,* a brilliant new book by my good friend Gene Lees; a biography of Bertrand Russell; and Tolstoy's *Anna Karenina.* After some deliberation I decided on the Tolstoy. I had read *Anna Karenina* before, but I was in a 19th-century-Russian sort of mood, ready to dream my way back to St. Petersburg at the time of the tsars.

"Waiter!" I called. "A glass of fresh-squeezed orange juice, please."

"Absolutely, sir!" Getting pampered is what ocean liners are all about.

I looked up from *Anna Karenina* about forty-five minutes later when I detected the inviting aroma of food coming from the cafe by the swimming pool. Long tables had been arranged to invitingly hold sandwiches, fruit, and pastries—a delectable midmorning buffet. It was at that moment I saw the young stowaway from the lifeboat. He still wore the shapeless sports coat and had his duffle over his shoulder. I could see him better now. His dark hair was tied back in a small ponytail, and he had a gaunt poetic face and narrow nose. There was a day's growth of beard on his chin, but this was fashionable among young men these days, whether stowaways or not.

I watched him casually amble past the pool to the buffet

table, where he unzipped his bag and quickly stuffed it with three sandwiches, two oranges, a banana, and a Danish pastry, the sandwiches and pastry he had wrapped in paper napkins. He started away, but changed his mind and slyly grabbed another sandwich and an orange. At last he carried his booty up to the Sun Deck, where I was so pleasantly ensconced, found a chair a dozen feet away from mine, and began to tear ravenously into his food. I watched three of the sandwiches disappear in record time.

"You'll get indigestion if you eat so fast." Chelsea, the young woman traveling with her grandmother, stepped out from behind a metal air vent. Perhaps she had been hiding there, spying on people. She was dressed in shorts, sandals, and a dark blue silk blouse, but the young man seemed more interested in ripping an orange apart and cramming the pieces into his mouth than in appreciating her fresh prettiness. We do not live, alas, in a romantic age.

"Didn't you eat breakfast?" Chelsea asked him.

"I'm a hungry guy," he said with his mouth full. When the orange disappeared he got to work on the Danish pastry. The girl studied him as if he were a specimen in a jar.

"My name's Chelsea Eastman," she declared. "I'm a sophomore at Vassar."

"Swell." He unwrapped the last sandwich.

"I'm going with my grandmother to England. I didn't want to, but my parents said I must because my grandmother is old and you never know when she's going to die."

"Is she rich?" the young man asked, suddenly interested.

"Loaded."

"They just want you to kiss up to the old lady so you'll inherit her money."

"You're very cynical."

"I've got to be, in my profession."

"What profession is that? You're a safecracker, I bet."

"Nope."

"A gigolo?"

He laughed.

"A professor of eighteenth century poetry at Sarah Lawrence?"

"You're getting colder."

"Well, you've got to give me a clue then," she said.

"Hey, I don't have to give you anything."

They were only young people doing the age-old dance of the sexes; I tried to tune them out and return to *Anna Karenina*. But they were difficult to ignore as their conversation gradually became more interesting.

"*I* know what you are," Chelsea taunted.

"What?" he smirked. At least he had finally stopped eating.

"You're a stowaway."

"You're crazy," he said, but his smirk was gone.

"And I know what else you are," she told him.

"Look, I'm not really in the mood for playing this game."

"You're a journalist. You're spying on Mudgie and probably all the other celebrities on board. Couldn't you get a stateroom?"

"Is prying the sort of thing they teach at Vassar these days?"

"No, but it's how you *really* learn what you need to know. Anyway, it's been nice talking to you. Goodbye, Larry Goldman, columnist for *Trend* magazine. Incidentally, I liked your book—*Celebrimania*—although you're a bit too glib, you know."

Chelsea Eastman made her exit, her schoolgirl nose somewhat in the air as she stepped haughtily down the steps toward the pool, leaving the poor stowaway sputtering in his chair. He quickly brushed orange peels from his lap and went after her.

"Hey, wait a minute," he said.

She turned and nailed him with her green-eyed stare. "Don't worry, Larry," she said. "I'm not going to turn you in." She walked away from him, across the pool deck, and disappeared inside the ship.

The young man stared after her, then saw me looking at him and shrugged. "Crazy college kids."

I watched him as he walked back to tidy up his debris. I remembered when *Celebrimania* was on the best-seller list. Larry Goldman was one of those bright new journalists who make a splash from time to time by presenting themselves as more hip than the poor celebrities they quickly dispatch. It was not my favorite form of journalism. I guess you have to be a fan of the Me Generation to appreciate journalists who write chiefly about themselves.

"I have to say I'm curious too, Mr. Goldman," I said to him. "Can't *Trend* afford to buy you a proper ticket?"

He gazed at me with a sour expression. "I can't believe that chick's blown my cover!" he complained. Then he sighed dramatically. "Money had nothing to do with it. This tub has been sold out for months. I called too late to get a ticket."

"But you decided you weren't going to be left behind?"

"You kidding? This is the greatest boat story since *The Titanic!*"

I watched him steal two more sandwiches on his way past the pool. His last words left me with a sinking feeling, no joke intended. But Goldman did not seem concerned. After all, he had the best stateroom possible should nautical history repeat itself.

chapter 8

You can see a lot from a deck chair if you keep your eyes open. Late in the morning as I was bounding over the waves with Gene Lees's book open on my lap, a momentary glare of light made me look up. I noticed a pale man in Bermuda shorts and a colorful Hawaiian shirt sitting about twenty feet away, nestled close to the side wall of a bar that had just opened up. His stomach rolled in a moderate paunch over his belt, and he sported black socks and black city shoes that didn't go well with the tropical look of the rest of his costume. Clearly he was not one of the beautiful people. He was hidden in the shadows; I suspected he might be avoiding someone.

At first I had no idea what had caused the glare that made me look up, but then the man lifted a small pair of field glasses to his eyes and the lenses momentarily caught the sun. He was looking up at something at about a forty-five-degree angle. I turned to see what he was studying with such interest: It was the tycoon's eldest son, Dicky, who was standing by the smokestack on the highest deck—where Jayne and I had stood the night before. There was a man with Wilmington. I could not see his features well from such a distance, but he was tall, with dark hair and round eyeglasses. Dicky and the man were having an angry, animated conversation; I wished for a pair of binoculars like those of my friend in the Bermuda shorts, and perhaps a listening device as well. It's frustrating trying to spy without proper equipment.

When I looked back, the man had lowered his binoculars and was writing something in a small notebook. Apparently I was not the only spy on board *The Atlantis*. What with Chelsea Eastman, we might have a Spy Convention in one of the lounges some afternoon. Meanwhile, Wilmington and his friend were obviously upset with one another. Dicky finally walked away, throwing up his hands in disgust. He jogged angrily down a flight of steps, and I momentarily lost sight of him. Then he appeared on my deck, walking purposefully toward the stairs to the swimming pool. When he saw me, however, he reversed his direction and came my way.

"Ah, Steve!" he said with a big but insincere smile, pulling a deck chair close to mine as though we were buddies. "Just the man I wanted!" There are few things more discordant than someone who is upset pretending to have a great time.

"Having fun so far?" he asked brightly.

"Yes," I said.

"I'm pleased," he responded.

"You're very easily pleased," I retorted.

"Great weather," he said.

"Couldn't be better."

Dicky sighed. "Too bad we're heading into a goddamn storm."

It's not pleasant to see a human being collapse. All at once it was as if the man's chest had caved in; he seemed inches shorter.

"A storm?" I prodded speculatively.

"A goddamn storm!" he repeated.

"Are we talking about a figurative storm in which one's emotions are tossed to and fro, or the literal variety with wind and rain and sliding furniture?"

"Oh, there'll be wind and rain," he said gloomily. "I mean, you'd think the weather would cooperate, for God's sake."

"Looks fine right now," I said hopefully. "When are things supposed to change?"

"Tonight, if we're unlucky. Maybe the ridge of high pressure will keep it to the north of us, but it doesn't look good. The barometer is already starting to fall."

"Surely a ship like *The Atlantis* can weather a little spring storm."

He had a desperate look in his eye. "We could have thirty-foot swells by dawn," he said. "Seventy-mile-per-hour winds—maybe worse. *The Atlantis* isn't in danger physically, but we don't need everyone losing their lunch for the next three days and swearing they'll never travel by ship again."

"Could we turn back to New York?"

He shook his head. "Suicide. Pure suicide. Can you imagine the publicity? We might as well sign everything over to our creditors right now."

"That much depends on *The Atlantis* being a success?"

"Yeah. Dad should be shot for putting so much money into it. The banking side of the business still hasn't recovered from the eighties when a whole lot of questionable real-estate loans didn't pan out. Then the Hollywood studio made that sixty-million-dollar bomb last summer—did you catch *My Mom the Alien*?"

"No, I'm afraid not."

"Well, no one else did either. As for the newspapers we own, they're folding right and left. Americans would rather get their news on television."

"I know," I said. "I mentioned that in my book *Dumbth*."

"Oh? Well, *The Atlantis* is just the last string in a series of bad luck and bad judgment moves."

"Don't write her off yet," I told him. "This is only the first morning. Maybe the storm will blow off to the north. Weather reports have been wrong before. Or we could alter course."

Dicky looked at me as if he wanted to believe there was hope, but he was not a happy sailor. "So how was your talk with Dad last night?" he asked.

"Fine."

"He seemed . . . okay?"

"His health?"

"Well . . . his mind. He didn't seem bonkers or anything?"

I was about to say something pleasant, but then I had an image of old Wilmington as the sole passenger riding this huge liner through the Panama Canal; the words stuck in my throat. "He seemed chipper for his age," I said diplomatically.

Dicky sighed. "He didn't say anything about Mom or me and Alexis?"

"Not that I remember," I lied. "Why don't you ask him yourself?"

He sighed again, morosely. "Well, that's the problem. He won't see any of us. He's become such a recluse he communicates only by memo."

"When's the last time you actually saw your father?"

"A year and a half ago. As CEO of his company, that's damned embarrassing! That's why I was hoping you'd put a word in for me, Steve. Maybe you could convince him to see me. Not because I'm his son—we can leave family out of it, if he likes—it's just a straight business matter. If I could only meet with him face-to-face I'm sure I could bring him 'round."

"Bring him around to what?"

"It's complicated," Dicky admitted, looking ever glummer. "I can't talk about it."

"Does it have anything to do with that man you were fighting with up by the smokestack?"

Dicky looked at me sharply. "What man?

"Hey—"

"And I thought you'd be on my side!"

I tried to calm him, but he turned and fled, jogging quickly down the steps toward the swimming pool and disappearing inside the ship. I thought of going after him, but there was no point.

I saw it was time for lunch and was glad to forget the Wilmington clan for a while. Gathering my books and papers, I was about to walk away when I noticed that Mr. Bermuda Shorts had positioned himself by the rail and was studiously looking out to sea just a few feet from where I had been talking with Dicky. I was sure he had heard at least some of our conversation.

I was getting a little tired of all the cloak-and-dagger business aboard this ship, so I walked boldly over to the man. "So tell me," I said rudely, "who are you?"

He turned my way with a professionally cynical expression I recognized all too well.

"Ah," I said. "The fuzz."

chapter 9

Pink may have been the color for breakfast, but now the main
dining room had been transformed to pale yellow, from the ta-
blecloths to the maître d's jacket. Color motifs seemed important on board *The Atlantis*, and everything had been coordinated
with great care.

Jayne, Cass, and I were at 177, a round table with yellow
linen napkins folded like little hats and a small cut-glass vase
filled with tiny yellow roses. On either side of the heavy china
plates was enough silverware for a dozen courses. The table was
set for six, and we speculated as to who our eating companions
might be for the next three-and-a-half days. We would have
preferred to dine with the Sidney Sheldons or Michael Viners,
but we hadn't known they would be aboard until it was too late
to make such arrangements. Breakfast was open seating—
meaning we could graze at will—but table 177, First Seating,
was our assigned spot for the rest of the way to England.

We had already met Giorgio, the maître d', and Christophe
our waiter. When we'd first arrived in the dining room, Giorgio
had offered us a table by ourselves, but on an ocean voyage, you
might as well go whole hog; eating far too much in the company
of utter strangers is part of the tradition.

Scores of serving people walked about with almost military
precision, all in crisp light yellow jackets, black trousers, white

shirts, and black bow ties. The guests were a mixture of high-profile Hollywood and social, East-Coast-money types. I waved at a famous actress I knew, and then a television executive and a screenwriter. Jayne whispered that our son Bill, who is president of MTM studios, had just made a deal with the screenwriter, one of the hotter new talents in Hollywood. The story was to take place aboard an ocean liner, so this was undoubtedly a working vacation for the woman.

"I'm starved," I said, glancing through the menu choices for the five-course luncheon.

"It comes from spending such an energetic morning," Jayne said. "At least Cass learned how to tango." Cass had already demonstrated a few slinky steps as we'd waited for the elevator, and I had to put my hand on his arm to stop him from leaping up and showing us more now.

"By the way, I met my competition today," I said, to distract him.

"Another comedian?" Cass asked.

"No, another investigator, although not a private one."

"What's he doing aboard?" Jayne asked.

"Actually he has every right to be aboard; he's with the FBI."

"Have I met him?" Jayne quickly surveyed the other diners.

"I don't think so," I said. "His name is Lawrence Schwartz. So far I've only seen him wearing ill-fitting Bermuda shorts so I think of him as Bermuda Schwartz."

"Who was doing the interrogating in your little exchange?" Cass wanted to know.

"We both were," I admitted, "and neither of us came up with much. He wanted to know why I was talking to Dicky Wilmington."

"Why *were* you?" Jayne asked.

I was in the process of telling her and Cass my morning adventures when an elegant, single gentleman dressed in a well-cut gray suit and ascot arrived at our table. He appeared to be in his fifties, a trim fellow with graying hair and a mustache.

"How nice to see you," said Jayne in her best hostess voice. "I'm Jayne, this is my husband Steve, and our friend Cass."

The man made a helpless gesture with his hands. *"Je suis désolé, madame, mais je ne parle pas anglais."*

The Frenchman smiled politely, but I had a feeling he would not be a scintillating dinner companion; such is the luck of the draw on ocean crossings. I looked up expectantly as our other two dining companions stopped beside the table, tried to hold on to my smile as I saw the green eyes of Chelsea Eastman look at the number written on the little flag in its center, then at me, then back to the flag again, as though she could not quite believe her bad luck. "Here we are, Grandmother," she said in an exasperated voice. "With *these* people."

The Frenchman and I stood up to greet the older woman.

"You had that television show, didn't you?" she asked suspiciously after I introduced myself, Jayne, and Cass. I confessed to the crime. "Of course, I don't watch television much, except for 'Masterpiece Theater' and 'MacNeil/Lerher,'" she said quickly.

"You're fortunate," I said.

Her name was Gladys Moffet. I sensed the Moffets went way back and were wary of people who had television shows. Nevertheless, she appeared thrilled to meet Jayne, and as it turned out, "I've Got a Secret" was perhaps the one show she had enjoyed that was *not* on public television.

Chelsea seemed to be another matter entirely; unfortunately she took the vacant seat directly to my left.

"It was cute the way you slam-dunked Larry Goldman," I told her.

"You *are* in the habit of eavesdropping, aren't you?" she said.

"Not really, but sometimes you can't help hearing what others are saying."

"So why did you pretend to be reading *Anna Karenina?*" she asked.

"I wasn't pretending," I said. "And your noticing the title of my book suggests that you're not above a bit of observational intrusion yourself."

"Why do you read novels anyway? If they're good you can see the movie, and if they're not, you can avoid wasting a lot of time."

"I will assume your question arises from genuine curiosity. I read novels because I also write them, and I find I can learn a great deal from people who are better than I am, at any sort of task."

At that point her grandmother joined in the conversation, for which I was profoundly grateful. "I see you two have already met," she said.

I found myself with a growing respect for the old lady. To have a granddaughter like Chelsea Eastman, you would need nerves of steel.

Our waiter, Christophe, came by, and we all ordered. As I finished reciting my selections, I noticed the full Wilmington entourage sweep into the dining room. Gertrude led the charge, followed by Alexis, Candy L'Amour, Dicky, and a prim blond woman I guessed was Dicky's wife. The final member of the group was a tall, suntanned man with silver hair.

Gertrude moved through the dining room bosom-first, like a ship's bow breaking water. She ignored two film stars who tried to catch her attention, though I noticed she nodded primly to Tony Newley. When she was about a dozen feet from our table, she suddenly stopped and headed our way. I smiled in greeting, but she didn't seem to notice.

"Aunt Gladys!" she said to Gladys Moffet, giving the word *aunt* an upper-crust pronunciation. She kissed the old woman enthusiastically on the left cheek. "How nice to see you! And this must be little Chelsea."

"Little" Chelsea looked as if she'd like to push Mrs. Wilmington over the side. Meanwhile Gladys introduced Jayne, Cass, and me to the matriarch of the Wilmington family—it impressed me that she remembered our names—and the Frenchman stood and introduced himself. "Michel Duclerc," he said with Gallic charm. *"Enchanté, madame."*

"Are you staying in London long, Aunt Gladys?"

"No, dear. Chelsea and I will take a week to see some plays and then catch the Concorde back to New York. Chelsea has to be back in school, of course, and I hate to be away from my cats too long."

"Let's get together for a good chat. Call me later this afternoon—I'll leave word with the operator to put you through," Gertrude said. With a wave, she resumed her parade across the dining room.

It had been only a brief table-hop because the Wilmington entourage hovered nearby, blocking the progress of several waiters.

I found myself looking at Aunt Gladys with new respect. I wished now that I had listened more closely to Rusty's gossip and the genealogies she'd mentioned. "You must be a Baltimore McEagle?" I ventured.

"You mean the Philadelphia McEagles, perhaps?"

"Yes."

"No, I'm not. The family connection is on the Van Gelder side. My sister, Clara Van Gelder, was Gertrude's mother."

"Yes, now I remember. And how is Clara these days?"

"Dead sixteen years."

"Ah, well," I said, staring at my lobster appetizer that had just arrived. "I suppose you know old Marcus pretty well?"

"I shouldn't think anyone knows him terribly well. I went to the wedding, of course—'forty-two, I think it was. One of those war years. You'll never believe it now, but at the time we all thought he was marrying Gertrude for her money!"

I smiled encouragingly. "And now he's a billionaire several times over."

"Too much money," said Gladys with a frown. "It's bad taste."

"Well, as long as the family is happy."

"Ha! They hate each other. That's what too much money does to families."

"Perhaps you're right."

"One should have just the right amount of money," the old woman decreed.

"And the blond woman with Dicky Wilmington . . ."

"That's his wife Wendy. She's very social. I think she wishes Dicky had more drive."

"And the last man in their group? The one with the silver hair and Palm Springs tan?"

"Will Sanders. The family lawyer."

"I see. Probably a good idea to keep your lawyer handy."

"Well, he's the one who really runs things, you know. That is, when Marcus isn't around. The children aren't allowed to do much, though they have rather grand titles."

"Really? Doesn't Marcus get along with his children?"

"He thinks they're idiots. And he's right, of course. If it weren't for Gertrude's insistence they wouldn't be working for the company at all. She's gaga about her boys and wants them to have the best of everything."

"Then Gertrude and Marcus must have some terrible—"

"Areas of disagreement? I should say so! He's quite a bully, but she's not exactly a dormouse herself. Tough as nails! That's what we always used to say about Gertrude."

Grandma turned to the busboy to ask for a glass of water and then began speaking to Jayne. Meanwhile Chelsea was studying me in a disapproving way. "You wouldn't make a very good detective," she whispered.

"I beg your pardon?"

"It's so obvious you were pumping my grandmother for information."

"I thought I was being quite subtle."

"So why are you so interested?"

"Because you have a fascinating family," I said diplomatically. "Doesn't everyone ask you questions?"

"Yes, and it's boring."

"I find that the word *boring* is one of the most misused in our language. Generally when people say they're bored, they're really annoyed, perhaps even furious.

Chelsea pursed her lips in annoyance, but did not contest the point. "Well," she said, "I find both money and talking about it boring. Personally, I'm a socialist. When I get my inheritance, I'm giving most of it away to people who need it."

"Very commendable," I said.

It was an excellent lunch. I had only meant to have a bite or two of each course, but the plates had a way of emptying themselves before I remembered my resolution. Jayne, Cass, and Gladys Moffet got on well and began to tell each other stories about their childhoods—Jayne about China, Gladys upstate New York, and Cass Wyoming. Michel Duclerc smiled modestly from time to time and concentrated on his lunch.

As for Chelsea and myself, we reached a sort of truce. She was eating even more than I was, and I didn't know where she put it since she was girlishly trim. She kept calling the waiter over and batting her eyes at him, asking for more. "Oh, Christophe, do you think I could have a few rolls? And perhaps another plate of the Chicken Tangiers. And you know, Mr. Allen's salmon looks so scrumptious, I think I'll have some of that as well. It's okay to have three main courses, isn't it? Oh, Christophe, what a darling you are . . . and why don't you bring us *three* plates of cheese and crackers."

Christophe, I should mention, was a handsome young man with blond hair and a French accent. She had him running in circles, but he didn't seem to mind. Personally I was getting suspicious, and I soon saw where she was putting the extra food—in a large beach bag on the floor.

"You're very kind," I said, catching her at it.

She shrugged. "He'd be a good writer if he weren't so glib, especially about love and sex."

"I'm glad to note you make the distinction," I said.

"I don't believe in love anymore," she told me, seriously. "Anyway, I don't even know if I'll be able to find him to give him the food."

"Try lifeboat number nine," I suggested.

She grinned mischievously. "You're pretty hip for an older man."

That was a compliment. I guess. Since we were friends now, more or less, there was something I wanted to ask her. I had noticed a man sitting about five tables over who looked very much like the fellow I had seen arguing with Dicky Wilmington. Chelsea seemed to know a lot of people so I asked who he was.

"That's Peter Moon," she said. "The Wall Street lizard— wizard—whatever."

"Ah, yes, I didn't know what he looked like."

So that was one riddle solved. But what, I wondered, was Dicky doing having secret meetings with Peter Moon? And why was Bermuda Schwartz of the FBI so interested in their conversation?

When you're thinking about someone, sometimes that person is thinking about you. The psychologist Carl Jung called this synchronicity. Just as I was pushing away my desert Christophe slipped me a handwritten note. It was from Dicky.

Mr. Allen,
Sorry about earlier. I can't tell you the pressure I'm under. Please meet me at the smokestack after the lifeboat drill. Maybe you can help.

D.W.

After lunch, Jayne and I walked around the Promenade Deck to work off some of the calories. A dark cloud had crossed the sun, and the wind had picked up considerably. A storm was indeed on its way.

chapter 10

The phone by the bed woke me from my nap. The ocean breezes, the rocking of the ship, and a big lunch had made a midday siesta irresistible. Hell—inevitable. I was dreaming of something pleasant, but couldn't remember what it was as I shifted from one world to another and reached for the phone.

"Mmm," I said, yawning loudly into someone's ear.

"Sorry to wake you, Steve, but I thought you might like to get a load of— Whoa!"

"A load of whoa? What's whoa, Cass?"

"You'll see if you come down to the casino."

"How much did you lose?" I asked.

"It's not me. I'm ahead six and a half bucks. It's Candy L'Amour. She almost lost her shirt, literally. And I think we're about to have a fist fight between her admirers."

"Tell you what, Cass, you can tell me all about it at dinner. I'm going back to sleep."

"It's Alexis Wilmington and Peter Moon," Cass said. "They're really going at each other. . . . Holy cow, he just threw a drink in his face!"

"Who threw a drink in whose face?" I asked. "Never mind, I'll be right there."

Jayne, wearing earplugs and sleep mask, had stretched, rolled over in bed, and was apparently asleep again. I looked at her enviously as I hurriedly put on my clothes, patted down my mussed-up hair, and stepped into the hall. There was a new motion to the ship now. Earlier we had been rocking almost imperceptibly from bow to stern, but now we were yawing from side to side as well, in a somewhat sickening motion. I had to steady myself against the corridor wall a few times, and at one point an elderly woman and I did a little dance getting past each other.

"You'd think they'd *do* something about this motion," the woman complained.

"I'm sure they would like to, ma'am. But the ocean usually has the last word."

On the Upper Promenade Deck, I saw that the sky was now a patchwork of quickly moving dark clouds. The wind had picked up greatly, stirring the steel gray waves into whitecaps, and the sharp chill in the air made me wish I had put on a sweater. It was hard to believe this startling difference had occurred in just a few hours. This morning we might have been on a Caribbean cruise; now we could be headed to the North Pole.

I was contemplating the awesome power of wind and water when I heard a gunshot, not my favorite sound. I turned and walked quickly toward the point where the sound had seemed to originate. I heard a second report and a third in close succession, each louder than the last. I broke into a run. More shots rang out as I leaned over the rail and saw below a TV actor I knew shooting skeet from the lowest deck at the stern. I watched, feeling like a fool, while a crewman fed another disk into the machine and sent it flying.

"It's getting too windy, sir," I heard the crewman say. "We have to stop."

"Ah, just keep sending 'em up, son," the actor said. "I spent enough money to come on this tub, I should be able to do any damned thing I please!"

The actor, Tracy Devine, portrayed a detective on one of the gritty new cop shows, so perhaps he thought he had a natural right to play with guns. I left him blasting away at little flying plates and jogged down two flights of stairs to the casino. Except for the yawing motion of the deck, I might have been magically whisked to Las Vegas. There were the same neat rows of slot machines, with their cherries and oranges and eternal promises of free money. Bright lights flashed, colorful roulette wheels spun; it made losing money seem like fun. Tables of green felt shone in pools of light, and pretty waitresses in short skirts walked the aisles carrying drinks.

I passed the blackjack tables and a poker game. Cass was at a distant table with a Coke. I was heading his way when I saw Candy L'Amour. She was sitting at the bar in a tight silver dress, Alexis Wilmington on one side of her and Peter Moon on the other.

"No-o-o," I heard her whine in two octaves. "I don't wanna go. . . . I wanna stay and have fun."

"You heard her," Peter said. "The girl wants to play."

"Shut your bloody mouth!" Wilmington told him.

"Alex, you're not being very nice," Candy pouted.

I sat down with Cass. "What's up?"

"It's calmed down for the moment," he said. "Candy's drunk or stoned—or something. She started to do a sort of striptease. That caused a commotion! Alexis got her buttoned up quick, but Peter's been encouraging her to cut loose. When I was talking to ya on the phone, Alexis threw a margarita in Peter's face and they sorta danced around a bit looking like they were going to start slugging, but then they relaxed."

It was a sickening spectacle. Peter Moon, the Wall Street takeover artist, seemed to be doing his damnedest to take over Wilmington's girl. From up close, I could see that Moon was a thin man in his late thirties with a pale wolfish face, a thin mustache, and predatory eyes beneath the round glasses. I had a feeling he was just using Candy to prove to Alexis Wilmington that he could take whatever he wanted.

"You gotta do a show tonight, honey," Wilmington was telling the girl, in the sort of hopeful voice kindergarten teachers use on bad children. "Why don't you come back to the cabin and take a little nap?"

"I don't wanna go back to the cabin, Alex," she said. "And I don't wanna do the show tonight. I just wanna have fun."

"But you have to, honey. You agreed to do the show a month ago, remember? Everyone will be awfully disappointed if they can't hear you sing."

I won't, I wanted to say.

"Look, you're paying her nothing," Peter chimed in. "Candy's used to getting half a mil for concerts in stadiums. Isn't that right, sweetheart?"

"I got nearly a million in Tokyo," Candy said dreamily. "They really love me there."

"They love you everywhere," Peter assured her. "You don't need to play this boat, baby. Just let me take care of the details. I'll buy out your contract—if it's even valid."

"Look, Butthead, she's doing the show as a personal favor to the Wilmington family," Alexis said angrily. "Money's got nothing to do with it. So get lost, Moon."

"You get lost, sonny boy. Candy's bored with you. She's ready to play with the grownups now."

Wilmington turned red in the face and jumped on Peter Moon again, fists flailing. They tumbled over a barstool and landed on the floor—the deck at sea—where they kicked and pulled each other's hair and shouted every four-letter word they knew. Stewart Hoffman, the security man, entered the fray, doing his best to pry Moon and Wilmington apart; he had his hands full. Candy L'Amour, meanwhile, climbed up on the bar, and with a dreamy smile was about to strip to the old Beatles song that was playing over the PA system. To add to the general nonsense, I noticed the stowaway journalist sitting calmly across the room with a 35mm camera, taking picture after scandalous picture.

"Tell you what, Cass," I said. "You get the film from Goldman—tell him you'll turn him in to the captain if he doesn't hand it over. Meanwhile I'll do something about the girl."

"You always have all the fun," Cass complained.

It had been ages since I had seen a girl dance on a bar.

"Come on down here, Candy," I said from the deck.

"You come up here." She giggled.

"Naw, it's more fun on the floor."

"I don't wanna come down."

"Sure you do," I told her.

She bent over, hiccuping as she peered bleary-eyed into my face. "Hey, you're the TV guy." It was all I could do not to step back.

"That's right," I said. "I run a repair shop on Forty-seventh Street. We fix Sonys, Mitsubishis—"

Her response was an outburst of words once reserved for teamsters on strike, but since she sometimes addressed her adoring audiences in the same way, perhaps I should have considered myself flattered. Realizing that if our exchange escalated into an actual argument I could do very little to improve the situation, I said, "Listen, I have friends in high places, and if you come down from there like a good girl, I think I may be able to wangle a special citation for you on next year's Oscars."

"Oh, yeah? What citation?" she said.

"It's the Audrey Hepburn Award for Ladylike Behavior Under Stress," I said.

"Oh, I get it." She sneered. "I know your type—always making cracks about there bein' too much sex in the movies, but at night you're out lookin' for it." She bent even closer, hiccuped again. "Hey, how'd you like a little skeetledee-wheedledee right now?"

She made a vulgar gesture and did a wobbly impersonation of a burlesque dancer's bump.

"Now you're talkin'," I said. "But that means you're going to have to come down off the bar. I'm not an exhibitionist. And we'll have to lose the two chaps fighting over you."

"Yeah?"

"Yeah. Fighting's dumb. People should love one another."

"You know, that's my philosophy too. Where you wanna go?"

"How about my stateroom?"

"Yeah?" she giggled. "Well, okay. Let's take a bottle of champagne along."

"We'll order from room service," I said.

And so I found myself leading the platinum-blond pop "icon-arina" back to my cabin for fun and games and nostalgic conversation while Stewart Hoffman, with the help of the black bartender wrestled with Wilmington and Moon, and Cass unwound the film from Goldman's camera. You never know what's going to happen on an ocean voyage; that's part of the fun. As I guided Candy through the casino, a woman with a small Instamatic tried to take our picture, but I looked at her and said, "Don't even think about it." Fortunately the casino was not very crowded at that time of the afternoon.

In the elevator, Candy wrapped her arms around me, but I told her we had to be discreet or there might be a scandal. She giggled. I'm sure I wasn't her type if she could see straight, but seeing straight was not exactly her problem at the moment. She wasn't my type either, but I was sober enough to know it.

"What's your real name?" she said, making goo-goo eyes at me as we staggered down the corridor.

"Edgar Kennedy," I said, giving her the name of a film comic of the 1930s. "What's *your* name?"

"Candy L'Amour," she giggled.

"I know that. What's your *real* name?"

"Promise you won't tell anyone?"

I nodded.

"Bernice Esposito."

"And where did Bernice Esposito grow up?" I asked.

"South side of Chicago. Can't you tell?"

"Actually yes, I can."

Jayne was lounging in the sitting room, reading a book, as Miss L'Amour-Esposito and I more or less fell through the door together.

"Wow," my new companion said. "You got a chick here already. Edgar, you're somethin' else."

"Edgar?" Jayne asked.

"Yes," I said. "I'm sure you remember Edgar Kennedy, the funny man who used to do the slow burn?"

"Oh, wow," Candy said suddenly. "You're Jayne Mansfield!"

"I used to be," Jayne said.

"But now," I explained, "she's Jayne Meadows, and being the motherly type, she'll be glad to order some black coffee for you. You do have a show to do tonight, remember?"

But the coffee turned out to be unnecessary, for the party girl suddenly ran out of steam, dropped to the sofa, and immediately fell asleep.

"It's settled then," I said optimistically to Jayne. "Get her sobered up, maybe give her some coffee and a cold shower, and take off all that horrible makeup and reveal the real girl underneath. Then get her talking about herself and Wilmington. Find out all her secrets."

"What if there is no real girl underneath? Steve, I have other plans for the afternoon."

"You want me to give her the cold shower?" Jayne was a little exasperated, but I smiled nicely.

"All her secrets, you say? Her life story?" she said, warming to the task.

"No, that would be too sad," I said. "Just the past few months, and her connection with the Wilmington family."

"You're going to owe me, darling."

"And when you're bosom buddies, you might ask her why

everybody's feuding. She'll love to confide in you, Jayne. Everybody does."

"And where will you be while I'm doing your dirty work?"

"Talking to a Wall Street specialist, I hope, about a nasty takeover attempt."

chapter 11

Peter Moon was not at the casino bar when I returned. Nor was Alexis Wilmington, Stewart Hoffman, Cass, or Larry Goldman.

The gentlemanly bartender, recognizing me as the one who had spirited away the blond bombshell, evidently saw me as a man of great prowess to be back looking for more action so soon. Unfortunately he could not tell me where anyone had gone. I used a phone in the casino and asked the ship's operator to connect me with Peter Moon's cabin. The telephone rang and rang, but there was no answer. Then I dialed Cass's room. No answer there either.

I stepped outside, onto the aft deck and stood there pondering my options. *Boom!* A gunshot. Devine was still massacring skeet set in flight by a bored crewman. *Boom . . . Boom . . . Boom.* I was standing so close I *felt* the sound: percussive waves rattling my eardrums as if someone were hitting a bass kettle drum inside my head. It was beginning to get on my nerves. I walked toward the front of the ship, where people were engaged in more pleasing activities.

I wondered what Dicky Wilmington was going to say to me at our rendezvous after the lifeboat drill. His note had been somewhat melodramatic; I was starting to get a bad feeling. I even considered beeping the old man with the electronic device in my jacket pocket. But what would I tell him? Except for the weather turning bad, all my fears were vague. The other passengers, apparently having adjusted to the rocky seas, seemed to be having a postcard-lovely time: lounging in lounges, gaming in game rooms, shopping in shops.

I spent most of the next hour roaming the ship, looking for Peter Moon. I checked the library, the lounges, game rooms, salons, sun rooms, swimming pools, even the stores in the Galleria. The Wall Street whiz kid was nowhere in sight. I would have preferred to spend the afternoon doing something else. Old Marcus Wilmington, whatever one thought of him, at least had made his fortune building things—such as this very liner. The Peter Moons of the world did just the opposite. They made their money by tearing things apart, leaving broken companies and huge debts behind, as well as a lot of unemployed people. I couldn't believe Moon was taking this cruise for his health; I wanted to know what he was up to.

I was deep in suspicious thoughts when bells went off around the ship and the horn began to sound in long, urgent bursts. I figured we were on fire or were sinking, or maybe both. Then I looked at my watch and realized it was only the four-o'clock lifeboat drill. I made my way back toward our suite, passing people with bright orange vests around their chests. Entering our sitting room, I was surprised to see a strange, dark-haired young woman wearing one of Jayne's silk robes. She was skinny, quite plain, and had a bad complexion; it took me several heartbeats to realize that this was the glamorous Candy L'Amour, teen idol and sex goddess, *sans* makeup and wig. At the moment she was drinking coffee and chewing her nails.

"How are you feeling?"

"A little shaky, but okay. Your wife's a good egg."

"One of the goodest," I said. At just that moment Jayne came into the sitting room from the bedroom, carrying his and hers life vests in glow-in-the-dark orange. She put hers on. She's the only person I know who can make a life vest look like the latest fashion statement from Rodeo Drive. From the way

Candy was looking at her with puppy-dog adoration, I could tell they had had a good heart-to-heart.

"We'll walk you back to your cabin so you can get your life vest, too," she said to Candy. "Then we'll go to the drill together."

"If it's all right, Jayne, I'll just hide out here for a little while and sleep."

"Dear, you really should go to the drill. It's obligatory, you know."

"I can't let people see me like this! You can tell me about it later. I'm sure *The Atlantis* isn't going to sink right away."

"Okay," Jayne said. "But do get some sleep."

"I will."

Jayne gave me my vest, and we headed to the drill.

"Well?" I asked in the corridor. "Have a good chat?"

"Oh, Steve, I'm so glad you're not a rock star. That business eats people alive. The poor girl doesn't know whether she's coming or going."

"I'd feel sorry for her if she had any real talent or originality."

"But that's what's so sad! She knows she doesn't, though she can't quite admit it. She's just a pathetic, lonely young woman who happened to be at the right place at the right time. Only none of it turned out to be right at all. A lot of people have used her to get rich. That's why she was so attracted to the Wilmington family."

"Now you've lost me."

We had arrived on the Lower Promenade Deck where lifeboats were dangling above our heads, held in place by pulleys and winches, ready to carry us into the cold sea were this a real emergency. Hundreds of passengers were milling about in their orange vests, everyone looking a bit self-conscious, like kids on their first day at a new school. Jayne and I headed toward lifeboat number nine.

"You have to imagine the Wilmington family from Candy's point of view," Jayne continued. "They're classy, solid, secure.

Not at all like the show-biz people she knows. Candy thought she'd found a safe harbor."

"Safe like Normandy Beach on D-Day," I suggested, not as ready as Jayne to buy this "poor Candy" line. "And what does she think about the Wilmingtons now?"

"She's disillusioned."

"Well, she can always go back to her trendy Hollywood crowd."

"She's confused, Steve. But she thinks she's in love with Alex."

I grinned. "That was not entirely apparent when I last saw her dancing on the bar for Peter Moon."

At lifeboat number nine, Jayne and I were separated. People were grouped according to sex and age. On this luxury liner it was still women and children first. I stood in the back with the guys, while Jayne went up closer to the rail with the women and small fry, and found myself standing next to Monsieur Duclerc.

"*Comment ça va, monsieur?*" I asked, quickly using up most of my French vocabulary.

"*Ça va bien, merci,*" he answered. "*Et vous?*"

"I'm having a bon voyage so far," I ventured. But he only looked at me as though I were a little *fou*. Crazy, that is.

Cass came running up, out of breath.

"Whew," he said. "I thought this boat was going to sink without me."

"Let's hope not." I was going to ask him how the brouhaha in the casino had ended, but it was time to pay attention to the drill.

One of the crew members began to address us, a ruddy-faced, redheaded officer with clipboard in hand. "Ladies and gentlemen, you are standing at life station number nine," he said patiently. "Your correct life station number is posted on your cabin door. Does everyone here *belong* at life station number nine?"

There were two lost souls—a youngish couple—who were

supposed to be at life station thirteen, which was around the bend on the starboard side of the ship. They went off looking a bit mortified and the redheaded officer began to call roll. One of the good things about being an Allen is you get through your part early on. There was only one other person ahead of me and that was my wife.

"Allen, Jayne Meadows . . ."

"Here I am."

"Allen, Steve . . ."

"Present."

"Ardeman, William . . ."

"Here."

And so it went. . . .

Fifty-five of us were supposed to fit into lifeboat number nine should the worst happen. This seemed crowded to me, but I supposed if *The Atlantis* were sinking none of us would care about luxury accommodations. The names droned on. Some of the passengers tried to be clever and answer with things like "Aye aye, sir" when they were called, but most responded with a simple "Here."

"Lawrensen, Ernie . . ."

"Yo."

"Lawrensen, Sandra . . ."

"Me too."

"Moon, Peter . . ."

There was no response to the name. In the quiet I heard the boom of a gunshot, but it was not close and none of us thought much about it since we'd been hearing the explosions all afternoon.

"Moon, Peter . . . Has anyone seen Mr. Moon? No?"

"Where's Moon?" I whispered to Cass.

"I don't know. Last I saw he was leaving the casino in a lousy mood."

"Quiet back there, please," said the officer mildly. Cass and I looked properly chastised. When the roll call was completed, the officer went on to explain how to don and use our life vests, and where we could find our individual whistles in them and even the little light bulbs that were supposed to turn on automatically in water. We learned that it was "highly unlikely" we would ever need such gadgetry, but international regulations required a drill within the first twenty-four hours of any ocean voyage. At the end of his speech, the officer solicited questions.

"What's happening with the weather?" someone asked, a good question since the sky was still steel gray, the same color as the ocean, and the wind continued brisk.

"There's a bit of a front coming through," the officer admitted cheerfully. "But we're hoping to miss the worst of it."

"Will it get rough?" someone else asked.

"Not at all. If the seas pick up, the captain will use the stabilizers—those are fins below the water line that keep us from rocking too much. Or perhaps we'll alter course a bit. Any other questions?"

I had a feeling the officer was not telling everything he knew, but presumably he had orders not to alarm us. At last he bade us good day, and the group dispersed. Cass and I wandered toward Jayne, who was talking to the skeet-shooting Tracy Devine I had noticed earlier at station number eight. He had walked over to say hello.

I had a nagging feeling that something was wrong with this. Then it came to me. If the gun-happy actor had been at the drill, who had fired the gun I had just heard? All passengers were required to attend drills, so activities had been shut down for the half-hour; even the casino had been closed.

So who'd been shooting skeet out of season? And then I remembered something else: the blast I had heard had not come from the same direction as the earlier ones. Sound waves can be confusing, but I could swear that the last gunshot had come from somewhere above.

Jayne, Cass, Tracy, and I were standing in a small circle by the side of the ship. The actor was telling us an anecdote, but I wasn't listening. The bad feeling had crystallized into an even worse image.

"Cass," I said, "come with me."

Jayne shot us a questioning look as I jogged up a flight of steps to the deck overhead, Cass grousing that I should slow down. One deck up, I broke into a run over the polished wood, moving quickly toward the midsection of the ship and then up two more flights of stairs to the small deck by the rear smokestack. Cass was huffing and was several dozen paces behind me when I arrived at the site of my rendezvous with Dicky Wilmington.

He had gotten there first, but being the early bird had not brought him any luck. The deck was slippery and dark red . . . as if wine had been spilled on the polished wood. But I knew it was blood. Marcus Wilmington's oldest son was sprawled against the smokestack, his head hanging cockeyed on his chest—or what was left of it. The midsection of his body had been destroyed by a close-range shotgun blast. I noticed that his right foot was bare, which seemed strange. But the sight was too much for me to take in for more than a moment or for my brain to comprehend all at once.

Feeling sick, I turned away, faced the stormy ocean. I kicked something as I stepped toward the rail. It was a pack of *Atlantis* matches. I bent over without thinking and put them in my pocket. I don't know why I did that, except that I hate to see litter. I was like a sleepwalker, hardly aware of what I was doing. But as I slipped the matchbook into my pocket I felt the old man's beeper. This woke me from my stupor, and I knew it was time to call in the cavalry.

I had never looked closely at the device before, and it did not appear particularly impressive: just a single red button set in cheap black plastic. As I held it in my trembling hand and looked at the vastness of the ocean in front of me and felt the ugliness of death behind me, it seemed absurd to imagine that this little button was going to do any good, but I pushed it anyway. I pushed it so hard the plastic box fell apart in my hand. I stared at the broken pieces and started to laugh. A "sophisticated" electronic device, old man Marcus Wilmington had told me. But he had lied. It was only a piece of cheap junk.

I wondered what other lies the man had told me as I tossed the plastic pieces into the gray waves below. It was a foolish gesture, and I later regretted it, but I was beginning to get angry.

chapter 12

Captain James R. Mellon was a mild-mannered fellow with short graying hair getting sparse on top, wire-rimmed spectacles, and a rather high voice. Had it not been for his erect posture and crisp white uniform with officer's epaulets, one might have taken him for a high-school biology teacher or a dentist rather than someone responsible for several thousand lives. He nodded his head at me and said mildly, "I see . . . and then what happened?"

"That's pretty much it," I told him. We had been going over the same ground for several minutes. "I found a crew member and told him what I'd seen."

The captain sighed. With a storm coming, I imagine he wished his employer's older son had found a more convenient time and place to die. We were sitting around a long table in a small conference room just off the bridge, the working part of the ship that passengers normally do not see. There were maps and charts on the walls and a coffee urn on a side table. Everything was clean, modern and functional, but the luxuriousness of the passengers' quarters was lacking here. From somewhere down the hall, I could hear the rhythmic dots and dashes of Morse code coming in on a radio. *The Atlantis* was pitching and yawing in the heavy seas now, and outside the gray sky had darkened to a premature night.

The captain was at the head of the table. To his left sat a young officer taking notes. Then in clockwise order were Cass, myself, Stewart Hoffman, FBI Agent Schwartz, and Will Sanders, the Wilmington's attorney. The captain had first turn at me, but it was obvious that the others were waiting impatiently to get their chance.

Captain Mellon had had me run through how I came to find Wilmington dead, then had asked Cass to add his version of events. The captain was thorough, but it was obvious he was not an experienced investigator.

Schwartz cleared his throat. "Captain, if you're finished . . ."

"Certainly, Agent Schwartz."

The FBI man turned an unfriendly stare on me. Earlier in the morning, he had been a vaguely comical and out-of-place figure in his Bermuda shorts and sports shirt, but now, dressed in neat gray suit, he didn't look funny at all. He just looked like a cop. His voice was languid, almost sleepy, but his slightly bulging eyes were predatory.

"Mr. Allen, when did you first meet Richard Wilmington?"

"It was in Los Angeles, a few months ago. He invited me to lunch at the Polo Lounge to discuss my performance on the boat."

"Your performance? Was Mr. Wilmington familiar with theatrical matters?"

"Not that I know of," I said.

"Couldn't such an exchange have been handled through a simple phone call to your agent?"

"It already had been actually. I suppose Wilmington just wanted to have lunch with me to become better acquainted. It was his idea that we get together."

"And what did you two talk about?"

"Oh, we discussed the sort of show I do. I explained that I have never done the same show twice because I answer actual questions written by people in the audience. I think the subject of my piano-playing also came up. I might have asked him who led the ship's orchestra, so my office would know who to send the musical arrangements to. Just things of that sort."

"He had come to Los Angeles just to see you?"

"No. He indicated he had other business in town. We soon drifted into small talk."

"Just kind of shootin' the old bull, eh?" Schwartz's tone did not disguise his disbelief. "And when did you see him again?"

"Last night, on board the ship."

"Doesn't it seem strange that someone you hardly knew would send you a note asking to discuss apparently quite intimate matters? He asked you to meet him on the upper deck by the smokestack at four o'clock, you say?"

"After the lifeboat drill, yes. As I told the captain."

"Well, you can tell *me* now, sir. Do you have this so-called note, by the way?"

"Why do you say 'so-called note'?" I knew my voice was sharp, but I didn't like the man's manner.

"Just show me the note, please."

"I don't have it on me. It must be back in my cabin—if I didn't throw it away."

"You're telling me you threw away a vital piece of evidence?"

"Agent Schwartz, at the time no crime had been committed and it was *not* a vital piece of anything. Once I'd read it, it was just a scrap of paper. I'm not in the habit of keeping every piece of paper handed to me."

"In other words," Schwartz said, "you can not actually prove that Mr. Wilmington sent a note requesting to see you. For all we know, you could have found him walking on the upper deck, shot him, and then thrown the weapon into the ocean."

"For all you know," I said, mimicking his tone, "I could be an alien from outer space simply pretending to be a television comedian and looking for a way to get my name into the *National Enquirer*. If you want to talk nonsense, I'll be glad to produce an unlimited supply."

"Mr. Allen," Schwartz said, his voice not rising at all, though mine had, "we're conducting a serious investigation here."

"Good for you," I said. "But may I suggest that you stop throwing out farfetched theories and stick to digging up the facts?"

Will Sanders broke in. "Mr. Schwartz, with all due respect, I don't think suggesting Mr. Allen might be the murderer is going to get us anywhere."

"And besides," Cass cut in, "I saw the note. It all happened just like Steve said."

"You work for Mr. Allen, don't you?" Schwartz said.

Cass, the Wyoming cowboy, reddened at Schwartz's implication. "Hey, listen, Schwartz, if this is a case of good cop/bad cop, I think it's time to bring in the good one."

Sanders held up a hand. He had an aging Ivy Leaguer's charm. I could imagine him as the conciliatory voice at many a board meeting. A distinguished-looking man, he had a lanky body and a pleasant smile; his silver hair grew over his ears and collar in a school-boyish way, and he wore his clothes well—at the moment a tan suit with a button-down blue shirt and wide, yellow paisley tie.

"Let's try to keep this amicable, sir," the attorney said.

Schwartz, to my surprise, flashed me the barest suggestion of a smile. "I'm only trying to establish the facts," he said. "Sometimes it helps to throw witnesses—or suspects—off guard." At this he reached in the pocket of his jacket and withdrew a cigar. "Anyone mind if I smoke?"

We all minded strenuously. Fortunately the captain backed us up.

Schwartz put away his cigar, looking mournful. "Now, Mr. Allen," he said, "I have a witness who saw you leave the Cafe Cabaña last night in the company of Richard Wilmington. You were just going off somewhere to discuss . . . what?"

"He was taking me to see his father."

Schwartz's eyes widened. "The old man? I understood he never sees anybody."

"I know," I said, somewhat wearily. "Compared to Wilmington, Howard Hughes was as accessible as Richard Simmons. Nevertheless, I did see the man."

"On board this vessel?"

"Of course not."

"Then how?"

"I went in a helicopter," I said, feeling a bit foolish.

"A helicopter," Schwartz said. "Forgive me for sounding skeptical, but you have to admit that sounds pretty farfetched."

"The entire history of Western civilization sounds farfetched," I said. "I didn't say I had reservations or plans of any kind. I was simply transported in a helicopter, which took off from an upper deck, to some big estate—I was blind-folded so I can't tell you where. But I spent about thirty minutes with Marcus Wilmington."

"Really . . ." Schwartz said, with a half-sneer.

"For God's sake, we're wasting time here. If you don't believe me, ask Mr. Hoffman. He set the whole thing up."

Schwartz turned to Hoffman, who had been silent thus far.

"Well, Mr. Hoffman," the special agent said, "*now* we're getting some place. Did you, in fact, go with Mr. Allen in a helicopter to some country estate to meet old Mr. Wilmington?"

Stewart Hoffman answered quietly, but his words shook my world worse than any earthquake.

"No," he said calmly, "I did not." He sounded like the epitome of sanity and reason. I almost believed him myself.

chapter 13

For a moment I was speechless, which is unlike me. "Hoffman," I said at last, trying to be calm, "why the hell are you lying about this?" In my semipanic I had a foolish impulse to say there was a witness to my abduction . . . but then I remembered the witness was now dead.

Hoffman turned his cold, blue-gray eyes in my direction and moved his arm slightly, so that the shoulder holster beneath his dark suit was not altogether concealed.

"Everybody knows no one sees Marcus Wilmington," he said tonelessly. "I've never met him myself."

"So you are saying you did *not* take Mr. Allen to him last night?" Schwartz repeated.

"That's what I'm saying."

I was baffled by Hoffman's lie and stared at him angrily, but his gaze was impassive.

"This is ridiculous," I muttered as I turned to the captain. "Surely *you* must have seen the helicopter take off or return?"

The captain seemed uncomfortable. "Well, there were several helicopters coming and going last night. That's how a number of passengers arrived," he said. "But I'm sure the authorities will look into all these questions in more detail when we get to England. At the moment I'm simply trying to establish the facts in an informal way, and I can't see how your meeting or not meeting Mr. Wilmington is relevant. By the way, Will, have you informed the old man about the death of his son?"

"Of course. I telephoned Mr. Wilmington as soon as I heard," the attorney said. "Naturally he was very upset."

"You *telephoned* him?" Schwartz asked, turning his attention to Sanders. "That means you have a phone number for the guy."

"Of course. I'm his attorney."

"I see. And would you give me this number?"

"I'm afraid I can't do that. Privileged information and all that."

"Great. I suppose I'll have to get a court order to talk to the man."

"You can try," Sanders said mildly. "Meanwhile he asked us to do whatever possible to find out who killed his son, provided we do it quietly so as not to upset the passengers."

"And how do you propose to do that?" Schwartz asked.

"By keeping them in a state of ignorance, of course. There's no reason for them to know there's been a murder on board. It could cause unnecessary panic." The attorney flashed his best Ivy League smile, which narrowed his eyes to slits.

"I'm not sure we can keep this hushed up," the captain said. "What do you think, Stewart?"

"Sure we can," Hoffman answered. "At least enough to keep it from disrupting the voyage. We sealed off the area immediately. A few passengers might have gotten a glimpse of the body, but we can put out a rumor that the death was accidental, by gunshot."

"Good idea," Sanders said. "People will find out the truth eventually, but it's vital that our passengers have the best possible time during these three days at sea."

"Meanwhile there's a killer loose on board," I reminded everybody.

"All the more reason that no one panics," Sanders said smoothly.

"I agree," the captain said. "The weather's going to cause enough concern without people worrying about a murderer lurking under the bed." He turned to Hoffman. "You really think you can keep a lid on this?"

"I'll tell the cabin stewards and head waiters to tell just a few people, confidentially, that Wilmington died accidentally. It'll start just the sort of rumor we want."

"Where's the body now?" I asked.

The captain gave me a wary look. "Mr. Allen," he said, "all major ocean-going vessels have the ability to preserve the bodies of passengers who die at sea. We keep them in a freezer compartment prepared especially for that purpose."

"Really," I said.

Schwartz cleared his throat. "Maybe we can get back to Mr. Allen's story," he suggested. "There are a lot of things here that don't add up."

"Like what?" I said.

"Like why you were spying on Richard Wilmington this morning."

"Spying!" I cried. *"You* were the one who was spying, sir— and not doing a very good job of it, if I may say so."

"Gentlemen, please," said the captain wearily.

The meeting was breaking down into bickering. I'm not certain where it would have gone had we not been interrupted by Gertrude Wilmington, who came into the room looking very aristocratic in a gray cashmere dress, a string of pearls around her neck.

"I heard there was some trouble," she said. "And I got a message to come to the bridge."

I was surprised that she had not yet been told about her son's death. But she was so imposing perhaps no one had found the nerve. I felt unhappy about the coming scene and noticed that the others, too, did not dare to look at her.

"Won't you have a seat, Gertrude?" Sanders offered kindly,

but she seemed to sense something ominous in our collective embarrassment and remained standing.

"Tell me what has happened." She spoke in an imperious tone that tolerated no contradiction.

"Well, it's sad news," Will admitted, rubbing the back of his neck.

"Tell me," she commanded.

"Mr. Allen, perhaps you'd best tell Gertrude exactly what happened, since you were there."

I was dumbfounded that Sanders passed the buck, and to me. After all, I hardly knew Gertrude Wilmington, or her dead son for that matter. But the woman was studying me gravely and I didn't want to add to her distress by keeping her in suspense any longer.

"There's really no kind way to say this, Mrs. Wilmington. Your son is dead."

"Alexis?" she cried.

"No. . . ."

"Oh, no . . . Dicky!"

"Yes. He's been shot."

She had turned away from me and was facing Sanders.

"Will," she whispered. "How did this happen?"

Under her gaze, the attorney lost most of his New England poise. "Gertrude, you must calm yourself. We don't know how it happened yet, but we'll find out. It might have been an accident. You know how badly—I feel terrible about this, Gertrude. Perhaps if you sit down . . . Does anyone have a bottle of brandy?"

While Sanders babbled, I heard a noise I couldn't at first identify, a sort of low moan that seemed to be coming from the room itself. Then I realized it was coming from Gertrude Wilmington, though her lips were closed. The unbearable sound seemed to well up from the deepest part of her, rising in volume and pitch until it was a wail. I had never heard a sound so horrifying. It rose to a kind of breaking point until it turned into a scream. Then the stunned mother seemed to go wild. She began tearing at her clothes and hair. She ripped the pearls from her neck and sent them scattering across the room. Captain Mellon and Sanders were immediately at her side, holding her hands to keep her from doing any damage to herself. I was surprised at this intense, primitive show of grief; the woman had always seemed so prim and impenetrably Brahmin. I was deeply moved and wished I knew something comforting to say, but wisely said nothing.

Sanders got her to sit down while Hoffman picked up a telephone and called the ship's doctor. Even Agent Schwartz was unnerved. He was scurrying about, looking for some water to give her.

Cass and I felt out of place in the context of such intimate agony. I gestured toward the door, and we took our leave. Gertrude Wilmington's pitiful screams followed us from the bridge. We went on deck to get some air, but had to duck inside fast because the first rain of the storm was coming down in hard, pelting drops.

chapter 14

Rusty O'Conner spotted us in the reception area outside the dining room as Jayne, Cass, and I arrived for the first seating. We pretended not to see her, but she lowered her head and charged our way, nearly trampling a young couple in her path. She was wearing a shimmery black, off-the-shoulder dress that showed a lot of leg—and lots of diamonds. She spoke in an ecstatic whisper.

"Did you hear about Dicky Wilmington?" she gulped. "He's dead, poor darling!"

"Really? How did it happen?" I asked innocently.

"It was a terrible accident—he slipped on the stairs coming down from the top deck. You can imagine why they're trying to cover it up! Bad publicity."

"But how did *you* manage to find out, Rusty?" I asked.

"My steward, Leonard," she whispered happily. "He made me promise not to tell anyone."

"Then perhaps you'd better not," Jayne said sternly.

"Oh, I wouldn't think of it!" Rusty said, scurrying off to friends—some elegant people from Santa Barbara—to give them the shocking news of Dicky Wilmington's "accident." I saw that one of the women she was hailing was Beverley Jackson, a journalist with whom, in the mid-seventies, Jayne and I had made a fascinating trip to China.

Catching my eye, Beverley pantomimed a sort of hi-love-'n-see-you-later message.

"I guess they call that 'damage control,' " Cass observed, stepping from behind the potted palm he had used as conceal-ment from Rusty.

As we made our entrance into the dining room people turned briefly our way, admiring Jayne's red silk Yves St. Laurent gown that went so nicely with her hair, and I was surprised, after the horror of Dicky Wilmington's death, to see life going on as usual. The women were dressed in elegant gowns and wore jewelry, the men had on well-tailored suits or dinner jack-ets. Among this well-turned-out crowd waiters bustled about, carrying great trays of food with acrobatic derring-do, while the maître d' smiled and bowed, and busboys filled glasses with ice water. All was as it should be. Except for the weather. The ship was heaving noticeably, and some chairs were empty. A few passengers apparently had succumbed to the scourge of ocean travel.

Monsieur Duclerc was at our table munching on a bread stick when we arrived. There was no sign yet of Chelsea or her grandmother. Duclerc rose politely as we approached, and Jayne surprised me by carrying on a brief conversation with him in French. Then I remembered that she had lived in Paris for several months long before we'd met.

At one point, lapsing into English, Jayne said, "Did . . . you . . . have . . . a . . . nice . . . day?" As if slowness would help.

The Frenchman shrugged helplessly.

"A . . . bon . . . jour?"

"Ah, oui!" he cried. "Bonjour!"

Christophe, our waiter, handed out the night's menu, but I was not particularly hungry. Jayne went along with the vegetar-ian fare I ordered, though I had spared her the knowledge of what was in the meat locker. Only Cass went whole hog—all five courses with beef Wellington in a special béarnaise sauce as the main event. It would take more than stormy seas and a gruesome murder to dampen the old cowboy's appetite.

Peter Moon, I noticed, was not at his table. Neither was the Wilmington entourage at theirs. Nor was there any sign of Candy L'Amour, but of course she was probably getting ready for her show later in the evening.

"Well, gang," I said after our waiter walked away, "I believe it's time for us to get organized and do a bit of detecting."

"You don't think we should leave this to the authorities?" asked Jayne with a twinkle in her eye, since she knew I wouldn't.

"What authorities?" I cried. "Stewart Hoffman? He's a damned liar. Bermuda Schwartz? Scotland Yard? They'll be all over us once we reach England, but that's not for three more days. Meanwhile there's a killer on this ship, and I have a very personal interest in finding him. Or her. I can't help thinking Dicky was going to tell me something important—and that's what got him killed."

I glanced at Monsieur Duclerc to see if he was following any of our conversation, but he was tasting an avocado prawn cocktail with an abstracted air of pleasure; I went on.

"We'll have to find out what Wilmington was up to. Somehow I think Peter Moon will know, and I'd say it's suspicious that Mr. Moon has been absent since before the life drill."

"Do you think Moon could have killed Dicky?" Cass asked.

"Why not? He and Wilmington were obviously in collusion about something. Remember Marcus's complaint about leaks to the press? Dicky could have been working with Moon to destabilize the family business so it was ripe for a takeover."

"But why would Dicky work against his own father?" Jayne asked.

"Perhaps because he wasn't getting any respect from the old man. His father wouldn't even see him for the last year and a half. A smart operator like Moon could flatter Dicky a little and easily bring him around to playing the traitor. Maybe that's what got him killed."

"H'mmm," said Cass. He had just polished off his first course—grilled salmon with a cucumber-dill sauce. "If what you're saying is true, Steve, then the killer could be someone in the Wilmington family."

"Yes, but doesn't have to be. It could be Stewart Hoffman, say. Or even Sanders, the family lawyer—someone who was supposedly protecting the family's interests."

"My nominee would be Hoffman," Jayne said. "He gives me the creeps."

"A lot of people could have done it," I went on. "This ship is a small city. There are twenty-one hundred and thirteen passengers on board, and nearly eight hundred crew members. I read that in the brochure while you were getting ready for dinner. So it'll take some narrowing down. It's fortunate we had the lifeboat drill."

"Why's that?" asked Cass.

"Everyone who was there had his or her name checked off a list. Anyone at the lifeboat drill has an alibi."

Cass broke a roll apart and began to smear it with butter. "You know, Steve, I don't want to be a wet blanket. . . ."

"Go ahead, Cass."

"It's just . . . well, it would be easy for someone who wasn't at the drill to have another person cover for him. All someone had to do was say aye twice. People really didn't know each other, and in that crowd who would notice?"

Cass was right, and there was another hitch, most of the crew members had not been part of the drill. Any one of those could have killed Wilmington while the rest of us were standing in our orange vests beneath the lifeboats. In other words, the possibilities were endless.

"I think we'll need to separate so we can cover more ground," I said. Crimes were often solved by patiently following leads and eliminating possibilities. This was not easy to do without the resources of a police force at one's disposal. During the soup course and the salad, I suggested ways we could organize what resources we had.

I asked Jayne to talk with Candy L'Amour at the first opportunity. We had to know the mysterious inner workings of the Wilmington family, and as Alex's fiancée, the young singer probably knew a lot. Following the same strategy, I also asked Jayne to approach Dicky's widow, Wendy Wilmington, the cool blond we had seen at lunch. I hoped she would have some ideas about what had happened. If she would talk . . .

I suggested that Cass concentrate, for the time being, on the murder weapon. There was a good chance it was the gun used for skeet. As far as I knew, the weapon had not been found. It probably had been dropped overboard, along with any other vital evidence that might point to the killer. In that case, the ocean would hide the secret forever.

I wanted Cass to question the crew member in charge of the skeet shooting and to learn where the shotguns were kept, who had access to them, and if any of the weapons were missing. After that, Cass could cozy up with any crew members he managed to befriend and could try to learn of anything unusual going on. He had a way of getting bartenders and busboys talking, so I was hoping he might be able to get a sense of what was happening behind the scenes on *The Atlantis.*

"And you, Sherlock? What will you be up to?" Jayne asked.

"I'm going to find Peter Moon. The great Wall Street takeover artist is in this up to his John Lennon glasses, and I'd like to find out how. Then I'm going to have some serious conversations with Will Sanders and Stewart Hoffman about their reclusive employer. I want to know why I was taken on that dumb helicopter ride last night, and why Hoffman lied about it this afternoon. All in all, I'd say there are enough mysteries here to keep us going for several voyages."

chapter 15

We were halfway through dinner when Chelsea Eastman arrived unexpectedly. To our surprise, she was accompanied not by her grandmother but by Larry Goldman, who was proving to be a rather bold stowaway. Chelsea, who was wearing a burgundy-colored knit dress bisected by Tibetan beads that served as a belt, seemed a little out of breath. Larry had on his only outfit, a shapeless sports coat and baggy pants, and there was a hungry look in his eyes. At least he had shaved. I wondered what sort of bathing facilities he had in lifeboat number nine.

"Damn! Have we missed dinner?" Chelsea asked as she and Larry sat down.

"I'm sure you can still get something," Jayne replied. "Where's your grandmother tonight?"

"Flat on her back in our stateroom, vowing never to travel by sea again. Personally, I think a storm's exciting. Don't you?"

"I hope not *too* exciting," Jayne said.

"I hope it rains and rains, with lots of lightning and thunder. I love nature," Chelsea said enthusiastically.

Larry reached for the bread basket and butter and began to stuff himself. I wondered how our waiter would react to his sitting in for Grandma. But Christophe approached as politely as ever and gave them both menus. It's amazing what you can get away with if you're bold enough. Larry Goldman was. He did not act like a stowaway. He ordered escargots, the cream of spinach soup, hearts of palm salad, and two main courses—the beef Wellington and broiled lobster tails with drawn butter.

Then the wine steward came over, and Goldman requested a good bottle of French bordeaux.

"How's the lifeboat?" I asked.

"I've moved," he said. The escargots had arrived, and he swallowed them down one after another.

"Did you find an empty stateroom, perhaps?"

"I wish! I found an empty storage room. It's all the way down on F Deck. Not exactly luxurious accommodations, but it'll do."

"Listen, Larry, I hate to bring this up, but aren't you going to have some trouble disembarking in Southampton?"

"Absolutely. The bobbies will probably throw my butt in jail," he said cheerfully.

"That doesn't bother you?" I asked.

"Not as long as I can write about it. I'm going to do my entire piece on *The Atlantis* from a stowaway's perspective. If they throw me in jail in England, it'll make a great ending. No matter how it turns out, I can't lose."

"I wish exciting things like that would happen to me," said Chelsea.

"You gotta *make* 'em happen, kiddo," Larry declared, attacking his soup. "Journalism is not for the faint of heart."

"Not these days certainly," I said.

"Christophe! Do you think I could have another order of snails?" Larry asked.

"Certainly, sir."

"And how *is* your article coming along?" Jayne politely entered the conversation. She would converse with an elephant escaped from the circus should one find itself at our table.

"Great," he said. He lowered his voice. "I got an exclusive interview with Mudgie this afternoon."

"Remarkable! But I'm surprised she consented," said Jayne.

"She didn't know she was consenting," the journalist said with a grin.

"What do you mean?" I asked.

Larry took a very small cassette player and headphones from his sports jacket pocket. It was the sort joggers use to listen to music as they trot about.

"See this?" he said. "It looks like an ordinary cassette player, right? . . . Wrong! It's a listening device. These things were developed by the CIA, but you can order them from catalogs these days. It has a very powerful directional microphone; point it across a crowded room, and you can listen in on any conversation. I zeroed in on Mudgie and that Captain Doodie guy while they were having tea this afternoon in the Cafe Cabaña. Man, did I get some great stuff! They were talking all sorts— Well, perhaps I shouldn't say."

"But you're not going to print that," Jayne said with a pleasant but firm manner. "It would be taking unfair advantage."

"Unfair advantage?!" Larry nearly choked on a snail. "Hey, all's fair in love, war, and journalism!"

"No, it isn't," Jayne said.

"You're nice, Miss Meadows, but kind of old-fashioned," Goldman said. The wine he'd ordered had arrived, and he was in a good mood. Too good to be put off by old-fashioned scruples. I have to admit that I stared at his listening device with some envy. Mudgie and Doodie could have all the private conversations they liked as far as I was concerned, but I would have enjoyed using Goldman's gadget when Peter Moon and Dicky Wilmington were going at each other.

"Say, what's this I heard about someone getting killed today?" he asked me, narrowing his eyes. "I should know about that."

"It's a complete mystery to me," I answered.

"I wonder who I can ask," he said thoughtfully.

"Try Rusty O'Conner," I told him.

"That's the ex-wife of that actor, isn't it? What's his name?"

"Exactly. She's has the lowdown on everything."

"Thanks. That's a good idea. I'll look for her. By the way, do you know who got killed?"

"Not really," I said vaguely.

"I saw Peter Moon this afternoon, and he looked so pale I thought *he* was a ghost!"

"Is that so?" I tried to keep my voice casual. "I was looking for Peter myself actually. I need to talk with him. What time did you see him?"

"About four, I guess. It was during the lifeboat drill. He was running down the passageway on F Deck looking scared to death. I thought the guy was going to have a heart attack!"

"F Deck, you say? He was supposed to be up on the Promenade Deck in his life vest with the rest of us. Did you talk with him?"

"No way. I was making a dash back to my storage room to get out of sight."

"Do you have any idea where he was going?"

"Haven't the foggiest," he said. "As I said, I was hurrying back to my hole. . . . Hey, is that Rusty O'Conner over there? The big lady in the black dress with all the diamonds?"

"Thar she blows," I said.

"Look, Chelsea sweetheart, don't let Christophe take my plate away. I'm just going to wander over and say hello to this O'Conner person. I'd like to see what she knows."

Chelsea watched Larry Goldman admiringly as he made his way toward Rusty, several tables away.

"Isn't he dreamy?" she asked.

"Dreamy isn't precisely the word I would use," Jayne said.

"He has so many wonderful adventures!" Chelsea stated with envy. "I can't wait to get out of school. Nothing exciting ever happens at Vassar."

"I'd stay in college if I were you," Jayne said. "You'll have time for adventures later, dear."

"You know, I think our young journalist is about to have an adventure now," I observed.

All the time we had been talking, the rocking and creaking of *The Atlantis* was getting harder to ignore. I saw one middle-aged woman stagger and fall into a gentleman's lap.

As for Goldman, he had sunk to one knee rather romantically by Rusty's table. I could see he was laying on the charm. They both glanced over in my direction, and I surmised that he'd told her I had sent him over. I waved at Rusty, and she waved back.

Then a curious thing happened. As they talked, a huge wave sent *The Atlantis* rolling sideways with such force that a waiter carrying a tray piled high with entrées for Rusty's table swayed and did a desperate jig to right himself. He might have regained control had he not tripped over Larry Goldman, who stood up at entirely the wrong moment. Goldman and the unfortunate waiter did a slow-motion waltz for several seconds, then both tumbled onto the table with a huge crash. Food rained down upon Rusty O'Conner, Goldman, the miserable waiter, the two ladies from Beverly Hills, and several other people I did not know. It was a truly spectacular mess.

Rusty had a lobster claw stuck to the bosom of her dress and half a chicken in her lap. The rest of the table was awash in a bouillabaisse, decorated with mussels, clams, prawns, and crab legs.

"Well," I said brightly to Jayne and Cass. "Anyone for dessert?"

chapter 16

Jayne was surprised when I said I wanted to go to Candy L'Amour's early show in the Grand Ballroom, maybe even catch the late show as well.

"I'm curious," I said, "to see what all the fuss is about. The lyrics are moronic and the tunes are worse, but that doesn't mean a singer with no talent might not bring them to life."

"Could be." She shrugged.

"How about you, Cass? You up for a little noise?"

"Well . . . normally I'd say no. But seeing as we're in the middle of the ocean and there's nothing else cooking tonight, sure. I'm curious, too."

The Grand Ballroom, on the same deck as the dining room, was nearly full when we arrived.

I assumed that, for reasons of her own, Miss L'Amour was contributing her services for the evening, since ordinarily performers of her stripe would never be booked to entertain the sophisticated, mature audiences who favor luxurious ocean travel. As a performer she was of no interest to them, but her status as a celebrity elicited their curiosity.

Apparently, tonight people were determined to see Candy L'Amour regardless of the weather, or maybe to take their minds off it. I even got a glimpse of the Princess and her captain. The room was impressive, nearly as big as a Vegas showroom and as glitzy, the stage large enough for a small Broadway revue. There was an orchestra area, a patch of wooden dance floor leading out into the room, and then a forest of small round tables, each with an elegant white cloth and a candle lantern. The tables rose up on different levels toward the exits in the back. A huge, modern, crystal chandelier hung from the ceiling, its light now dim in expectation of the show. The candles on each table gave the room a warm and intimate glow, and there was much laughter, talk, and clinking of glasses. Jayne had reserved a table for us earlier, and the maître d' now led us almost to the dance floor, three rows back from the stage. For better or worse, we would get a good look at Miss Depravity of the Year.

Candy L'Amour was not, of course, the person I had come to see. I was betting that Peter Moon would be in this audience, probably doing his best to steal Alexis Wilmington's girl. He was a man, I imagined, who simply had to have everything: the most money, the best car, the biggest house, and, if possible, someone else's woman. I very much wanted to talk with Mr. Moon.

But we didn't see him anywhere. I even excused myself to go to the men's room so I could walk around a bit and get a good look at the audience. I passed Alexis, who appeared grim and pale. He was sitting at a table with Stewart Hoffman, drink in hand. I saw Will Sanders and Rusty O'Conner—waved to Sidney and Alexandra Sheldon seated with Michael Viner and his actress wife Deborah Raffin—even pretty Chelsea Eastman, who was at a table with her stowaway journalist. Larry had managed to get somewhat cleaned up, but his sports jacket still bore a few culinary reminders of his recent debacle in the dining room, which didn't seem to bother him a bit. The room was full of people—but no Peter Moon. I wondered if he had gone into hiding or fallen overboard. Or perhaps I had simply missed him in the crowded, dimly lit room.

I got back to Jayne and Cass just as the show began. The performance was both better than I expected and worse. The small but professional orchestra started with a nice rendition of "Satin Doll." They were great. It always strikes me as remarkable—and a bit heartbreaking, too—how many wonderful musicians are playing on boats and in small venues, backing up other people and never quite finding their own places in the limelight. A piano, drums, rhythm guitar, electric bass, a miniature string section, a few horns, and a clarinet to represent the woodwinds—that was the lot. I listened to them closely because they would be backing me up for my own show on Tuesday night. The musicians, all men, were mostly in their fifties, and I was willing to bet they could play any tune forward and backward and in any key. I'd also have bet they were the best part of Candy L'Amour's show.

Halfway through "Satin Doll," the cruise director, Kevin Dobbs, came on stage. He was a clean-cut fellow, but I would not have bought a used car from him. While the band vamped, he said what a great pleasure and fabulous honor it was to welcome aboard *The Atlantis* that wonderful talent of international renown . . . the one and only . . . Candy L'Amour!

The music swelled, the curtains parted, and Candy came slinking into the spotlight in a black dress that was tight and bulging in all the right and wrong places. She had a cordless microphone which she managed, from time to time, to hold in a suggestive manner as she pranced about a bit before joining the band for a breathy, little-girl version of a novelty song from the 1930s called "Oh, Johnny."

She had a thin, Betty Boop sort of voice that would not have carried two feet were it not for the microphone. She wasn't terrible, but she wasn't great either. Though she couldn't sing worth a damn, she had a kind of sullen, imitation sex appeal and more stage presence than I would have thought. She held the audience's attention.

I was surprised by her next choice of material. She had, after all, made her reputation on absurd pop tunes like "I Wanna, Wanna, Wanna," but I suppose she was trying for legitimacy now that she was a multimillionaire. Nearly everyone comes around to the standards in the end. Candy sang "Misty" and "Lullaby of Birdland" and "The Way You Look Tonight." Then she went on to a medley of pop tunes and things got worse. At least the ocean cooperated, more or less. There was only one moment when the swaying of the ship nearly sent her flying, and when she managed to make a joke about it, the audience applauded helpfully. The band was good enough to cover her few mistakes, the soundman managed to add some presence and warmth to her voice with a little reverb, and Candy L'Amour was definitely famous. So the audience went wild, because most people don't care about talent, they care about fame. As for me, I was impressed that she could pull it off after being in such bad shape earlier in the afternoon. And she looked good too. I could hardly believe this was the same skinny girl with a bad complexion I had seen earlier in our stateroom. When the show ended, I was clapping along with the others.

"I wanna thank some special people for making it possible for me to be here tonight," Candy said into the microphone, and the applause died down. "First I wanna thank my boyfriend Alex. . . . Come on, stand up and take a bow, baby. . . . And also my very special friend, Jayne Meadows Allen . . . Jayne, where are you?"

This was unexpected, but Jayne is the sort who can rise into any spotlight—which was precisely what she did. There was more applause, and waiters brought three huge bouquets of red roses to the stage. Finally the houselights came up; people began to stand and make their way out. I tried to spot Peter Moon in the crowd, but there was no sign of him. I was beginning to find his continued absence disturbing. From the little I knew of Moon, I didn't imagine he would be shy about showing his face . . . unless there was a very good reason.

"Jayne, how would you like to go backstage and congratulate your new friend on her show?"

"Must I, darling?"

"It would make her happy. While you're at it, you might find out who the roses were from. And if Peter Moon shows up, stay close to him and try to page me."

Jayne gave a mock salute. "Aye aye, Captain."

"Now, Cass, I don't think you're going to have any luck at this hour in finding out about the shotgun, so why don't you come with me? We're going to find Peter Moon, come hell or high water, if he's aboard this ship."

"But where else could he be, Steve?" asked Jayne.

"It's a big ocean," I said. "Cold. And deep."

chapter 17

Cass and I joined the general exodus from the Grand Ballroom. I overheard a number of favorable comments about Candy's show, though most of the remarks had to do with how she looked rather than her performance. Some folks were discussing the weather and joking about friends and spouses who were lying in the cabins, unable to eat or move. Seasickness is always something of a joke . . . for those who are immune.

Cass and I made our way to The Seven Seas, a lounge not far from the Grand Ballroom. It featured huge aquariums filled with exotic saltwater fish of various neon-like colors. The largest tank was behind the bar; it must have been a good thirty feet long and ten feet high. In it, crabs, eels, strange rockfish with large prehistoric heads, and a few small tiger sharks swam about in a mysterious greenish gloom, and throughout the lounge the lighting was low and green-blue; you could sit in a booth and imagine you were underwater.

Across the room a trio of musicians played polite versions of rock tunes. I scanned the crowd for Peter Moon and thought I spotted him on the dance floor doing a fox trot with a young blonde, but when I looked more closely it turned out to be someone else with round dark glasses. Why do some men want to look like insects?

I had come into the bar only to look for Moon. Since he

wasn't there, while Cass ordered us mineral waters with lemon slices, I asked the ship's operator to connect me with Moon's stateroom. The phone rang and rang. No one answered. I hung up, punched *0* again, and told the operator that I wanted to make certain she had connected me to the correct stateroom. "Mr. Peter Moon . . . he's in The Virginia Suite, isn't he?" I asked disingenuously.

"No, sir. That is incorrect."

I knew that, since Jayne and I were in The Virginia Suite. I was simply trying to edge the operator toward volunteering the right answer. She volunteered nothing.

"Can you tell me what stateroom Mr. Moon is in?" I asked after subtlety had failed.

"I'm sorry, sir, but we're not allowed to give out that information."

"I understand. But this is important."

"I'm sorry, sir. I can take a message for you, and have Mr. Moon call you back."

"No. . . . I'll try later."

I hated to strike out yet again. Locating Moon was becoming an obsession.

"No luck?" Cass asked. "Well, maybe he'll be at Candy's second show."

I supposed Cass and I should go to the ten-o'clock performance in the hope that we might spot Peter Moon, but frankly the idea of sitting through Candy L'Amour's act a second time was depressing. I had thought I was very brave in making it through her first show. As I sat wondering what to do, I noticed Alexis Wilmington and Stewart Hoffman come into the bar and sit down together in one of the booths near the dance floor.

"I tell you what, Cass. Go back to the Ballroom and see if Moon has made a reservation for the ten-o'clock performance. I should have thought of that earlier. Ask about the first show as well. If he was actually there and we didn't see him, the maître d' probably crossed his name off a list. When you find out, meet me back here."

Cass took a big gulp of his mineral water and went back to the Grand Ballroom. I took my own glass and ambled over to Alexis and Stewart. The younger Wilmington brother was dressed in a white tropical suit, a dark shirt, and a flowery silk tie. I could tell as soon as I approached the table that he had been drinking. His wavy dark hair was in disarray, and his handsome face was flushed. He was young enough so that he didn't yet have the look of a hardened drinker, more of a college boy on a spree. He was unexpectedly friendly when he saw me.

"Mr. Allen, listen, I've been wanting to talk to you. Sit down," he said, "an' let me buy you a drink."

"I already have a drink."

"Well, join us anyway."

Alex Wilmington was used to getting his way, so I slid into the booth beside him, nodded at Hoffman across the table. The security man was dressed in his usual dark suit. He did not smile. He watched me guardedly and without comment. When I saw that he was drinking coffee, I realized he was here to keep Alex safe from harm.

"Have you met my keeper?" Wilmington asked. "Stu the Strong. Stu the Brave. Stu who is supposed to take care of all our problems, no matter what."

"We've met," I said.

Stewart Hoffman did not react to Wilmington's sarcastic introduction. He just stared at me, as if I were a fly he might have to swat.

"Tell me, Hoffman, why did you lie about taking me to see the old man?" I asked.

Hoffman shrugged. "It's quite simple. I have instructions to keep Mr. Wilmington's movements absolutely confidential. If I had mentioned your visit, the others would have known he was on the East Coast."

"Is hiding his whereabouts so important?"

"To Mr. Wilmington it is. He pays me very well to do what he tells me."

"Ah, yes, Stu the Loyal. What a guy! . . . In fact, let's all get stewed," Alexis said merrily. "Waitress! You can bring me another margarita. Steve, you gotta join me. What will you have?"

"San Pellegrino," I said.

"That's the problem with the world. No one drinks anymore," Alexis lamented. "Stu, can I get you a shot of cognac for your coffee?"

"Not tonight."

"You see what I mean? You'll have to excuse me, Steve. Normally I'm a very sober individual. But I'm having a little private wake for Dicky."

"I'm sorry about your brother," I said.

"Are you? Me too. The poor son-of-a-bitch. No one gives a damn about him except you and me, Steve. Stu doesn't care. Do you *care*, Stu?"

"I'm not paid to care," Hoffman said.

"And what *are* you paid to do, Stu? To protect us, that's what. You sure screwed that up, didn't you, Stu?"

Stewart didn't answer. He was colder than the tiger sharks swimming by the bar. He stood. "I'll be back in fifteen minutes," he said. "There's something I have to do."

Alexis shook his head as he watched the security man depart with purposeful, military steps. "There goes Frankenstein," he remarked.

"How long has he worked for your family?" I asked.

"About a hundred years. As long as anyone can remember. Ol' Stu knows where all the bodies are buried. He used to be a cop, you know."

"I didn't."

"A homicide cop. NYPD. Then one of my father's rivals had an unfortunate accident—fell out the window from his thirty-eighth-floor office—just when it looked like he might outbid Dad for a newspaper. Well, Detective Hoffman showed up to investigate a possible murder, but it took him only about a week to decide where his best interests lay. He ruled the death a suicide, quit the force, and went to work for Dad. Pretty nifty, huh? His salary went up about three hundred percent, and Dad bought him a nice condo on the Upper East Side as a kind of a welcome-aboard present."

"That's quite a story," I said.

"You hear a lot of stories when your father's a big tycoon— Oh, waitress! Another margarita, honey. And this time tell Fred to put some tequila in it. . . . Sure you don't want a real drink, Steve?"

"I'm doing fine," I said.

"I wish I were. Candy wouldn't let me come backstage after the show. She said it would make her nervous."

"Performers often don't like to see friends between shows."

"Yeah, but I noticed your wife going backstage."

"Jayne has a very calming effect."

"Well, so do I. When I'm not drinking. But tonight my brother is dead, so I have a right, don't I?"

"I'd say you had the right, Alex. Whether it'll help matters is another question."

"It helps tonight," he said stubbornly. "I'll worry about tomorrow another time."

It was clear that being the children of one of the richest men in the world had not made either Alexis or Dicky Wilmington happy or well adjusted. Alexis was the handsomer of the two and on the surface had all the grace and ease that Dicky had lacked, but it didn't seem to have done him much good.

"I wanted to ask you something," Wilmington said vaguely, scratching his chin. "About Dicky."

"Yeah."

"Stu told me Dicky was supposed to meet you up there. Where he was killed."

"That's right. Your brother sent me a note. I was supposed to meet him after the lifeboat drill."

"Why? That's what I was wondering. What did he want to say to you?"

"I don't have a clue."

"I mean, if he had a problem, why didn't he come to me? I'm his brother, goddamn it. Maybe I could have helped."

"Were you close, you and Dicky?"

"When we were kids we were. We had to be close because our childhood was so strange. We grew up in a huge house, and we weren't allowed to have any friends over. It was lonely so we had to get along, whether we liked it or not. We used to pretend we were firemen and cops, ordinary people who lived in little houses, without a whole lot of money, and maybe threw a football around with their children on little backyard lawns. That's all we ever wanted to be—normal. Dicky and I, we had a lawn half the size of a football field, but our father wouldn't play catch with us. He was too busy making money."

"I can see how that would make you close with your brother," I said.

"Then Dicky grew up and became a jerk. We went in different directions, Dicky and I. I was the playboy. Having so much fun you could hardly believe it."

"I believe it."

"And Dicky was the worker. He slaved so at school it used to make me want to cry. And he worked even harder when he joined good ol' Wilmex Corp., our little family gold mine. Dicky always wanted to impress Dad with what a sharp businessman he was; unfortunately Dad was never impressed by anyone except himself."

"But he made your brother CEO of his company."

"That was pretty much a joke. Don't think Dad relinquished any *real* power—particularly not to one of his children. God forbid! Most of the time, Dicky just played golf with clients and had a lot of lunches with people."

"Did he like that?"

"What do you think?"

"I don't know. Some kids might enjoy easy street."

"Not Dicky. He really wanted to do something that would measure up to the old man. That's what's so damn sad. He kept trying to dream up clever business strategies, but Dad would just laugh and tell him to stick to golf. It really burned Dicky up."

"This morning I noticed your brother talking with Peter Moon," I said. "They were arguing over something."

"*That* son of a bitch!" Wilmington grumbled. "Why would Dicky go to him?"

"I've been wondering that myself. Do you think your brother was so unhappy at work that he might have done something rash? Like turn traitor and feed confidential information about Wilmex to Moon?"

"Not Dicky."

"But say Peter Moon went to great pains to make your brother feel important. He might point out how unappreciated Dicky was at the company, and what a shame it was for someone so clever to be kept from doing anything vital. All Dicky had to do was feed inside information to Peter Moon, and when the takeover was complete, he'd get a nice reward—maybe CEO, but this time with real power. That would make your Dad respect him, wouldn't it?"

Wilmington was quiet for a few moments. Then he grinned and said sourly, "Maybe it makes sense. I'm not sayin' you're right, but it *could* have happened like you said, Steve. If someone flattered Dicky, he'd be putty in their hands. The poor guy was desperate for respect. And if Moon offered him a chance to get even with Dad, it's possible he'd go for it. Dicky *has* been acting strange recently."

"Oh? Like how?"

"Like nervous. Nothing I can put into words, but something was on his mind. And yet . . . it's still hard to accept the idea of Dicky selling out to a creep like Peter Moon."

"He did something that made someone angry enough to kill him, Alex," I mentioned.

"You think it was Moon? But if Dicky was working for Moon, why would he kill him?"

I looked up and saw Hoffman coming our way.

"Maybe it wasn't Moon," I said. "I thought so at first, but I'm not sure anymore."

"But who else could it be?"

I only shrugged because I wasn't ready yet to tell anyone what I was thinking. If Dicky Wilmington was playing traitor, the chances were he was not killed by anyone outside Wilmex Corporation but by someone from the inner circle. And the prime suspect, as far as I was concerned, was walking our way.

chapter 18

"It's time for you to call it a day, Alex," Stewart Hoffman said brusquely as soon as he returned to our booth in The Seven Seas lounge.

"You want to tuck me in, Stu?"

"Let's get going."

Wilmington winked at me. "Charming, isn't he?" He turned back to Hoffman. "I was telling Steve the old story about how Dad lured you from your cop gig with a cushy job and a condo."

"Let's go, Alex. Now."

I expected Wilmington to tell Hoffman to go to hell, but he stood up with a wry smile. "My keeper calls," he said. "Nice to talk to you, Steve."

I slipped out of the booth and faced the impassive Mr. Hoffman. "I want to see Marcus Wilmington again," I told him. "Or talk with him on the phone."

"That's not in my power, Mr. Allen."

"Just get in touch with him and tell him we need to talk. For *his* sake. That little beeper was a joke."

"I don't get in touch with Mr. Wilmington," Hoffman said firmly. "Mr. Wilmington gets in touch with me."

"I'm sure he'll want to hear what I have to say."

"Perhaps," he said. "Perhaps not." Hoffman gave me an inscrutable look, then left with Wilmington in tow.

Cass, who had returned to the bar a few minutes earlier and had been watching from a nearby bar stool, walked over and sat down. "I'd be careful with that guy, Steve," he said. "I wouldn't trust him any more than I'd trust a rattlesnake."

"Yeah, but I wish I knew what was going on with the Wilmington family," I said unhappily. "I was just getting warmed up with Alex when Hoffman came back."

"Maybe he didn't want you to ask any more embarrassing questions."

"How about you? What did you find out?"

"Peter Moon made reservations for both shows. But he didn't show up at the eight o'clock performance, so five minutes before the curtain went up they gave away his table. It's a house rule. The maître d' said he might have come in after the show started and stood in the back, but there's no way of knowing."

"Moon still has a reservation for the ten o'clock show?"

"So far."

"Well, then, I'm afraid we're going to see Miss L'Amour twice tonight. The longer Moon stays out of sight, the more worried I am."

And so Cass and I returned to the Grand Ballroom. It is not easy to be a private eye, amateur or otherwise. Sacrifices must be made. Since all the tables had been reserved, Cass and I stood in the back along with a few dozen curiosity seekers. We discovered the location of Peter Moon's reserved table from the maître d'—but it was given away to a happy young couple five minutes before show time, when Moon had not appeared. Cass and I remained close to the maître d's podium so we would see Moon if he arrived late. I noticed Jayne near the front of the room, sharing a table with Dicky's widow. I was surprised that Wendy was out and about only hours after her husband's death, and curious as to how Jayne had ended up at her table. But I didn't want to disturb the synergism of their new friendship so I stayed with Cass in the back of the room.

Candy had not magically acquired talent between shows. In fact, she was slightly the worse for wear. Her wispy voice began to get on my nerves, and since Peter Moon never showed up, the second performance was a waste of time for Cass and me. Three-quarters of the way through the show, when Candy was about to do the medley of pop tunes, I finally lost my patience. "Let's get out of here, Cass," I whispered.

"Gladly."

As we escaped. I said, "I've got an idea on how to find out which is Moon's stateroom."

"Great. Then what do we do?"

"We break in, naturally."

chapter 19

I dialed room service from a phone on a decorative marble table that was beneath a small Picasso lithograph near a bank of elevators.

"Good evening," I said. "I would like to send a bottle of champagne to my friend Mr. Peter Moon. I'm sorry, I don't know his stateroom."

"No problem, sir. It's in the computer."

This was so deliciously easy I wished I had thought of it earlier. But my smile evaporated when we began to discuss the prices of the different champagnes, which ranged down from five hundred dollars a bottle for a very nice vintage French—something with a long unpronounceable name—to a thirty-five dollar California Korbel Brut. Needless to say, I chose the Korbel. I would have sent Pink Thunderbird had it been available.

As it turned out, I could have saved myself the money since the room-service operator, bless his heart, let the cat out of the bag by accident. I told him my name and Atlanticard number, and then repeated Moon's name. The operator punched a few computer keys, thinking aloud. "Moon, Peter . . . Valkyrie Suite."

I was tempted to cancel the order now that I had the information I wanted, but didn't want to arouse suspicion. Anyway, the operator had saved Cass and me some trouble, and it seemed petty to be stingy. I had been planning to follow the room-service waiter to Moon's suite, but it was a large ship and I decided that might prove difficult.

"How long will it be before the champagne is delivered?"

"Less than ten minutes, sir."

"Very well. If Mr. Moon is not there, just leave it in his suite."

"Will there be any note?"

"Say it's from a secret admirer."

I hung up, and Cass and I asked a crew member for directions to the Valkyrie Suite. It turned out to be only two doors down from my own quarters. As is often the case, what we were seeking was closer at hand than we suspected.

Cass and I ensconced ourselves in my sitting room. With the door partly open, we listened for the waiter to deliver Moon's champagne. I saw that in the next room my bed had been made up for the night: blanket turned down, pieces of chocolate on the pillows, and a ship's newspaper. There was no sign of Jayne; I trusted she was pumping Wendy Wilmington for information.

Almost ten minutes had passed when Cass and I heard the waiter knock two doors down. "Room service!" he called. After a moment he knocked again. We heard him use his passkey to enter the suite and waited for him to leave. If we were really lucky, he might forget to remove the passkey from the lock.

After a few minutes, I dared to stick my head out the door and peer up and down the corridor. It was empty.

"To work, Cass," I said.

"B and E," he sighed. "Do you think they have a jail on board?"

"Certainly not. And if they do, I'll bet the food is excellent. Anyway, we're not criminals—we're on a quest for knowledge," I assured him.

Cass really does a lot for me, and I don't take it for granted. His skills are endless. He can shoe a horse, fix a car, repair furniture, cook gourmet dinners around a campfire, tail suspects without their knowledge, fish, track a herd of elk, and even survive the Los Angeles freeways with a sense of humor. We strolled rather casually down the hall and stood innocently before the Valkyrie Suite. Cass was about to set to work when two boys, about eight and ten, galloped our way with shrieks of laughter, the older one chasing the younger. We let them run past and around a corner.

Cass took out his Swiss Army knife. It was one of those models that has just about everything—a saw, scissors, punches and picks, and blades of different sizes. The Swiss Army, I suppose, must be ready for anything. Cass opened a very thin blade, got on his knees, and slipped the metal into the lock.

"Whoops," I said. "Company."

A young woman strolled toward us. Cass took the knife out of the lock and pretended that he was tying his shoe. But she hardly noticed his charade. "Have you seen two small boys?" she asked.

"They went thataway," I said, pointing down the hall.

"Some vacation . . ." she muttered.

We watched the woman disappear. Then Cass got back to work. His face was intent as he concentrated on probing the inner workings of the lock. "It's a kind of Zen thing," he told me once when I asked him how to do it. "You have to feel in tune with the lock." Cass had been in California a number of years.

"I don't know, Steve. This is a pretty good lock," he said after a while.

"I have great faith in your skills, Cass."

"Damn . . . Almost had it!"

"More company," I hissed.

This time it was a ship's officer. Cass hurriedly began working on his shoelace again.

"Good evening," I said, the very image of a model passenger. "How's the weather holding?"

"It's holding," the officer replied grimly.

"It doesn't feel quite as rough as it did at dinner," I mentioned politely.

"We shouldn't get the full brunt of the storm until tomorrow afternoon."

"It's going to get worse then?"

"We'll see," he said guardedly. He wished us a good evening and disappeared in the same direction as the two boys and the woman. Cass got out his knife once again and continued to work at the lock. Every minute we lingered in the hallway increased our chances of getting caught. I was on the verge of calling the whole thing off when Cass grinned, turned the handle, and let us in the suite. I closed the door behind us and breathed more easily.

Peter Moon's suite was almost a mirror image of ours, except that it was done in a pastel orange. And it wasn't nearly as neat. Shirts, pants, socks, and underwear were scattered about on the chairs and deck. Papers covered every surface, and a laptop computer sat on the dressing table. The bottle of Korbel was in an ice bucket on the coffee table along with two glasses. Beside it was a clutter of belongings—a tennis racquet, a Walkman, cassette tapes, a paperback mystery, and a small stack of business papers that were full of figures. I glanced at the papers, but they could have been the national debt of China for all I knew.

Now that I was here, I was forced to acknowledge that I had no idea what I was looking for. Nothing I saw brought Peter Moon into sharper focus. I'm not sure what I expected. Perhaps a handwritten diary entitled "The True Story and Intimate Revelations of Peter Moon." That would have come in handy.

Cass and I walked into the bedroom. The covers of the bed were pulled down, like my bed two doors away. Other than that, the bedroom was even more of a mess than the sitting room. Pajamas, a silk bathrobe, jogging pants, more underwear, stray socks, and other bits of Peter Moon's wardrobe had been tossed in every direction. Cass explored the bathroom.

"Looks like he takes sleeping pills to get his forty winks," Cass

mentioned. "Other than that, there's nothing out of the ordinary." He looked around. "God, what a slob!"

I went through each of the two closets, where a dozen cus-
tom-made shirts, suits, and slacks hung side by side. Moon had
come aboard *The Atlantis* ready for every occasion. In the back
of the closet I noticed a bag of golf clubs. I presumed these were
for use in England since golf was one of the few activities not
offered on the ship. From all these belongings, I derived an
image of a rich, self-indulgent Baby-Boomer-made-good. *But
where the hell was he?* That was what I desperately wanted to
know; and nothing in the Valkyrie Suite provided a clue.

I was about to close the closet door when my eye was attracted to the glint of metal behind the golf bag. I curiously
pulled the bag aside, and my heart nearly stopped beating.
There was something frightful about the shotgun leaning there,
an inanimate object gleaming with evil intent. Despite my having gone through basic training in the infantry during World
War II—heavy weapons—I don't know much about guns, but
this one did seem similar to the one Devine used for skeet.

"Cass, come here," I said.

He whistled when he saw the gun. "My, my! Maybe Mr.
Moon doesn't like to lose at golf."

"I doubt if he likes to lose at anything. Don't touch it, Cass.
I'll bet it's the murder weapon. Peter Moon is going to have
some explaining to do."

We stared at the gun for a while, mesmerized, unable to
move, then I heard a key turning in the lock of the door to the
corridor. Someone walked into the sitting room. Cass and I
looked at each other in alarm. We heard footsteps on the carpet
in the next room and then a weary sigh as someone settled onto
the sofa. My heart was beating, and my lips were dry. If the
gleaming object at the back of the closet was the murder
weapon, then Moon was almost certainly the murderer, and he
would not be pleased to find us here.

I heard papers rustling in the next room and gestured to Cass that I would stand on one side of the bedroom door, and he was to stand on the other. When Moon came into his bedroom we would jump on him from behind. It wasn't so easy explaining all this in sign language, but Cass got the general idea. The only risky part was that the bedroom door was slightly ajar and if Moon was looking in the right direction he would spot me getting into position. I slipped off my loafers so I could walk without a sound and moved cautiously toward the door.

I listened to the rustling of papers, hoping Moon was concentrating on what he was reading. I couldn't see him, so it finally came down to luck. I stepped quickly to the other side of the door. Thankfully, the papers continued to rustle; I had succeeded.

The phone rang, almost causing me to fall out the door in surprise.

"Yeah?" A man spoke gruffly in the next room. "Okay. . . . No. . . . We'll see. . . . Maybe tomorrow." It was a woefully inexplicit conversation. Then he spoke my name, and it caused a chill to run through me. "Steve Allen? . . . He *did?* . . . Well, doesn't that beat everything? Yeah, I see it on the table. Hold on, there's a note. . . . 'From a Secret Admirer'—thinks he's funny, I guess. But I'm going to nail that bastard."

Just wait 'til you come to bed, Moon! I thought savagely. We'll see who nails whom.

I heard Peter put down the phone and yawn loudly. *That's right. Come to beddybye,* I called in my mind. And he seemed to hear me. He stood up, wandered about the room, and moved our way.

I glanced at Cass to see if he was ready. He nodded. Normally he and I are mild-mannered gentlemen who would not even consider carrying out this sort of ambush, but he looked as revved up as I was by the prospect of battle. Then the door opened wide, and Moon stepped into the bedroom. He moved past us toward the bed.

"Now!" I cried. I threw myself on his back with a banshee

yell. Cass charged, too. The responding cry of surprise sent my adrenaline pumping. He swung around, stronger than I imagined, and his arm knocked my glasses loose. I could barely see without them, but vision isn't very important in this kind of close fighting. For a while the three of us spun around together—a tangle of legs and arms— gasping and grunting and letting out little cries.

"Son-of-a-bitch!"

"I'm going to kill you bastards!"

"Oh, no you're not, Moon!"

Cass and I succeeded in wrestling the figure face down onto the bed and pinning him there. Cass had hold of one of his arms, and I was sitting on the other.

"Give up?" I asked.

"Go to hell!" The voice was muffled but angry.

Cass pushed his arm upward at an angle that nature did not intend for it. Moon screamed in pain. "All right!" he cried. "What do you want?"

Cass watched him carefully and I found my glasses as our victim turned over. We stared, not pleased at what we saw. The man we had jumped and wrestled onto the bed was, alas, not Peter Moon.

"Whoops," I said, "Agent Schwartz!"

"In person," he grouched. "And you two idiots are under goddamn arrest!"

chapter 20

While Cass and I were headed for jail—the "brig" at sea—
Jayne, as she later told me, remained in the Grand Ballroom.

She has always had a maternal, caring side that could have
been put to more use if she had become a mother superior. At
any rate beneath the surface toughness, she saw something vulnerable in Candy L'Amour and therefore enjoyed her performance more than I, by watching the show the way you might
watch your granddaughter perform in a high-school play.

Anyway, after Cass and I left, Jayne made her way backstage,
where a crew member was turning away enthusiastic well-wish-
ers. Jayne saw Alexis Wilmington sent away and supposed this
would be her fate, so she asked only for a piece of paper to send
a note to Candy telling how much she had enjoyed the performance. But when the crew member saw Jayne, he said, "Oh, Miss
Meadows. Good. Miss L'Amour asked for you. Just follow the
hall to the first dressing room on the left."

Candy had already shed her expensive gown and lay
stretched out on a small sofa, draped in an oversized robe,
drinking Perrier. "So whaddaya think? Was I okay? Was I
awful?" she asked all at once.

"You were wonderful, dear."

"Really? I know a lot of those songs are probably not your
bag, but I was hoping you'd like some of the standards."

"I loved them all."

"Really? You're not just being nice?"

"Candy, you should feel more confident. You're a big star."

"Yeah, I guess so." She sighed.

Jayne had spent much of her life in dressing rooms like this one: a makeup table, a mirror ringed with bare light bulbs, a couch, a chair or two. Dressing rooms generally are impersonal, sometimes lonely places where you summon your nerve to face a theater full of strangers and then retreat afterward to mull over how you did.

"Those are lovely roses, dear," Jayne observed, noticing the three bouquets Candy had received on stage.

"Yeah. One of them came from Alex. The other two are from that creep Peter Moon. I guess I haven't been awfully nice to Alex. That's why I mentioned him out there on stage. But I really couldn't see him right now. He's so . . . so . . . needy, ya know? It's exhausting."

"I'm sorry. Of course, you must be tired," Jayne said. "I'll leave you to rest for the next show."

"Oh, you don't exhaust me at all. You're so different from my so-called *friends*. They're along for the party—know what I mean? If tomorrow I suddenly stopped selling records they'd be gone."

"Everyone in show business is besieged with people like that; you just have to become more discerning, dear. How did you meet Mr. Wilmington?"

"Alex? I met him in Palm Beach. I had just done a big concert in Miami, and Sol, the promoter, invited me to Palm Beach to see a polo game. I was bored so I thought, What the hell.

"Alex was one of the players. You should have seen him galloping up and down the field on this big black horse! It was like something out of an old movie. After it was over, Sol took me to the clubhouse, and Alex invited me to a party at one of those old mansions on Ocean Boulevard. Real fancy, ya know? I thought he was some kind of Prince Charming."

"That's understandable," said my understanding wife.

"It all seemed so romantic, and suddenly everything in the record business seemed sort of fake and sleazy. I mean, this was the real thing—butlers, chandeliers, all the trimmings."

"But it didn't turn out quite as you imagined?"

"Well, Alex is sweet, but he's not very strong, ya know? His mother pulls all the wires."

"You don't like his mother?"

"She scares me to death!"

"What did you think of Dicky?"

"Weird." She laughed, not humorously. "The whole family is nuts. Well, I've never met the old man, but he sounds more sideways than the rest of them put together."

Jayne laughed. "None of them seem very happy, do they?"

"God, no! They're fighting all the time!"

"Really? What about?"

Candy shrugged. "Money and power, I guess. Everyone's nerves have been strained because of *The Atlantis*. If it isn't a big success, they're done for." She laughed again, one short laugh. "Maybe that wouldn't be such a bad thing. . . . Well, except for the prison part."

"Prison! What have they done?"

"I don't know everything," Candy said. "They shut up when I come into a room. But I'm not as dumb as they think, and I've picked up a few things."

"I'll bet you have," Jayne observed.

Candy leaned forward and lowered her voice. "They had to do some illegal stuff to get *The Atlantis* in the water, you know."

Jayne leaned forward too, and lowered her voice. "What sort of stuff?"

"They raided the pension funds of some of their companies. Alex told me that one night when he was drunk. It made me mad to think of all those people—I mean, what are they going to do when there isn't any money for their old age? The Wilmingtons have fine ways, but they really aren't much better than some of my Hollywood friends, ya know?"

"I should say not," said Jayne. "Which pension funds have they been . . . er . . . stealing from?"

"Practically all of them, according to Alex. It's why he drinks so much. He said that a year ago they realized they were about a billion dollars short of what they needed to finish *The Atlantis* and their credit was stretched to the limit. Can you believe that? A *billion!* But Alex said if everything goes well, they'll put the money back before anybody knows it's gone."

Jayne was deeply shocked. "Incredible!" she said. "I can see why they're so concerned that the ship does well!"

"That's really why I agreed to do this show tonight for no bread. Normally I wouldn't play anything less than an amphitheater, but I figured I'd better do my part—for Alex, and for all those people who want to retire one day."

"That's very thoughtful of you, Candy. But what in the world are you doing accepting roses from Peter Moon?"

"Oh, that was just a dumb mistake. I didn't really mean to lead the guy on—or maybe I did," Candy said miserably. "I was just feeling bored and resentful. Sometimes I don't even know why I do things. It's just . . ."

"Just what, dear?"

"I don't know. I sacrificed a spring tour to come on this cruise. I could have made a ton of money, and my agent thinks I'm crazy. It's not that I want everyone to bow down in gratitude and treat me like I'm some sort of saint, but Gertrude—that's Alex's mother—she makes me so mad! She treats me like a whore. Like I'm not good enough for her precious son. Like I'm after him for *money*, if you can believe it! Ha! I have a lot more money than he does! Anyway, Peter kinda hit on me at just the right moment. I didn't go to bed with him or nothing, but I guess I flirted a lot. . . . God, he's such a vulture."

"Have you seen Mr. Moon tonight?"

"No." Candy chuckled. "Maybe he picked up on the fact that I was gonna tell him where to get off."

"You were? Well, good for you." Jayne patted the girl's hand in encouragement. "Candy, will you do me a favor?"

"Sure."

"Keep your eyes open. There are a lot of strange things going on, and some desperate people who . . . Well, I want you to promise to come to me if you run into any problems."

"I don't know anyone I'd rather go to," Candy said. "God, I don't deserve a friend like you, Miss Meadows." And then Candy L'Amour burst into tears.

chapter 21

Wendy Wilmington was trying to get past the man at the stage door when Jayne came out.

"But I only want to say hello to her," she was insisting loudly. "I'll just be a moment."

"I'm sorry, Mrs. Wilmington, but I have strict instructions not to admit anyone. Miss L'Amour wants to rest between performances."

"Who does she think she—" Wendy stopped in midsentence, and her eyes flashed glints of steel as she saw Jayne. "How'd *she* get in?"

"Miss L'Amour left instructions that—"

"Oh, to hell with *Miss* L'Amour and her instructions!"

Wendy Wilmington was making such a fuss that Jayne looked at her more closely. The woman was in her early forties. Her straight blond hair hung severely to her shoulders, and nothing on her face came together right. The chin was weak, the nose too sharp, and the eyes too small. Still, had Wendy been a nice person, it wouldn't have been a totally unpleasant countenance. Unfortunately, she was not nice. In fact, she was in the process of writing down the crew member's name so she could report his impudence to her mother-in-law.

Jayne decided to step into the fray.

"You're Wendy Wilmington, aren't you? I'm so sorry about

your husband," she said. "You must forgive Candy—she really is exhausted and performers often don't like to see people between shows. It destroys their concentration."

"She saw you," Wendy said sullenly.

"Well, yes, she did," said Jayne, quickly making up a white lie. "But it was only because I brought her some vitamin C. She's on the verge of feeling ill, poor darling. In fact, I advised her to cancel her ten o'clock show."

"Oh, she mustn't do that!" Wendy said quickly.

"Exactly. She doesn't want to. So why don't we let her rest?"

"Let's sit down someplace and have a drink," Jayne led Mrs. Wilmington away. "You must have had a terrible day."

"Atrocious. Simply atrocious." Wendy's eyes filled suddenly with tears. "Poor Dicky! He was such a horse's ass. Still, it's terrible to be a widow. I don't look at all good in black, and now I'll be an extra woman at dinner parties. If anyone invites me anywhere." She was almost blubbering. Jayne told me later it was not a pretty sight.

"That *is* sad," Jayne said. Wendy was too taken with her own predicament to notice the tinge of sarcasm.

"I was hoping Candy would say something about Dicky's . . . passing."

"Well," Jayne said, as kindly as possible, "I think it might be better if as little was said about that sad subject as possible. I know old Mr. Wilmington wanted the passengers to have the best possible time, so . . ."

"Perhaps you're right."

They sat at a table near the stage. A waiter came over, apparently prepared to tell them that they were not yet seating people for the second show, but when he noted the presence of a Wilmington, he quickly changed his mind. Wendy asked for a double vodka martini on the rocks; Jayne requested one of her fruit juice drinks with an umbrella.

"Do you have any idea why someone would want to murder your husband?" Jayne asked when the drinks came.

"It was probably that horrid Peter Moon. Did I tell you Dicky knew him at Harvard?"

"No, I didn't know that."

"We-e-ell," Wendy said moving closer. "He wasn't calling himself Peter Moon then. His name was Minovsky. From the Bronx, if you can believe it. A scholarship student! His father was a tailor."

"Were Dicky and Mr. Minovsky friends in college?" Jayne asked.

"Not really. Peter hung around Dicky because of the Wilmington name, but they had a falling out after Peter stole one of Dicky's girlfriends. They had a tremendous row about it. You'll never imagine what Peter had the nerve to say!"

"Please tell me."

"Peter said that someday he'd have twice as much money as the Wilmingtons! He said—and I quote— 'I'll bankrupt you one day and dance on your grave!' "

"Goodness! Did they ever run into each other after Harvard?"

"Not until six months ago. But I'm afraid I can't tell you about that, Jayne. Dicky made me promise."

"Of course. I wouldn't think of asking you to go back on your word."

Wendy continued anyway. "You see, he was worried about Wilmex. He knew Peter was trying to make a raid, or whatever it is these silly businessmen call it, on the company. Peter offered Dicky a one percent commission if Dicky helped him. Well, one percent of Wilmex—that could be *many* millions of dollars. He also said he'd install Dicky as the new CEO, with *real* power. You can understand why Dicky made me promise not to tell anyone!"

"I certainly can. What else did he make you promise not to tell, Wendy?"

"Well, it was all very hush-hush, you know. They telephoned each other from public booths and met at midnight under street lamps. That sort of thing. If you ask me, they were acting like a couple of little boys playing spy. Dicky was giving that bastard all sorts of confidential stuff! I wish I could tell you what else he was doing, but that was the part he *really* made me promise not to tell."

"Then perhaps you shouldn't," said Jayne.

"Well, it can't hurt now. . . . This was the clever part: He was giving Moon *false* information!"

"Really? That is clever."

"Dicky got the idea out of a spy novel. Disinformation, I think they call it. Or counter-something. Anyway, the point was, Moon was in for a few surprises."

"So Dicky was loyal to the family after all?"

"Naturally," she said breezily. "He was a Wilmington. He'd never turn his back on his own kind."

"But perhaps he was too clever for his own good," Jayne said.

"Well, he wasn't very bright. Poor Dicky! I think I'm going to cry."

But she did not. Instead she finished her martini and ordered another. Meanwhile, as she and Jayne talked, the doors to the Grand Ballroom opened and the place filled up quickly with those who had reservations for the ten-o'clock show. Wendy, flushed and effusive from the alcohol, insisted that Jayne sit with her through the performance.

And so Jayne watched Candy's second show in the company of Wendy Wilmington, while Cass and I were watching less comfortably from the back. Wendy was the sort who talks a great deal during a performance—performers hate this—and normally it would have annoyed Jayne, but since she'd already seen the show, she didn't stop her. Wendy talked about such things as how difficult it was to find a decent servant these days, how dreadful to pay income taxes in her bracket—it was getting so that a person was hard put to become a billionaire—and how she had no sympathy at all for young people who didn't appreciate the value of hard work. Wendy wanted Jayne to know that *she* worked very hard indeed—one afternoon a week on the social committee of her country club—so she knew the meaning of the word. It wasn't until nearly the end of the show that Jayne managed to steer the conversation back to matters of more substance.

"Tell me, did you by any chance mention Dicky's clever scheme to anyone else?"

"Naturally not! I promised. The only people I told were in the family."

"Ah."

"I wanted them to know what a clever thing Dicky was doing. None of them ever really appreciated him, you know."

"So you told . . ."

"Only Gertrude. And Will Sanders, of course. And I wrote a little note about it to old Marcus, because *I* felt Dicky deserved a raise. But I didn't tell Alexis. He's a horrid man, and I talk to him as little as possible."

Jayne was glad she had never told Wendy Wilmington any secrets.

As the show was ending, a waiter came up to Jayne to deliver a message—from me. It was a waiter she had never seen before—and would not see again. The message was that I wanted Jayne to meet me, in fifteen minutes, down on F Deck, at the inside swimming pool. It seemed a strange and deserted place to meet anyone so late at night, so Jayne had the waiter repeat the message to make certain she had it right.

"The swimming pool? Well, I suppose so," she said uncertainly. "Mr. Allen gave you this message personally?"

"Yes, madam."

"Well, then I'd better go."

Good loyal Jayne. Unfortunately I had not sent any message to her.

chapter 22

Jayne made her way through the well-dressed crowd that lingered in small groups outside the ballroom, talking and laughing. It was hard to believe this was still only the first day of our voyage. It seemed the ship had been sailing for weeks and life on land was a distant memory.

Rain on the black portholes made the inside of the ship glow in a cozy way as Jayne pressed the button for the elevator, which promptly came up from a lower deck and disgorged Monsieur Duclerc.

"Bon soir, madame," he said politely, as he stepped out of the elevator and she stepped in.

"Bon soir, monsieur," Jayne replied. There is a certain fun in speaking a foreign language, even if one only remembers a few useful phrases, and she was pleased with herself as she punched the button marked *F*. The elevator doors closed, and the car descended.

Seconds later it stopped at F Deck, far from the staterooms and glamorous lounges. The doors hissed open, and Jayne peered out. She could feel the throbbing of the engines vibrate upward from the bottoms of her feet. Long, empty hallways stretched out from the elevator in geometric lines. There was a hum from the fluorescent lighting. Jayne found it all a bit eerie. Worst of all, the ship in these lower reaches creaked and groaned as it made its journey over the waves. She shuddered nervously, and would have immediately returned to the gaiety and laughter above were it not for the fact that I had sent for her. She feared, she later told me, that I might be in some sort of trouble. So she took a deep breath and stepped out of the elevator.

A sign on the wall said POOL, and an arrow pointed down one of the endless corridors. Jayne told herself she was being silly, then headed off in the advised direction. Still it was not an altogether pleasant feeling to hear the elevator door hiss shut behind her and know she was now stranded. The corridor's deck was linoleum, and her red high heels click-clacked as she walked along. She passed doorways that seemed to lead into storage areas and other mysterious places. There were cryptic signs on some of the doors, like REC ROOM 3 and CGX AREA. Jayne recalled that the brash stowaway, Larry Goldman, had made a home for himself in one of these places. An entire warren of cubbyholes where one might hide from view was located down here.

Jayne walked along the dimly lit maze of corridors, turning left and right as arrows directed. "This is a little too cloak and dagger," she muttered. Her mouth was dry, and she began to hum a few bars of "This Could Be the Start of Something Big" to prove to herself she was not afraid. She smiled when she at last came to a door marked POOL, and below that: POOL HOURS—8 A.M. TO 10 P.M. It was after ten now, of course, and Jayne expected the door to be locked. Perhaps the waiter who had given her the message had gotten it wrong after all. Perhaps she was supposed to meet me at the much more hospitable outdoor pool upstairs. She tried the handle of the door, partly hoping it would be locked. But it was not.

With some effort on her part, the heavy metal door opened and Jayne stepped inside. Surprisingly, all the overhead lights were blazing, and she found herself almost blinded by the lights reflected off the walls of the large white room with marble columns in the style of a Roman bath. She jumped nervously as the metal door swung shut of its own weight behind her.

The blue-green pool water sloshed from side to side with enough motion that water sprayed against her feet.

"Steve?" she called. "Steve!" Her voice did not sound as confident as it usually did. "Darling, I'm here. I— *Ahhh!*"

Her words turned into a low scream when she noticed the man floating face-down at the far—the shallow—end of the pool, his corpse washing to and fro like a clump of kelp as the ship rolled in the sea. For a wild second, Jayne thought the body was mine, but then she saw that it had on jeans, a blue polo shirt, and white tennis shoes. This man was tall and lanky, and his hair was dark.

What she did next was simply instinctive. She kicked off her high heels and stepped into the pool to see if the man could be saved. Water dragged at her gown as she fished about, finally grasped the man's arm, and pulled him back toward the steps. He was too heavy for her to pull out of the pool, but she managed to flip him onto his back in the vague hope that he could then breathe. At once she saw that he could not—ever again.

The dead man was Peter Moon.

Jayne suddenly felt cold and frightened. She hurried out of the water, scooped up her shoes, and ran to the door. But now the heavy metal would not budge. She tried to open the door several times, and found there was no mistake. It was locked. Someone did not want her to leave this Roman bath of a tomb. Neither Jayne nor Peter Moon were going anywhere.

chapter 23

Cass and I inaugurated the brig aboard the gleaming new ocean liner. I suppose this was a singular honor, but the pleasure of it escaped me at the time.

Muttering dire warnings about the penalties for breaking and entering, not to mention assaulting a federal officer, Bermuda Schwartz had two beefy crew members lead us to jail, a ten-by-fifteen-foot cabin with no portholes and with four bunk beds hanging from the walls. There was a wash basin at one end and a small, open cubicle that contained a cramped toilet. The deck was hard, cold linoleum. There were no metal bars, which was nice, but the door leading to the corridor was locked from the outside. It was clean and not too uncomfortable, but it was a jail just the same. At least they didn't take our shoelaces or wrist-watches.

Cass and I passed the time by playing the casting game until Agent Schwartz arrived and all games ended for the time being. I glanced at my watch and saw that we had been imprisoned for less than an hour.

"Come with me," Schwartz said grumpily. His gray suit was wrinkled, and he looked a bit the worse for wear, with a day's growth of beard.

"Are you certain we've paid our debt to society?" I asked.

Schwartz muttered something that had a few choice four-letter words in it—very un-FBI, I thought—and led the way to the small conference room near the bridge. I had a glimpse of the bridge itself as we passed by. It was dimly lit, with green glowing screens and strange nautical devices, dark glass facing the open ocean ahead. It was actually thrilling to see it.

Cass and I continued behind the rumpled agent toward the conference table, where Schwartz motioned us to sit. "Coffee?" he asked.

It seemed a sort of peace offering, so I said, "Sure." Cass said he'd have some as well. Schwartz filled three Styrofoam cups from an electric urn, asked like a proper host if we wanted cream or sugar, then joined us at the table.

"Now then, Mr. Allen, Mr. Cassidy . . . suppose you tell me what the hell you think you're doing," he demanded.

"We're on our way to England, just like everyone else," I told him.

"Please, no jokes—if that's what that was. Look, leave the detective business to the professionals, okay? There's serious stuff going down here, and amateurs could get hurt."

"I'll remember that," I said. "But isn't it a pity that you professionals couldn't keep Dicky Wilmington from being killed?"

Schwartz ignored that. "Let's back up a little," he said evenly. "I want to know everything about your meeting with Marcus Wilmington."

"Then you finally believe I saw him?"

"We'll pretend I do, okay?"

"I'll pretend anything you want. But you'll have to tell me something in return."

"Like what?"

"Like what the FBI is doing on *The Atlantis*. And what authority you have to lock Cass and me up. These are international waters; I *could* tell you to take a hike."

He smiled dangerously. "You're talking technicalities, Mr. Allen. Sure, these are international waters. Sure the captain is in charge. But this vessel is registered in the United States, and the captain hopes to dock in New York harbor on his return, so he's anxious to accommodate me. If you'd like a smooth return to sunny California, you'd better do the same. Do I make myself clear?"

"Thoroughly."

"Good. Now suppose you answer my questions, and then maybe I'll tell you a few things in return."

"All right. What do you want to know?"

"Start from the beginning—when you left the ship with Dicky Wilmington."

"I didn't. It was Stewart Hoffman who took me."

Schwartz raised an eyebrow, just slightly, then asked about my helicopter ride, the blindfold, and the room where I met Marcus. He was interested that I had tried to count the time we were in the air, and he went over this carefully, trying to make a guess as to where we were.

"It could be the old man's house in Poughkeepsie. He has one of those huge mansions overlooking the Hudson."

"It smelled and sounded like a forest," I mentioned.

"He has about five hundred acres of trees behind the house."

"Well, maybe that was it then. Is it important where we were?"

"Everything's important. Now, what did he look like?"

"Don't you know?"

"No one but the family and a small inner circle have seen him for ten years," he admitted. "And they're not talking. That he met you in person has made me very curious. So let's start with his appearance."

I did my best to describe the odd old man, from his fuzzy ears to his ageless face. "He was like an elf. I couldn't tell if he was sixty or one hundred sixty."

"He's ninety-three, according to his birth certificate. Born in Cedar Rapids, Iowa, in nineteen hundred and one."

"Ninety-three! He seemed in good shape for that age, very trim and coherent. I even had the feeling he could be dangerous if he chose. Maybe there *is* some truth to the rumor that he went to a Greek island for some miracle rejuvenation."

"He did that in eighty-three, Mr. Allen. He spent two months on a small private island between Rhodes and Mykonos. We sent one of our agents there to check it out."

"You *are* curious, aren't you?"

"You bet. A man that rich—it's like having a small independent country in America. Rumors about his health can make the stock market rise or fall twenty points."

"Which brings us to what you're doing on this ship," I reminded.

He flashed his sour smile and asked me to continue with my account. I decided to be forthcoming in the hope that Schwartz would return the favor. I mentioned that the old man had offered me one hundred thousand dollars to keep an eye on things. Even that he had said to keep an eye on his children and his wife.

"It's getting late," I said finally. "And I'm weary. Now it's your turn to do some talking. Why are you on this boat?"

"For a lot of reasons," he said. "But mostly intuition. We're on the same side here, Mr. Allen, and I'd appreciate it if you'd let me know if Wilmington contacts you again."

"Of course," I said.

Cass yawned. "Look, I'm going back to my cabin and get a few winks."

"I'm calling it a night as well," I said.

The agent walked us to the door and wished us pleasant dreams.

"One more question," I persisted. "I'm so exhausted I almost forgot. Did the shotgun in Peter Moon's closet kill Wilmington?"

"We won't know that until we run some tests. We do know it was the missing skeet gun."

"How about Moon? Have you found him?"

"No. Now good night!"

Cass and I yawned all the way to my suite. He said good night outside, and I slipped inside quietly, so as not to disturb Jayne. But she was not in the sitting room or in bed. In fact, there was no sign that she had returned since Cass and I had last seen her at Candy's show.

Puzzled and worried, I picked up the phone, wondering which of our friends I could disturb so late to ask if they had seen my wife. I was dialing the Sheldons when I saw a small white envelope I had not noticed as I came in. It had been stuck under the door. I hung up the phone, opened the envelope, and read the computer-perfect capital letters on the note inside:

CHECK THE SWIMMING POOL IF YOU'RE FEELING LONELY. LET THIS BE A WARNING TO STAY OUT OF AFFAIRS THAT ARE NOT YOUR BUSINESS. THE NEXT TIME YOUR LONELINESS WILL LAST FOREVER.

chapter 24

I pounded down the hall, vaulted two steps at a time to the upper-deck swimming pool. The rain outside stung my face, but I hardly noticed.

The pool was drained and covered with blue canvas, the area was deserted. I looked at the abandoned tables by the poolside cafe and the deck chairs that had been folded, stacked, and tied down for the coming storm.

"Jayne!" I called. *"Jayne!"*

There was no answer but the wind. A sudden terror churned the pit of my stomach, and I was about to untie the canvas that covered the pool to see what might lie beneath when I remembered there was a second pool, indoors someplace. Was *that* where I was supposed to find Jayne? I thought of calling Cass for help but was too frantic to take the time.

Running inside, I consulted the map of the ship that was mounted by the elevators, though I was in such a panic, at first I could find no meaning in its colored lines. I forced myself to take a deep breath and calm down. Almost immediately I located the reference to the Indoor Swimming Pool, Deck F. I summoned the elevator and descended into the depths of the ship. Then I followed the arrows through the maze of long, gloomy corridors to the door marked POOL. It was locked, but a key had been left in the lock. I turned that, opened the door, stepped into the brightly lit, cavernous room—and saw Jayne at once. She was sitting calmly on a chair beside the deep end of the pool.

"Jayne! Are you all right?"

"*I'm* fine, dear."

"What are you doing here? Did someone attack you?"

"No. I just got myself locked in this dreadful place."

"What's so dreadful about—*Oh!*" I exclaimed, noticing for the first time what was half hanging, half floating in the shallow end.

"It's Peter Moon," she said.

"Did you— ?"

"*I* didn't do it, darling. He was like this when I arrived."

"And why *did* you come here?"

"I was delivered a message—by a waiter—to meet you here. What brought you?"

"I got a message, too. I think we'd better get out of here," I said.

I took Jayne's hand and led her out of the pool and into the corridor. Someone was leading us on a merry chase. Someone who knew where to find us and how to set us in motion. But we knew nothing about him. It was maddening. Frightening.

Seeing a telephone by the elevators, I called Agent Schwartz. The switchboard operator was reluctant to put me through to his stateroom at such a late hour, but I assured her it was an emergency.

The FBI man answered in a groggy voice. "Yeah?"

"This is Steve Allen," I said. "Guess what?"

"It's too late for guessing games, Mr. Allen."

"My wife found Peter Moon," I told him. "I think you'd better come down to the F-Deck pool right away."

He did. Jayne and I answered questions until I reached such

a state of exhaustion all I cared about was getting into bed. That finally happened, shortly after three A.M.

And so ended our first full day aboard *The Atlantis*. It wasn't a boring day, but I was far from certain that I would recommend the ship to my friends.

chapter 25

I yawned and stretched like a waking tiger. With the curtains closed, the bedroom was dark, but I could hear Jayne moving about in the sitting room.

"Morning, dear," I called.

"Oh, good. You're awake." She breezed in with a glass of cold orange juice in one hand and a cup of hot coffee in the other.

Sitting up on my throne of pillows, I felt lazy and luxurious, which led to my yawning again, rather loudly.

"I've got a couple of bran muffins," Jayne said. "Do you want one?"

She was wearing a frilly white robe, and her red hair spilled beautifully over her shoulders, but when she opened the curtains, no sunlight came flooding in. The sky outside was dark gray with low-hanging clouds. And there was something different about the motion of the ship I couldn't quite put a name to it, since I was hardly an old salt and was not yet entirely awake.

"I feel as if I'd slept for a month. It must be after eight," I said.

"It's ten-fifteen."

"Damn, we've missed breakfast!"

"Don't worry. I called room service. Breakfast awaits you in the next room."

Jayne left me to rouse myself. I had been so tired the night before it took several minutes to shake off the lingering shrouds of sleep. For a moment I couldn't even remember what day it was and had to count forward from Saturday night, the last date I was sure of, the day we had come aboard *The Atlantis*. That meant yesterday was Sunday, and this—logical deduction— was Monday. When you are on vacation it's easy to lose track of such simple facts as the day of the week. Today was Day Two of our voyage. Ergo, tomorrow would be Day Three—Tuesday— and I was glad to remember that because I had two shows to do Tuesday night, murders or not. The show, as they say, must go on.

On Wednesday afternoon, Day Four, we would arrive in Southampton. Those of us who were still alive, that is.

I contemplated the threatening note I had received the previous night and how Jayne had been so easily trapped. I didn't like the way someone was manipulating us. We were in the middle of the ocean, in an unfamiliar, enclosed world, at the mercy of . . . well, many things.

As I stood up, I realized what had struck me about the motion of the ship: There *was* no motion. I pressed my nose to the porthole and studied the dark, ominous sky. The strange, unnatural calm of the sea seemed more frightening than the earlier tossing.

I joined Jayne at the cheerful room-service table. Breakfast— oatmeal and whole wheat toast—was accompanied by a special shipboard distillation of *The New York Times*. I tossed the paper aside. One of the joys of a sea voyage is that you can let the world go to hell on its own for a few days.

"Well, darling, what's on the agenda for today?" Jayne asked.

"Ping-Pong," I said. "I'm challenging you and Cass to a tournament."

"You're kidding."

"And of course there's horse racing this afternoon. Cass mentioned the ponies as we were leaving New York, and I'd kick myself if he missed it. Then there's a matinee of that new movie we wanted to see in Los Angeles but didn't have time for. And you know, I'm really looking forward to hearing Bobby Enriquez in The Seven Seas lounge tonight. A little of his magic on the ivories should calm our nerves."

"Steve . . ."

"I also thought we could go to the gym and work off some calories. Maybe even join that Ship Shape aerobics class."

"Steve, I know why you're doing this."

"Hmmm?"

"It's that threatening note. It's very chivalrous of you to worry about me, but you needn't. We'll just be careful."

"Look, we don't have a chance against whoever it is that's killing people. So let the FBI take care of it—that's what I say. Let Scotland Yard nab our killer when we get to England."

Jayne delicately held a bran muffin in midair. "So we're just going to play Ping-Pong?"

"We have to be reasonable, dear. And it's not only you I'm thinking about, it's Cass and myself as well."

Jayne chomped down on her muffin in a decisive way. "Meanwhile we have nearly three days left at sea. What if someone else gets killed? It isn't like you to give up."

"It's a new me," I told her. "From now on, you'll find me in a comfortable deck chair, finishing Gene Lees's book and snoozing my way across the ocean."

"Mmm," said Jayne, with a thoughtful pout. "What if the killer decides to get rid of us anyway, even if we *are* minding our own business?"

"That," I said, "is the one thing we must not do, under any circumstances."

"What?"

"Haven't you ever noticed that when we hear about terrible things happening to people—accidents, murders, drive-by shootings—there's always one factor the reports have in common?"

"And that is?"

"All the victims were *minding their own business.* Think about the comments of witnesses, or the victims themselves if they survive: 'Well, I don't know, Officer . . . I was stopped for a red light and this guy walks in front of me, just walking along *minding his own business,* when all of a sudden—*Wham!*' Or on some TV news show, a guy with a microphone up his nose says, 'We'd just gotten off the plane and were walking toward the terminals, just *minding our own business,* when all of a sudden—' "

"I get your point," Jayne said. "But tell me the truth. Aren't you scared?"

"Nah," I said.

"Good. I'm not either."

At that moment a loud rap on our door caused Jayne to nearly jump out of her skin.

I grinned. "Who is it?" I called.

"Radiogram, sir."

I walked to the door and, peering through the little peephole, saw a man in a white uniform. The peephole glass distorted his face like a funhouse mirror.

"Just leave it by the door," I said.

"Yes, sir."

I watched him disappear from the range of the peephole. After a moment, I unlocked the door, grabbed the white envelope, then locked the door again fast. I tore open the envelope and pulled out a radiogram form.

"Read it aloud," Jayne commanded.

" 'Dear Mr. Allen, Due to the serious nature of events on board *The Atlantis,* I now believe it best to leave the investigation to the proper authorities. I trust you will have a pleasant voyage. Best wishes . . . Marcus Wilmington.' "

I sat down with the radiogram in hand. Jayne took it from me.

"How do we know this even came from Mr. Wilmington?" she asked. "It's nothing but a piece of paper from a computer printer."

"It looks official."

"Wouldn't it be easy to get a radiogram form like this by passing through the radio room?"

I smiled at my clever Jayne and picked up the telephone on the coffee table. "Give me the radio room, please. . . . Radio room? Hello, this is Steve Allen. Do you keep a log of the messages you receive? . . . You do? Good. Can you tell me if I've gotten a radiogram in the past twelve hours? . . . That's right. Steve Allen. . . . Thank you."

I hung up the phone.

"Well?"

I shook my head. "You get an A-plus, dear."

We gazed uneasily at the bogus message that lay on the breakfast table between the butter and the raspberry jam.

There was a loud knock on the door, and this time we both jumped. I picked up a butter knife, the first weapon I could find.

"Who is it?" I called, threateningly.

"It's Cass."

His voice was muffled by the closed door. I approached cautiously and peered through the hole. I didn't see him.

"Where are you? Step in front of the door."

A fishlike image of Cass's face swam into view.

"Geez, what's going on in there?" he asked. "It's me, Cass."

"Are you alone?"

"Of course."

I opened the door.

"What's the deal, Steve? I missed you guys at breakfast."

Cass came into the sitting room, and I bolted and chained the door, then sank onto the sofa with a sigh. It was both exhausting and depressing to be this paranoid.

"We can't live like this, Steve," Jayne said simply. "Not for three days. Not even for fifteen minutes."

She was right, of course. If we were going to get killed, we might as well go down fighting.

"All right," I said. "But we stick together. I don't want any of us walking down lonely corridors late at night. Cass, I think you should move into our sitting room.

"Good idea," Jayne said. I believe the sofa can be converted into a bed.

I gave them a determined look.

"Okay, gang, from this moment, we're on the offensive!"

chapter 26

The sea was calm, but we were in motion.

I got Stewart Hoffman on the phone and told him, just for the record, that Marcus Wilmington had hired my services as a private detective and that I planned to keep on detecting until I learned who killed Dicky Wilmington and Peter Moon. And why.

Hoffman made no comment. Not a sound.

I also told him I had just received a radiogram, supposedly from the tycoon, taking me off the case, but since I had ascertained that the message was bogus I didn't intend to pay it any mind. If Wilmington no longer required my services, he would have to tell me personally.

"And what do you want from me, Mr. Allen?" Hoffman finally asked.

"Nothing much. Just that you stay out of my way."

"I hope you know what you're doing," he said. And then the line went dead.

I put down the telephone, a satisfied smile on my face.

"Well, you sure told him! You've got to bully a bully," Cass said encouragingly. "It's the only thing they understand."

Next I tried to phone Gertrude Wilmington. When she didn't answer, I left a message with the operator requesting an appointment with the matriarch. After that I called Will Sanders.

He was not in his stateroom, so I left a message for him as well. To tell the truth, I had no idea what I was doing, except stirring things up and making it clear that the investigating team of Allen-Cassidy-Allen was still in business.

Allen-Cassidy-Allen finished breakfast and walked together out on deck. The weather was very peculiar. The ship was enveloped in a thick wet mist, gliding through a motionless sea. At the stern, I looked down several decks to where a crewman was cleaning the skeet machine. Behind him, the wake of the great ship disappeared like a wide, flat highway into the fog. I asked Cass and Jayne to wait for me and jogged down to speak to the young man.

"Hello!" I called. "I need to talk to you!"

"I'm sorry, there's no skeet shooting today, sir. The visibility is too bad."

"I'm not interested in shooting. It's information I need."

He stood up from his work, a cloth in one hand, an oil can in the other. He smiled pleasantly as I read his name tag: CHRIS OBRECHT.

"I saw you here yesterday, Chris, with Tracy Devine," I said.

"Yeah. What a kick to see him in person. He gave me his autograph."

"That's nice. He was shooting skeet all afternoon?"

"Until the life drill, yes, sir," Chris told me. "He's a pretty good shot."

"When the drill began, do you remember what he did with the gun?"

Chris's smile faltered. I was not asking the sort of questions passengers were supposed to ask.

"I don't quite understand, sir."

"I'm interested in what happened to the shotgun. You realize there was a . . . an accident yesterday?"

"I'm not supposed to talk about that," he said cautiously.

"My name is Steve Allen. Marcus Wilmington asked me to

keep an eye on things, as a personal favor. So you can feel free to talk to me."

"Naturally I recognize you, Mr. Allen. But I already told everything I know to the FBI guy, and Mr. Hoffman asked me not to speak to anyone else."

"Perhaps you should call Mr. Hoffman again," I suggested. "He'll give you the okay to talk to me now."

A frightened look crossed the young man's eyes. I suspected he would just as soon not telephone Hoffman. After a short inner battle, Chris decided in my favor. I was glad; I had no idea what Hoffman would have told him, had he made the call.

"I guess it's all right then," he said. "Although there isn't much to tell. Mr. Devine was shooting up until the alarm sounded for the drill. Then I took the gun from him—you know, to put it away."

"You keep the guns down here?"

"Oh, no. That's against regulations. All weapons are kept in the arsenal on the bridge. Only the captain, Stewart Hoffman, and the first mate have the key. I have to sign out the shotgun from one of them, and then have them sign it back in."

"I see. So you took the gun back to the bridge?"

"I was about to, but Mr. Wilmington came by and said he'd do it for me."

"Which Mr. Wilmington?" I asked, with more than moderate interest.

"Dicky."

"Did that seem peculiar to you?"

"Well, yes. It *was*. But he's the boss. He said he was headed to the bridge anyway, and it would save me the trip. He seemed . . . Well, I probably shouldn't say. . . ."

"He seemed what?"

"Upset. He was very pale."

"Was he angry?"

"I would say frightened. I worried about the gun and told

him I had to go back to the bridge myself so it might be easier if I signed it in. But he got mad and—Hey, he was the boss."

"Did he take any shells?"

"No, but the gun was loaded. I told him that so he'd be careful. I even offered to unload it, but he said he'd do it. And that was all. He took the gun and I . . . uh . . . never saw him again."

I wondered why Wilmington had wanted to get his hands on a shotgun before his meeting with me. Who was he frightened of? Peter Moon? Stewart Hoffman? Someone else? He could not have been afraid of me, certainly.

"Did you hear the shot that came later—during the drill?"

The young man nodded. "Yeah. It came from up on deck somewhere, maybe ten minutes after I gave Mr. Wilmington the gun."

"What did you think?"

He shook his head unhappily. "I didn't know what to think. I knew it meant trouble, though."

I thanked Obrecht and walked slowly up to where I had left Jayne and Cass. I had a pretty good idea now how the shotgun had arrived at the murder scene. But how did it get from there into Peter Moon's closet? And if Moon had been the killer, how did he end up taking his final midnight swim?

I would have to find out from Agent Schwartz how Moon died exactly. There were so many mysteries. And so little time in which to solve them.

chapter 27

When we got back to our suite the telephone message light was blinking. Jayne called the operator.

"This is Jayne Meadows Allen. You have a message for us? ... I see .... Really? ... And you have such a charming Southern accent. ... You grew up in Baton Rouge? Oh, perhaps you know our very good friends. ..."

Jayne was off and running. She is the only person I know who can chat for ten minutes to someone she's never met and end up with intimate details of that person's life. Cass and I relaxed on the settee and patiently waited for her to finish.

"Isn't that extraordinary?" she said, putting down the receiver. "The operator grew up in Baton Rouge, the youngest of eight children—"

"Jayne, what was the message?"

"Message?"

"The light was flashing. Remember?"

"Oh, yes! It was Gertrude Wilmington. She asked us to drop by her cabin any time before lunch."

"Let's go," I said, jumping up.

"I've got to get dressed," Jayne said.

"Sweetheart," I pointed out, "you're already dressed."

"I know that," she said, "but I want to make a good impression. How do you like this pants suit?" She removed a flowery outfit from the closet.

"I think it's sensational."

"Good," she said, "then I'll wear this other one."

And with that she lifted out a floor-length, turquoise blue gown that we had picked up a couple of years earlier on a visit to Maui.

A short time later we took the stairs to A Deck, walked toward the bow of the ship and through a door that said CREW ONLY. An officer made a phone call to make certain we were expected, then pointed us toward a private elevator that had no buttons to push. The doors closed behind us, and a moment later, we were deposited directly into Gertrude Wilmington's grandiose suite.

"Hello, hello!" Will Sanders said, stepping toward us as we came out of the elevator. "Can I get you a drink? How about some fresh papaya-mango-cherry juice? It's my own concoction."

We said yes to the fruit drink, gazing about at all the splendor.

"Not bad, is it?" Will said.

It wasn't bad at all. The room's glassed section provided a panoramic view forward of the ship and the sea. The dark, polished wood floors were partly covered with Oriental rugs. We might have been in a Paris salon at the end of the last century. There was even a fireplace, and above its marble mantelpiece hung an original Rembrandt. A Picasso decorated the opposite wall. My eye moved across the room to a gleaming black concert grand. The cabin was so large the piano seemed small.

"It's a nineteen twenty-five Steinway," Will told us. "Used to belong to Rachmaninoff. Vladimir Horowitz was kind enough to give Mr. Wilmington a few lessons."

"Piano lessons from Horowitz!" Jayne said. "How amazing! Mr. Wilmington must play very well."

Will chuckled. "Actually, not much more than 'Chopsticks.' But it keeps him amused. Sit down, please."

Jayne and I arranged ourselves on a sofa while Cass sat gingerly on an antique chair. He seemed afraid to lean back.

Sanders brought our fruit drinks. He was being quite the charming host.

"Yes, it's a lovely ship, *The Atlantis*," he said happily. "I'd say the loveliest of all time. Certainly the most expensive."

He sat down across from us on a Louis XV chair. The attorney was beaming so brightly, and everything about the moment was so pleasant, I hated to remind him that two people had been murdered on this beautiful vessel. So I went along with his chatty manner.

"What's happening with the weather?" I asked. "It seems unnaturally calm."

"The calm before the storm, unfortunately. I'm afraid we're in for it tonight. Tomorrow morning at the latest."

"Will it be bad?" Jayne asked.

"Well, it won't be life-threatening—*The Atlantis* could sail through a lot worse—but the passengers aren't going to like it. Captain Mellon has advised us to turn south and try to miss the worst of it, but that would make us a day late in reaching Southampton."

"I doubt if anyone would mind," I said. "As long as you keep feeding us so splendidly."

The attorney smiled. "Yes, but that's part of the problem. An extra day changes the economics of the voyage. With the crew's wages, food, fuel, late-docking charges, and overtime for the people waiting to service the ship, we'd be losing a great deal of money. One extra day and costs could rise by as much as thirty percent."

"Money be damned!" said a regal, booming voice from behind our sofa. It was Gertrude Wilmington. Cass, Sanders, and I rose to greet her. Gertrude had regained her composure since I had last seen her. She was dressed in becoming black, with diamond broach on her left breast and a string of diamonds around her neck. They were small gems, probably only her daytime gems. Her gray hair was pulled severely back into a bun. She glided into the drawing room like Queen Elizabeth inspecting her troops, touched my hand, did the same to Cass, shook hands with Jayne more affably, and—oddly—glared at Sanders.

"What are you saying about money, Will?" she demanded.

"Only that an extra day at sea would cause some nasty red ink, Gertrude."

Mrs. Wilmington chuckled. "Actually," she said, seating herself gracefully, "it doesn't matter what any of us might think advisable. My husband has made a final decision."

"Oh?" Sanders said, turning his head sharply toward her.

"Yes," she said. "I've just finished talking to him on the telephone. I'm afraid *The Atlantis* will be passing directly into the eye of the storm."

chapter 28

Mrs. Wilmington and Will Sanders sat across from Jayne, Cass, and me, at a rococo gilt-edged coffee table. Gertrude sat with her spine stiff. Will crossed his legs and managed to look relaxed in his lanky way.

"I wanted to see you," I said, "because I received a radiogram this morning. It purports to be from your husband canceling his request that I do some secret sleuthing during the voyage. Are you aware, Mrs. Wilmington, that your husband met with me on Saturday night?"

"I heard that from Stewart, naturally. Frankly I do not approve of Marcus's theatrics. I trust you survived being blindfolded and those other games he plays when he invites guests to see him?"

"I'm willing to let the man enjoy his eccentricities," I said. "However, the message I received this morning, according to the radio room, was *not* sent by your husband. This means it came from someone on the ship—someone trying to frighten me off."

"And have they succeeded?" Gertrude asked.

"Not a bit. We're much too involved to quit this case, even if your husband had sent that message. After all, I found one of the victims, and Jayne the other. I'm not going to stop until I've brought the killer of your son and of Peter Moon to justice. I want you to know that, just for the record. If anyone thinks he can frighten us off this investigation, he's very wrong."

"Spoken bravely," Sanders said, "but do you really think you can do more than the authorities?"

"We all know there isn't going to be a full investigation until we reach England. And by then it could be too late."

"Well, personally I think you should leave this to Hoffman," the attorney said, smiling condescendingly. "Security is his department. Anyway, it isn't the best idea, Steve, for you to be going about, uh . . . disturbing the guests. Particularly if there's any personal danger involved for you and Jayne."

"Will, stop talking like an idiot," Gertrude said. Everything that came out of her mouth sounded like a royal decree. "I'm determined to find the murderer of my son." She turned toward me. "I would like to engage your services myself, Mr. Allen."

"Gertrude, Stewart is not going to be pleased—"

"I don't give a fig what pleases Mr. Hoffman!" Gertrude interrupted. She turned to me. "I want to learn who murdered my son a great deal more than you do, Mr. Allen. In fact, I'll pay you whatever my husband was offering—though at the moment I don't actually have any cash to speak of. Perhaps you would settle for a nice Picasso?"

"I'm not certain at this point that I want to work for anyone but myself. For all I know, Mrs. Wilmington, *you* could be involved in these murders."

"Don't be impertinent, sir. Explain yourself."

"I'm talking about pension funds. The ones that have been shifted around to finance this ship."

"That's ridiculous!" cried the attorney.

"Shut up, Will," said Gertrude, studying me calmly. "It's horrible, I suppose, gambling with the lives of thousands of little people, but great fortunes are often built on a throw of the dice, Mr. Allen. In any event, we had no choice. Peter Moon would have had us a year ago if it weren't for the fresh infusion of cash—and Dicky's little double cross. You see, Mr. Moon believed Dicky was spying for him, but my son was actually giving him false information, a strategy that bought us time. And we unlawfully took some pension money—temporarily, of course—to tide us over. Personally, I'd rather be in prison than lose the game to an unsavory upstart like Peter Moon."

I had a certain wary respect for Gertrude Wilmington because she had admitted the crime so freely.

"And now Moon is not around to trouble you anymore," I mentioned.

"Yes. And I'm not sorry. Nevertheless, I had no part in his death."

"Mrs. Wilmington, your son wanted to talk with me after the life drill. He seemed worried. Do you have any idea what was on his mind?"

"My son was not a very happy person," Gertrude admitted. "He felt his father did not appreciate him or give him any real responsibility."

"I've heard that."

"And recently, of course . . . well, he suspected his wife was having an affair."

"With whom?" Jayne asked, surprised that the drab and snobbish Wendy Wilmington would do anything so dramatic.

"We don't know. But she lied a few times, saying she had gone to a woman friend's house when she had done nothing of the sort."

"How do you know?" I asked.

"Dicky always confided in me, particularly when he was unhappy. He suggested divorce, but of course I told him that was out of the question."

"But why?" Jayne asked.

"You Hollywood people may do as you choose," Gertrude said majestically, "but we Wilmingtons do not allow our marital problems to get in the newspapers."

I decided to steer the conversation in a different direction.

"I'm not sure divorce was what was bothering your son yesterday, Mrs. Wilmington. He was so frightened of something that he took the skeet shotgun. Do you think he was afraid of Peter Moon?"

"He was frightened of everything and everybody, Mr. Allen. My Dicky was sweet, but . . . I know the gamble we were taking with the pension funds caused him some concern."

"Was there anything else? More recent? A person he was afraid of?"

"Not that I know of. Perhaps he didn't tell me everything. A mother always thinks so, but . . ."

"Tell me what you think of this scenario, Mrs. Wilmington. Say Peter Moon killed your son—perhaps he found out Dicky was double-crossing him and he became angry. Then let's say Stewart Hoffman found out somehow and took care of Peter Moon as an act of vigilante justice."

Or perhaps it was an execution ordered in revenge, by the Wilmington family, I thought to myself. I didn't say it, but I watched Gertrude Wilmington carefully, knowing she was probably capable of anything.

She apparently saw what I was driving at. "Stewart would let the law take care of the matter. And so would I, Mr. Allen. Not because either of us is faint of heart, but because it's stupid to take an unacceptable risk. Neither of us is stupid."

"I'm certain you're not. Is there anything else you can tell me?"

"Will," she said, "bring Mr. Allen that photograph."

The lawyer stood to do her bidding, and brought back from a desk drawer an eight-by-ten, glossy black-and-white picture of a man whose face I recognized immediately.

"Who is he?" I asked, keeping my face blank.

"You don't know him? He's the chairman of the board and major stockholder of Trans European Airlines, one of the largest carriers between London and New York. This is very possibly the man who killed my son. I know he hates the Wilmington family." She paused a moment, and her voice and eyes filled with ice. "If he did have any part in this, I want his head."

For a moment I pictured a butler carrying a severed head to Gertrude Wilmington on a silver platter.

"*Why* does he hate the Wilmington family?"

"It's an old story, Mr. Allen, and I don't wish to rehash the past. It's the present that concerns me."

I passed the photograph to Jayne. She looked at it and stifled a sharp cry of surprise.

It was Monsieur Duclerc. The funny little Frenchman from our table. Perhaps he was not so funny after all.

chapter 29

I closed my eyes and lifted my face into the warm rays.

Yes, the sun! While we had been talking with Gertrude Wilmington and Will Sanders, there had been a dramatic change in the weather. The mist had thinned and become translucent with light, a shimmering white shroud hovering on the water. Then *The Atlantis* burst out of the enclosing cloud into sharp clear sunlight. You could almost hear a collective "Ah!" rise up from the passengers. Both sky and ocean were suddenly a romantic blue. A fresh breeze came up, which sent our ship once again gently rocking over the waves. There was a chilling bite to this wind, but if you found a spot behind one of the glass windbreakers, as Jayne and Cass and I had done, the lulling, sleepy warmth of the sun made you want to curl up and go to sleep.

We decided to have lunch outside at the poolside cafe. Because so many seemed to have the same idea, the deck was crowded. There was a buzz of conversation and laughter, and a three-man Jamaican reggae group provided highly rhythmic music fortunately at low volume. Children swam in the pool, shrieking with delight. With the sunshine, a happy vacation mood had returned to the ship.

Lunch was served buffet style—but what a buffet! Jayne and I contented ourselves with the salad bar, where we found dozens of luscious selections, all served on huge clam shells by attendants in white aprons and chefs' hats. There was even sushi, that recent addition to the polyglot salad bar. Not the raw fish on rice, but the sliced rolls—rice and seaweed wrapped around bits of avocado and crab or tuna. It sounds strange if you haven't tried it, but California rolls are delicious. I plucked a few for my overcrowded plate, along with a pinch of *wasabe*, the nuclear-powered, green Japanese horseradish, which I mixed with a bit of soy sauce for dipping.

"Yuck! How can you eat seaweed and bait?" Cass made a face and continued past me toward long tables heavily laden with the more traditional ham, turkey, and roast beef, then to a cook preparing omelets to order. Jayne and I stared at our thin, wiry friend's heaped plate enviously, trying to figure out where all the calories went.

Sun and food occupied us for the next forty-five minutes or so, driving out of our minds any thought of murder and financial intrigue.

"I could get to like this," I told Jayne.

Alas, at that moment Bermuda Schwartz, back in casual attire, wandered our way. He was disheveled, as if he had been trailing a suspect for too many hours, sleeping in his car, and living on coffee and doughnuts. He settled down at our table with a heavy sigh, and Jayne, because of her warm mood, doubled her efforts to be charming.

"Agent Schwartz, where have you been keeping yourself?" she inquired. "You should make yourself up a plate of lunch at the buffet."

"My ulcer says no," he confided.

"Imagine that," I joked. "A talking ulcer."

He did not smile. "It's the stress of the job and the odd hours. People watch TV and they get the idea this is glamorous work. But the stress is no fun."

"Are you married?"

"Divorced."

"Oh, how sad."

"Well, it's probably for the best. I'm always out of town or busy on one case or another."

"Where is your home?"

"I grew up outside of St. Louis. But these days I'm based in D.C. Listen," he said, cutting the small talk, "I understand you folks saw Gertrude Wilmington this morning."

"How did you hear that?" I asked.

"Never mind how I get information. What did you talk about?"

"Oh, Rembrandt . . . Picasso. We had a very cultural morning." Mr. FBI was not amused, so I hurried on. "Then we talked about young Wilmington and Peter Moon. Money. Murder. Things like that."

"I want details," he said, pulling a notebook and a pen from his shirt pocket.

I went through the events of the morning like a good citizen, leaving out only that the Wilmingtons had been stealing from pension funds. I wanted Gertrude Wilmington to believe she could confide in me without my immediately running to the police. I wanted to keep my line of communication with her open.

Schwartz seemed particularly interested when I mentioned Monsieur Michel Duclerc; he wrote down the name.

"He's a big-shot businessman in Europe, but I don't know if he's legit," he admitted.

"Will you tell me what you find out?" I asked.

"Certainly," he said with a slight smile. "Tit for tat."

"Good. So tell me what killed Peter Moon. Was he shot?"

Schwartz shook his head. "From the ship's doctor's preliminary examination, it looks like he simply drowned."

"Just drowned?"

"There's no sign of a struggle. No contusions. No marks on his body—of any kind. No poison we can find. But his lungs were filled with sea water—"

"Which the pool is filled with," Jayne offered.

"How curious," I said slowly. "Particularly with the shotgun in his closet. I wonder how it all adds up."

"I've been wondering that, too," Schwartz said. "Don't go anywhere—I think I *will* make myself a plate of food."

While Schwartz was at the buffet tables, I tried to sort the puzzle out in my mind. Dicky Wilmington . . . Peter Moon . . . the pension funds . . . the shotgun that ended up in Moon's closet. There were various ways all these factors could fit together. A shadowy picture of the killer began to develop.

Agent Schwartz came back to the table with a huge plate of food. Despite his ulcer, he wasn't going to starve. All-you-can-eat buffets bring out the greed in all of us.

"You know," I said, "only one person can move about this ship as freely as he likes, has the opportunity to kill people and send crew members with fake messages, and can get in and out of locked pool areas or any other locked areas on board. I think we both know who that is."

"Maybe," Schwartz said. "But there isn't a shred of evidence against him."

"What if we prod him a little? Maybe set a small trap."

"Like what?"

"Like make him believe I've found some key evidence and I'm hot on his trail. Bait him a little. Then when he comes after me, you step out of the shadows and arrest him. Simple as that."

"That could be dangerous," Schwartz said. "And possibly illegal. Those of us in the Bureau have to be more careful than you civilians."

"I hope so," I said, smiling at him.

chapter 30

We briefly hobnobbed with the Princess that afternoon at the horse races. She was in the company of her two British escorts, Captain Dodsworth-Ellis—Doodie, to his friends—and the Earl of Donegall, whom everyone called Don.

Horse racing on board *The Atlantis* was not exactly Ascot, nor was it Longchamps or even Santa Anita. But it was fun nonetheless, and you could lose or win a bundle. The races took place on the dance floor of the Cafe Cabaña; six colorfully painted wooden horses stood at the gate ready to dash across the green felt squares of the course. The overly enthusiastic cruise director, Kevin Dobbs, was in charge of the action.

"Okaaay . . . is *eevvry*body ready?" he sang into his microphone like a carnival hawker. "Place your bets, ladies and gentlemen, right over there by the bar! Yes, siree, there's a bet for everyone! From two dollars to five hundred! Be quick, folks, the first race is about to begin!"

We decided that one of us would bet each race so we might feel the true thrill of the event. Cass read the names of the horses for the first race off a betting form. He thought he might put two dollars on horse number three, Dandy Dude, but I was urging him to back number one, Satin Doll, because as a friend of Johnny Mercer's, I liked the name. Jayne liked Nutcracker, since it reminded her of the ballet, but this was Cass's race and he went off to plunk his money down on Dandy Dude.

"Now I need some charming volunteers," cried Kevin Dobbs, dancing about with his microphone. "No, not *you*, sir —I said *charming!* Let's have your wife! I'll give her back, honest! That is if you want her! Ha! . . . What is your name, dear, and where are you from? . . . Susan from Lake Forest, Illinois? And how long have you been married, Susan? . . . Twenty-three years! Let's have a big round of sympathy for Susan!"

The cruise director needed six volunteers to man--or woman—each of the wooden horses, and another to pluck the dice from the spinning metal cage. As he was cajoling and pleading with the audience, Mudgie walked into the room with her two handsome escorts. All eyes, of course, immediately fastened upon her. I noticed Rusty O'Conner, at a table across the room, positively salivating.

"Your Highness?" the cruise director said. "How would you like to volunteer for horse number two, Uneasy Rider?"

Mudgie smiled shyly. I'm sure she wished she could decline, but as a proper young princess she had been taught a sense of responsibility toward us lesser mortals. "That would be just super!" she agreed.

"Wonderfully said! Your Highness, you may come and stand by your horse. And now, do we have any volunteers for horse number three, Dandy Dude?"

Clever Kevin Dobbs. He had no trouble getting volunteers now. Hands were raised all across the room—people eager to stand side by side with royalty. Even Rusty O'Conner had her hand up. Kevin Dobbs looked like a man who had died and gone to cruise director heaven. He peered about the room, ecstatically noticing Jayne's raised hand.

"Oh, how grand! Jayne Meadows, everybody! Miss Meadows, stand right there next to the Princess."

Jayne danced over to take her position on the green velvet,

standing so close to the Princess that it was natural for them to strike up a conversation.

"Isn't this absolutely cheery?" said the Princess.

"It certainly is," said Jayne. "Are you having a good time on *The Atlantis?*"

"Oh, quite! I haven't had such a good time since . . . since I don't *know* when!"

"Did you enjoy your stay in America?"

"Oh, yes, rather," she replied warmly. "We were in Arizona, you know. Such wide-open spaces. We don't have anything like that in England."

Meanwhile Doodie and Don sat down at the table next to mine. They were both in their early thirties, with fine ruddy complexions and the sort of military bearing you get from learning to ride horses correctly at a very young age.

"Oh, this *is* a lark!" Doodie said to me. "Aren't you that television fellow?"

"Yes, I am."

"Well, how extraordinary! Oh, look, we'll have to put some money down on Mudgie's horse to cheer her on. Be a good fellow, Don, and go bet a fiver for both of us."

The Earl of Donegall went off to the betting tables while the captain regarded me with a pleasant smile.

"I say, I heard there was some trouble on the ship yesterday. A chap got killed, I understand."

"Two chaps," I told him.

"They're keeping it very quiet, aren't they? Naturally I find myself concerned for the Princess when there's any sort of trouble about. Do you think the situation is well in hand?"

"I wouldn't worry, Captain," I told him.

"I understand you found one of the bodies. Did you?"

"I'm afraid so."

"How shocking for you. And it was an . . . accident?"

"At the moment, the entire thing's a great mystery," I told him honestly.

He nodded.

"I've spoken to that Stewart Hoffman fellow, of course," he said. "But he wasn't very forthcoming. I suppose he doesn't want to alarm us. So I was wondering, Mr. Allen, if by chance you hear of anything we should know . . . something that might affect the security of the Princess . . . if you would be so kind as to inform me at once?"

"Are you the Princess's bodyguard?" I asked, blunt American that I was.

He laughed. "Not officially. But I'm sure you can understand why I like to keep my eyes open."

Captain Dodsworth-Ellis gave me his card—his stateroom number was scribbled on it—and I promised to keep him informed. Then the Earl of Donegall returned from making his bet, the dice were rolled, and the horses galloped out of the gate. They tore up the green felt to the cheers of the crowd. Poor Mudgie got left behind nearly six squares, but she was a good sport. Jayne, bless her heart, came in ahead of the pack with Dandy Dude, and Cass won nine dollars for the two he had put down.

Mudgie returned to the table, to much applause, and she and Jayne continued to talk. The Princess was curious about our lives in California and what movie stars we knew, and she seemed thrilled to hear Jayne's stories about some of our show-business friends. All in all, her highness struck me as an exceedingly normal young woman.

The subject drifted to horses, real rather than wooden ones—and when Doodie discovered how knowledgeable Cass was on this subject, they were off and running, so to speak, discussing Appaloosas, Arabians, Morgans, and the qualitative differences between various British and American breeds. Cass was in his element, and not at all shy now that he had something interesting to discuss. I listened with half an ear until I saw Stewart Hoffman come into the room. Then I made my excuses and walked to the bar, where Hoffman was waiting for me.

He was the reason I was here. I had phoned after lunch to set up this appointment. It was nearly two-thirty now, and the horse-racing activity provided a safe cover.

When you meet with a killer, it's a good idea to choose a very public place.

chapter 31

Hoffman stood at the bar with a glass of something in his hand, staring at me with his icy, light blue eyes. He wore an expensive, well-cut, charcoal black suit, possibly of Italian silk. I suspected he made quite a tidy sum as security chief for the Wilmington family.

"So what can I do for you, Mr. Allen?" he asked, coming immediately to the point.

"It's what I can do for *you*, Hoffman," I said, putting on my best no-nonsense voice.

He raised an eyebrow. "I don't have time for games today."

"I think you do," I assured him. "I think you and I are going to play an interesting one—let's pretend."

"Let's pretend what?"

"Let's pretend you murdered Dicky Wilmington and Peter Moon, for instance."

He smiled coldly. "All right," he said. "Let's pretend I killed them. How did I do it? And why?"

"Well, first we have to pretend that Wilmington was in trouble, way over his head. He was double-crossing Moon, who found out about it and became extremely angry. He threatened dire consequences unless Dicky started giving him the real goods on Wilmex Corporation."

"What did Moon threaten?"

"Prison," I said. "And it wasn't a bad threat either, as threats go. Moon said he'd turn Dicky in for securities fraud, stealing pension funds, all sorts of illegal financial finaglings. I probably don't know the half of it. But Moon knew enough to blackmail Dicky. After all, as CEO Dicky was the one the authorities would haul away. So Dicky was caught between a rock and a hard place: Moon on the one hand and you on the other. He panicked, set up his secret meeting with me in the hope that, as a disinterested third party, I might be able to help."

"Interesting. But why would Dicky be afraid of me? I'm paid to protect him."

"No, you're paid to protect the interests of the Wilmington family. Moon had left Dicky no choice but to turn traitor—for real—so Dicky was as frightened of you as he was of Peter. That's why he took a shotgun to the top deck for his meeting with me."

Stewart Hoffman shrugged almost sleepily. "And then what happened?"

"Let's pretend," I said, "that you and your spies were keeping a very close watch on Dicky Wilmington and knew about his meeting with me. You could tell that he was ready to crack, so you got to the meeting first. Maybe you hid behind the smokestack to wait for him. You were surprised to see he was armed, although I doubt if that caused you much alarm."

"I disarmed him?"

"Could be. You probably only had to look him in the eye and say, 'Look, kid, let's not have any more nonsense. Give me the gun.' Maybe you pretended to be cooperative and told him that together you'd work out the problem with Moon. Dicky was not a strong person. Whatever you said, he gave you the gun."

Stewart leaned closer, staring intently into my eyes. "Then what did I do?"

"You looked about to make certain you were alone, and then you shot him."

"But why?"

"He was unreliable. It was safer to have him dead."

While we talked, I was vaguely aware of the continuing horse racing. Bets were made, volunteers coerced, dice rolled, and the wooden horses galloped on the green felt, accompanied by cheers and comic jeers. No one was looking at Stewart and me, our heads close together at the bar. It was strangely intimate. Hoffman's cold eyes twinkled; I sensed he was enjoying our dangerous game.

"All right, Steve," he said, "let's pretend I shot Dicky. Then what?"

"You left the shotgun by the body."

"Wouldn't it have been safer to toss it overboard?"

"Perhaps. But you thought it more clever to make Dicky's death look like suicide. You wiped your prints off the gun and then arranged Dicky's finger—"

"Big toe," he said.

"I beg your pardon?"

"With a shotgun, that's the best way to do it. Put the barrel in your mouth, or to your chest, and squeeze the trigger with your big toe. That's how Ernest Hemingway killed himself."

It was my turn to be surprised. "Well," I said. "I didn't real ize you were a literary man."

"I like action stories. Guns and derring-do."

"I'll bet you do. So you arranged it to look as if Dicky shot himself, with his big toe—"

"Go on," he said, because I had stopped cold, a faroff expression on my face.

The human mind is a funny creature, partly independent of the will. It's strange what you choose to remember and to forget. Yesterday I had been in a state of shock at coming upon Wilmington's body. I am not used to sights like that, thank God. Even now, the image refused to come into sharp focus. But one memory jogged loose: *Dicky Wilmington had one foot bare when I found him!*

I remembered I had thought it odd, but then it had passed

completely out of my mind. And there was something else I remembered now—the pack of matches near Dicky's corpse. *Good God, what had I done with them?*

"You look like a drowning man seeing his life pass by," Hoffman observed unsympathetically.

"I was remembering a few things. Dicky *was* barefoot, god damn it! Just like you said!"

"Well, it's only logical. If you're going to commit suicide with a rifle or a shotgun, that's the way you do it. Personally I'd use a pistol and save myself the bother."

I hated Stewart Hoffman for a second. But I got hold of myself; this was no time to lose control.

"So you killed him," I said. "Poor insecure Richard Wilmington. A rich boy who only wanted his father's love and respect. You shot him, and then tried to make it look like suicide. You're a real lowlife, Hoffman—you know that?"

"Well, let's *pretend* I am," Stewart agreed. "Let's pretend it went down just like you said. Then what happened?"

"Here's where fate took a hand. You thought you were safe—that everyone was at the life boat drill, all the way down on Promenade Deck. But someone saw you kill Dicky."

"Peter Moon?"

"Yes, Moon. He was suspicious of Dicky and had been following him that day. As soon as you were gone, Moon came out from wherever he was hiding and took the shotgun."

"But why would he do that?"

"Because *he* didn't want the death to look like suicide. He wanted it to look like murder."

Hoffman laughed. He seemed to be having too good a time. "Tell me," he said, "why would he want it to look like murder?"

"So he could blackmail you. As for the gun, it still had a few shells in it; perhaps he believed he might need it to defend himself if you got nasty."

"Sounds reasonable," Hoffman agreed. "I *can* get nasty. . . . But then, I guess we all can."

"Yes, we can. Unfortunately, Moon was not as terrified of you as he should have been because he approached you with a deal. Your response was to lure him to the indoor pool and hold his head under water. Simple as that. Case solved."

There were loose ends, but I thought I had the general details correct enough to scare Hoffman. Except he didn't look frightened.

"You can't prove any of this," he said with a grin.

"Not yet. But by the time we get to England, I'm going see you signed, sealed, and delivered to Scotland Yard."

He studied me in a good-natured way. "You know, I think I underestimated you, Steve."

"Maybe."

"But aren't you at all frightened? I mean, here we are, in the middle of the Atlantic Ocean, I'm the chief of security, I have guns, handcuffs, all sorts of people working for me—and informants too, you're absolutely right about that. I'm like a god on this boat. And what are you? You and your wife and that cowboy friend of yours—I'm not even certain you're a worthy opponent."

Strangely enough, now that the battle had begun, he didn't frighten me at all. Well, maybe just a bit. But I wasn't about to admit it.

"I guess, we'll just have to see who has the last laugh, won't we, Stu?"

"But I'm laughing now!" And he was, almost. Or at least his eyes were. "Look," he said, "I think we can make some sort of deal that might be mutually advantageous."

"You do?"

"I'm sure of it. I'll be in touch. Meanwhile, if I were you, I'd be *very* careful."

He tapped his index finger twice against my chest as he said "*very* careful," then smiled a smug smile and walked out of the bar.

My mouth was dry so I ordered a glass of soda water with

lemon. To my surprise, my hand was shaking when I raised the glass to my lips. But I was pleased. I had taken the offensive. Now I just had to protect Jayne, Cass, and myself—and wait for him to come at us. My plan was simple enough: When he tried to kill us, we would turn the tables on him and present him in a neat package to FBI-man Schwartz. We only had to be smarter, faster, and more dangerous than he. What could be easier?

But danger arrived sooner than I had expected. As I stood congratulating myself, the barrel of a small gun was suddenly jabbed into my back.

"Put the glass down slowly," said a voice in my ear. "Easy . . . Now let's take a walk on deck."

It was a familiar voice. Though I could not place it, the gun in my back convinced me to do precisely what the man said. I walked through the crowded bar, my abductor practically breathing on my neck. I had a glimpse of Jayne and Cass sitting at the table with their backs to me, cheering a wooden horse. They might as well have been a thousand miles away—for I could think of no way to attract their attention.

I stepped out on deck and walked toward the rail.

"You can turn around now. But the gun is in my pocket, so don't do anything stupid."

I turned. Standing in front of me, his hand aiming a small pistol through the material of his pocket, was the last person I would have expected to pull a gun on me—Tracy Devine, the TV detective.

chapter 32

Tracy Devine had apparently forgotten about the scriptwriters, camera technicians, and stunt doubles who made actors' feats seem so easy and had started to think he was really Frankie Brand, the cool, hard-living private eye who solved every case in less than an hour and got a lot of beautiful women besides.

Devine, in his early fifties, had broad shoulders, a square jaw, a strong nose, smoldering dark eyes, and lustrous black hair. Without makeup you could see bags under his eyes and other signs that life in the fast lane was working its damage. But he was still good-looking, if you like the aging matinee-idol type.

"What now?" I asked. "You're going to have to feed me my lines, Tracy, because the director forgot to give me a script."

"We're not on camera, Steverino. This is real life."

A young Yuppie couple in matching jogging suits came out of the Cafe Cabaña, and Tracy got nervous. "Stay cool," he hissed. "I'd hate to give you a second belly button."

I laughed, because I'd seen the show that line came from. I could tell I had hurt his feelings.

"Let's go up a deck where people won't disturb us," he said.

"Whatever you want." I walked ahead of him up the wooden stairs. Then, just as we approached the top, I tried a move I had seen in a movie once: I kicked out behind me with my right foot. Tracy went tumbling backward down the stairs and hit with a loud *oomph!* He lay in a heap at the bottom, and I ran down and pinned him under my knee.

He moaned. "I think I've sprained something," he whimpered.

"It's your own damn fault. Now let me have the gun."

"Jeez, it's only a water pistol. You think I could smuggle a real gun on this ship with all those scanning devices they had at the dock?"

I pulled it out of his pocket anyway. It was bright orange plastic with a rubber stopper on the back. Great summer fun for six-year-olds.

"You should be more careful, or you'll wet yourself," I told him.

"Jeez, man, you shouldn't have hurt me like that!" he complained. "I need a doctor."

"You're fine," I told him.

The promenading Yuppie couple had turned around to stare at us. I smiled at them as though we were just overgrown boys having a good time with a squirt gun, and they quickly jogged to a safer part of the ship. As I helped Tracy to his feet, he wiggled his matinee-idol nose back and forth to make certain it was still in one piece.

"God, if anything had happened to my nose, my career would've been over."

"You could always learn how to act," I suggested.

"Very funny. Am I bleeding?"

"Not yet," I told him. "But you *will* be if you don't tell me what this is all about."

"The man wants to know what this is about!" he cried, lifting his eyes to the heavens—heavens, I should mention, that were starting to look stormy again. *"I'll* tell you what this is about. They're canceling my series! Millions of good Americans aren't going to know what to do with themselves Wednesday nights at nine o'clock!"

"Maybe they'll read a book."

Devine was a baby once you took his water pistol away. He limped toward the nearest deck chair, groaning and nursing his wounds. I sat down beside him.

"Okay, they're canceling your show," I prodded. "What does that have to do with me?"

"They're canceling *every*body's show," he mourned.

"Who is?"

"Wil-Star—whad'ya think we're talking about, for chrissake?"

"Ah!" The light was dawning. Wil-Star was the television division of the studio owned by Wilmex Corporation.

"They're goin' belly-up," Tracy said gloomily. "The whole damn studio will be in receivership by the end of the month— that's the inside scoop."

"But certainly the new owner will continue the series."

"Not in this case, Steve. Some strange stuff has been goin' on. The financial picture is so tangled it's gonna take the Justice Department, the IRS, *and* the Securities Exchange Commission to figure it out. And by the time *that* happens, I could miss a whole season. And you know how fickle the public is. I might as well kill myself now and be done with it!"

"Wouldn't it be better to just take your show to another studio?"

He shot me an unhappy look. "It's a little more complicated than that," he said slowly. "A lot of my own money is invested in the studio. A few years ago, when my series started to take off, I took stock options instead of cash. I thought I was being smart. Like, how could I lose in a joint venture with Marcus Wilmington, right? Wrong! Then, to make it worse, about five months ago I went heavily into the theme-park thing."

"What theme-park thing?"

"With the studio. You know, we were going to have all sorts of rides. I had a great idea for a roller coaster called The Nielsen Rating. Goes up and down. Stuff like that. The son of a bitch convinced me to put ten million dollars into the thing—just about every penny I had. 'How can you lose?' the man said. And then the bastard robbed me blind."

"Slow down, Tracy. Who are you talking about? Marcus Wilmington?"

"I suppose so, although I never dealt with the old man. It's Will Sanders—that slick son-of-a-bitch! I'm gonna kill him!"

"Tracy, I would advise you not to voice threats like that. Not on this ship. You may regret it."

"I don't care. Look, I'm from the Bronx. Carlo Sappelli. The youngest of five kids who grew up in a crummy flat. I quit school in the fifth grade and got lucky in California. I worked hard for my money, and I'm not gonna lose it to some slick, Ivy-League bastard like Sanders. I lie awake nights thinking of what I'm gonna do to him! It ain't gonna be a quick death, man. . . ."

"Take it easy, Tracy. None of it's worth killing for. You're a star; you'll make more money."

"Steve, I know I don't look it, but I'm sixty-three years old. This beautiful black hair? A goddamned piece."

"I never would have suspected!"

"Well, it is. So how much longer am I gonna get away with acting like a kid on television, running around with a gun and getting all the babes? I invested my money with the Wilmington family so I could retire. Home, grandchildren—that sort of thing. I came on *The Atlantis* hoping I'd run into the old man, maybe work things out with him, get some of my money back. I'm tired of dealing with Sanders. And Dicky. But the old man is harder to see than God. I've written him letters, I left maybe thirty phone messages—he never calls me back."

"Well, he's shy. Howard Hughes didn't answer his mail either."

"Yeah? The old fox let some jerk journalist interview him last month! *That's* what really got me angry. He won't see me! Hell, I only invested ten million dollars in his damn theme park! And then, to add insult to injury, he gives an interview to *Trend* magazine!"

"Wait a minute. Are you sure Marcus Wilmington did an interview with *Trend?*"

"You didn't see it? I think it was his first interview in twenty years. With that Larry Goldman guy."

I was more surprised by the interview with *Trend* magazine than anything else Tracy had told me. It was hard to imagine the famous recluse exposing himself to the public—and with Goldman no less.

"So what does this have to do with me? Why the hell did you stick a pretend gun in my back and get me out here?"

"Because someone told me you were in thick with the old man. I thought if you were scared of me I could get to him through you."

"Sorry. I only met Mr. Wilmington the one time."

"Well, that's one more than most people. Christ, Wendy's only seen him once— about ten years ago—and she's his daughter-in-law, for chrissake."

"Wendy Wilmington? How do you know her?"

He looked away for a long moment. "Well, that's a bit of a story. . . ."

"You don't mean—"

"Yeah, I do. I'm sick of hiding it actually. You know, I don't usually carry on with married women, but I met her in L.A. about a year ago at some charity thing I was doing. I'd been lookin' for a ritzy woman like her for a long time. Someone who knows what fork to use at a five-course dinner."

My mouth was hanging open in surprise. The combination of Wendy Wilmington, the anemic, prissy blonde, and Tracy Devine, the big, not-too-bright hunk of a TV star, was an image I couldn't get in focus. But who can make sense of matters of lust and love?

"Dicky didn't know about it, though maybe he suspected," Tracy went on unhappily. "Wendy was going to tell him yesterday, as a matter of fact. She was all set to do it after the lifeboat drill. But she never got a chance."

I nodded, feeling like a sleepwalker in a strange land. I had a sudden suspicion. "Was Wendy the one who told you I was in thick with the old man?"

Tracy nodded. "Yeah. She and Dicky couldn't get over the fact that the old bastard actually saw you."

Listening to Devine, I had a dizzy sense of human complexity. The deaths of Dicky Wilmington and Peter Moon seemed suddenly part of a more complicated puzzle. I wondered how many other angry investors were aboard *The Atlantis*, how many secret lovers. For all I knew, Wendy Wilmington might have killed her husband.

"By the way, Tracy, has Wendy ever talked to you about, uh . . . Peter Moon?"

"That's been over for at least a year. She was feeling lonely, and it just kinda happened."

"Peter and Wendy?"

"Isn't that who we're talking about?"

I wasn't certain I could stomach any more revelations, and being worried about Cass and Jayne, I tossed Tracy's squirt gun into his lap. "Don't try anything like that again without your stunt double," I told him as I stood up.

"Look, Steve, if you run into old man Wilmington, ask him what happened to my money—okay?"

"You're sitting on it," I told him.

The actor wasn't bright. He thought I was making some obscure joke. He looked around for his money. He looked at his chair, at the deck. He didn't understand that the beautiful *Atlantis* had sailed off with his dreams.

chapter 33

I'd solved one mystery at least, talking to the TV hero. Ever since my conversation with Hoffman, I had been wondering what I had done with the book of matches I had found near Wilmington's body. Maybe they weren't important, but I certainly wanted to look at them. Pulling the squirt gun from Tracy's pocket made me remember putting the matches in my shorts pocket. My one thought now was to retrieve them.

The horse racing had ended. I spotted Jayne and Cass talking with Mudgie and her two companions. As I approached, I overheard Jayne inviting Mudgie to visit us at our house when she next came to California, and Mudgie was suggesting lunch together when we got to England. I suppose it was a big deal, but I had more important things on my mind.

"Jayne, do you remember what shorts I was wearing yesterday afternoon at the lifeboat drill?"

Jayne smiled apologetically at the Princess. "You'll have to forgive my husband. He's a little eccentric, but sweet."

"Come on, Jayne, Cass—we have to go. It was an honor to meet you, Your Highness—and you gentlemen as well."

I guided Jayne away from her royal friend. She waited until we were in the privacy of our stateroom to explode.

"Steve! That was *very* rude!"

Cass sat on the settee enjoying Jayne's description of the social heights we might have scaled.

"Hang social heights!" I said. "Was it the red shorts or the ones with sailboats on 'em?"

Jayne threw up her hands in resignation. "It was those blue-and-white checkered things. Why is that so important?"

"Where are they?" I was tearing through my drawers, making quite a mess, but I couldn't see them.

"Steve, stop throwing your clothes about like that. Your shorts are in the laundry, of course."

"*What?*"

"I gave them to our cabin steward this morning to be laundered."

"Damn!"

"Steve, you're acting like a loose cannon," Cass said. He's loyal to Jayne and gets very unhappy when I don't treat her properly.

I apologized, and the dark cloud hovering over our domestic bliss went away as quickly as it had arrived, unlike the dark clouds gathering over the ship. The wind had come up again, and *The Atlantis* was pitching and rolling even more than it had the previous night. One wave sent Jayne into my arms. But I had no time to enjoy the moment; I was on a quest for my checkered shorts.

After a number of phone calls to and from Matthew, our cabin steward, plus some to the laundry room, we discovered that my shorts could not be returned until the following morning, come hell or high water. I cajoled and pleaded, even intimated that I was a friend of Marcus Wilmington and that the old tycoon would be *very* upset if I could not get my blue-and-white shorts at once. When everything else failed, I bribed Matthew, giving him fifty dollars to take me to the laundry room and promising that I would iron out any difficulties with his superiors.

Leaving Jayne in Cass's care, I told them to lock the door and not open it for anyone except me. Then Matthew led me down halls and stairs, through a door marked CREW ONLY, and finally to a door marked HOUSEKEEPING. We passed hampers full of dirty sheets and towels and a group of noisy cabin stewards who were without their jackets, ties, and fine manners. They greeted Matthew by slapping palms and looked at me in a friendly, curious way. This was a world within a world, the backstage of the glamorous ship. We turned along a new corridor and came to a door marked LAUNDRY.

The huge room was filled with the hot smell of steam and suds. Giant hampers full of individual laundry bags stood in a line waiting to receive attention. A dozen people in white overalls were busy feeding washing machines. In another part of the room, other workers ironed and folded. Above the din of the machines, grunge-rock, sans melody—and short on harmony as well—blared from a tape player.

Matthew introduced me to Kitty LeMieux, who was a huge Polynesian woman with a child-like face, the Superintendent of Laundry.

"You really shouldn't be down here, Mr. Allen," she scolded good-naturedly as she proceeded to track down my small laundry bag in her queendom of dirty clothes. Like everything else on board, the laundry arena was computerized; she punched in my name and cabin number and in seconds came up with a specific hamper. Then we walked together toward the long line of washing machines. But, alas, we got there too late. I recognized Jayne's cream-colored blouse and my Jazz All Stars T-shirt swimming and bobbing behind the washing-machine window. For a second I even saw the object of my quest—then the shorts were swallowed by suds.

"Open the door," I cried. "I need those shorts!"

"I wish I could help, Mr. Allen, but the door locks until the cycle is finished," Kitty explained patiently.

I did not accept this gladly, but had to bow to the inevitable. It was too late anyway. The pockets and matchbook were already wet. I waited in a fractious mood, watching my clothes spin and rinse and spin again. At last the red light on the machine went off.

The moment Kitty opened the door, I grabbed my damp shorts. Not optimistic, I fumbled inside the pockets, and found the matchbook in the right-hand one. It was a messy tangle of damp cardboard and sulphur, although the stylized drawing of *The Atlantis* was still recognizable on the cover. I opened the cover carefully. There were some numbers written inside, but I had no idea what they signified. They were faded but still partially legible: 9267. Or perhaps the 9 was actually an *F*. Then again, the final 7 could have been a 9 or even a 4.

"So that's what all this fuss was about? What is that? Some lady's phone number?" Kitty asked, shaking her head in amusement.

"Yeah, I guess so," I told her.

But they might be a combination of letters and numbers, and that deepened the mystery.

chapter 34

We barely had time to make it to the captain's cocktail party at five. But then, it's always a challenge to keep up with the social events on a big liner.

"I don't have a tux," Cass complained. "Why don't I wait for you folks here?"

"We agreed to stick together," I reminded him.

"You'll look fine in your dark suit, Cass," Jayne said.

"But jeez, you know I can't make small talk worth a damn."

"You had no trouble with Captain Doodle," I said.

"That's true. But we talked about horses. On any other subject I'd do better talking to *Howdy* Doody."

"Cass, you have more charm than ninety percent of the people on this ship," Jayne said.

"You think so?" Cass fairly beamed as he picked up his suit and went into the bathroom to change.

We would get to the reception about half an hour late, which is when the fashionable people arrive anyway. Dressed in my white dinner jacket, black bow tie, and black pants with the stripe down the sides, I could have passed for the maître d' of any fine establishment. Jayne wore a classically styled, black evening gown that started low on her shoulders. For trimmings, she had added diamond earrings and necklace, and a scent that reminded me of a French garden at sunset. Cass managed to look a bit fenced in and awkward in his navy blue suit, white shirt, and bolo tie. At the last minute, Jayne had stuck a yellow rose in his lapel, and that had made him happy. As we got into the elevator I noticed he was wearing his pointed cowboy boots, a small act of rebellion; everyone would probably take him for a Texas oil baron.

The number F267 kept running through my head like a refrain to a song. Or was it 9267, or F269 or 9264?

If there were, in fact, four digits, it occurred to me that it might be a PIN number for an automated bank machine. But if the first figure was an F rather than a 9, that would indicate something else entirely.

We stepped out of the elevator near the Atlantis Room, the most posh of the ship's lounges, and I stopped at a telephone. Cass and Jayne waited nearby, watching curiously, while I dialed the operator.

"Can you tell me, is there a stateroom F267 on the ship?"

"No, sir."

"Is there any room at all on board with a combination of letters and numbers like that?"

"Not that I know of, sir."

I thanked the operator and hung up.

"Just another idea that didn't pan out," I told Cass and Jayne grumpily.

"It'll come, dear," Jayne said, taking my arm.

"Maybe it's a laundry code?" Cass suggested. "Or a date. Friday the twenty-sixth of July."

"It could also be a flight number. . . . Fuji Airlines, flight 267 to Bora Bora."

Wondering about such diverse possibilities, Cass, Jayne, and I walked into the gathering. Rusty O'Conner drifted by in a silver, floor-length gown, reflecting the light like a small star. She was wearing enough jewelry to excite the passions of any gentleman burglar. I saw Mudgie and her entourage, Candy L'Amour and Alexis, Tracy Devine and Wendy Wilmington, the

Sidney Sheldons, the Michael Viners, and Tony Newley waved from a distance. Everyone was dressed to the nines, and the murmur of conversation was often punctuated by laughter.

A string trio—violin, viola, and cello—played a lovely melody by Franz Lehár—I know it only by its English title, "Yours Is My Heart Alone"—as from a splendid multitentacled chandelier light shot out in every direction, and waiters circulated with silver trays laden with glasses of champagne and warm hors d'oeuvres.

Jayne, Cass, and I joined a reception line to shake hands with Captain Mellon, who, even in his crisp white uniform, reminded me of a high-school biology teacher.

"Are you having a good crossing, Mr. Allen?" the captain asked politely, although I thought his gaze rather stern.

"Except for a few unmentionable events, it's been a pleasure," I told him. "And how has *your* crossing been so far?"

His look turned suspicious—or was it just my imagination?—but he was saved from answering as the line continued to flow and others greeted him.

Despite our intentions to stay together, Jayne and Cass and I became separated. Doodie waved Cass over, and Jayne made her way to the Sheldons. I was about to follow her when a big friendly man with a Texas accent intercepted me, gushing about how much he had always enjoyed seeing my work on television. As he talked, he positioned himself between Jayne and me, and somehow pressed me up against a potted palm. I had a sense of being cut out of the flock by a clever sheepdog.

"Name's Moody. Dan Moody. I can't tell ya what a thrill it is to meet you, Mr. Allen," said the large man. "Why me and Mary Lou—we'd a-rather *died* than left the house the night your show was on."

"That's very nice of you, Mr. Moo—"

"Hell, the damn TV just ain't never been the same since you and Jackie Gleason and Red Skelton left the airwaves. Now it's all filthy language, hardly fit to watch."

The crowd surged around us, and the next time I looked, Jayne was halfway across the room and was talking with some people I didn't recognize. I couldn't see Cass anywhere. It concerned me, but I supposed we would be all right as long as none of us left the room.

"What part of Texas are you from?" I asked, my mind distracted.

"Dallas."

"I've always enjoyed working there."

"Yeah," he said. "Mary Lou and I caught ya when ya did that show with the Dallas Symphony a couple of years back. We're big supporters of the symphony. Incredible performance."

"Thank you," I said.

"In fact," he went on, "I remember one of your ad libs. Remember when you were reading that question from a woman in the audience who asked if you come from a rich family, and you said, 'Yeah, you folks have heard of patent leather? Well, my grandfather held the patent.' " He chuckled. "Funny stuff."

"You know," I said, "you can often tell a good deal about people by what they laugh at."

"How's that?" he said.

"Well, appreciating that line might mean you're wealthy yourself."

"I'm not as well set up as I might look," he said. "The government doesn't pay that well, you know."

"I see." I was honestly surprised. "What branch of government are you in?"

"I'm with the Company," he said.

I was aware that the term was sometimes used to mean the CIA, but it was unusual for an agent to reveal his identity to a relative stranger.

"If that's the truth," I said, "there may be as many cops on this cruise as there are robbers."

"It ain't the robbers that are worrying me." My Texas friend frowned. "It's the murderers."

"Oh." I deliberately played dumb. "I'd heard about the two deaths, but I didn't know murder had been established."

"There's a lot you might not know," he said. "But I've read some of your murder mysteries, and I'm sure you're keepin' your eyes open."

"It seems the thing to do." I tried to move away, but he was not to be brushed off.

"For example, when young Wilmington got shot, I understand you found him."

When you've been in show business as long as I have, you often get into conversations with strangers. I was smiling, my eyes half-glazed, and it took me a moment to realize that this particular conversation had veered way off course.

I looked at him more closely. The Texan had short, dark hair and a jowly, hound-dog sort of face. He was over six feet tall. I could imagine him playing football in college, about thirty years ago. He was smiling, but there was a deadness to his small brown eyes.

"So Wilmington was already dead when you got there?"

"Yup."

"That's too bad. I was hoping he might have had a chance to whisper something in your ear. You know, with his last breath."

"No, I'm sorry."

"Well, that's the way she goes, I guess," Moody said philosophically. "Hey, this is just a long shot, but you didn't *find* anything, did you?"

"Like what?" I asked cautiously.

"Hell, I don't know. A letter, a note . . ."

"And what would be on this piece of paper?" I asked, suddenly not trusting the man.

He was quick to laugh. "Well, hell's bells! If I knew, I wouldn't be askin', would I? To tell the truth, Wilmington and I were . . . in communication. I thought he might have somethin' for me. Somethin' he was hopin' to give me. To an untrained observer like yourself, Steverino, it wouldn't look like much if you saw it. A name, maybe, or just a few numbers."

"Like some secret code?"

"Maybe. Did you see it?"

"Not that I can recall. By the way, do you have any identification to prove you really work for the CIA?"

His laugh was starting to grate on me. "Hey, good for you. Be suspicious, I always say. But as it happens, we never carry Company ID when we're workin' undercover. You'll just have to trust my honest face."

I looked into his beady, dishonest eyes. "I wish I could help you out," I said.

"Well, think about it," he replied. "Maybe something will come to you."

"If it does, where can I reach you?"

He grinned. "I'll find you," he said. Then Dan Moody—if that was really his name—turned and lost himself in the crowd.

I was deep in thought when a waiter came over with a bottle of champagne.

"There are killers everywhere, sir," the waiter said.

"What?"

The waiter was a thin, middle-aged man with a pinched face and graying hair. He looked at me blankly. "Would you care for a refill, sir?"

"No, thanks."

Was I going crazy? I could have sworn the waiter winked at me as he turned and walked away.

chapter 35

As I scanned the crowd for Jayne and Cass, I heard the rapid whirring of a camera behind me and, having turned toward the sound, was not surprised to see Larry Goldman standing a few feet away. He was wearing a black dinner jacket that seemed a few sizes too big. Chelsea Eastman was by his side.

I wandered their way.

"How's life as a stowaway, Larry?" I asked.

"It's getting better," he said. "A few more deaths and a bit more intrigue and I'll be able to retire young."

A waiter came by with a tray of miniature quiche, and I saw that Larry's appetite had not decreased. He took three of the appetizers in one hand and two in the other, leaving his camera to dangle on the strap around his neck.

"So the article's coming along well?" I asked.

"Fabulous!" he replied, his mouth full. "I'm thinking now it'll make an entire book."

"You have that much material?"

"You bet! Glamour, murder, the adventures of the rich and famous—this book will have everything, if Sidney Sheldon doesn't beat me to writing it."

"Let's hope it has a happy ending," I said. "I understand you did an interview with Marcus Wilmington a short while ago?"

"Two months back, yeah. What a scoop! I don't think the old man had given an interview for twenty years."

"So how did you get to him?"

"He got to me. His attorney called me up."

"Will Sanders?"

"That's the guy. He said Marcus had liked something I wrote about Peter Moon, and he was willing to give me an exclusive interview. Maybe the old man was trying to upgrade his image and show the world his human side. *Trend* put it on their January cover."

"Where did the interview take place?"

"To tell the truth, I don't know exactly. I know that sounds crazy. . . ."

"Someone blindfolded you and took you to him in a helicopter?"

"In a limousine actually. But yes, I was blindfolded. The other condition was that there would be no photographs. I tried to bring along a miniature Nikon I use for undercover work, but his security people patted me down and found it. Man, that was a pity. He was one strange-looking dude! I would have loved to get a picture."

"What did you talk about?"

"His rags to riches story. *The Atlantis,* naturally. What he thinks about Japan and the new Europe, the Pacific Rim, America's place in the economic order—that sort of stuff. It was pretty dry, actually."

"It doesn't sound like your kind of article."

He grinned at me. "You didn't read it then?"

"I'm afraid I don't read *Trend* on a regular basis," I admitted.

"Tell him what he missed, Chelsea," he said, stuffing another quiche in his mouth.

"I can't. It was *too* sleazy for words!" Chelsea said sternly.

Larry only laughed. "It was great! You see, I found out something about him that no one knew. Do you remember Dawn Landry?"

"The movie actress from the fifties?"

"Right. The one who committed suicide eventually. Well, she had an affair with Marcus Wilmington back around 1952."

"How did you find out about that?"

The journalist looked very pleased with himself. "They had a child together. I made it the main focus of my story—dynamite angle, huh? The secret love-child of Marcus Wilmington! It was a lot better than all that dry stuff about international finance."

"*If* it's true," I said skeptically. "I repeat, how did you hear about this supposed 'love-child'?"

"Sorry, I never betray my sources."

"And generally I don't betray stowaways either, although there's always a first time. . . ." I let the sentence dangle as my eyes searched for the captain.

"Calm down, man. Peter Moon was my source, okay? When he found out I was going to write something about Wilmington, he sent me over a packet of letters the old man wrote Ms. Landry in fifty-two and fifty-three. Pretty steamy stuff. Marcus offered her fifteen grand a month for child support as long as she kept the baby a secret."

"That was a lot of money back in the fifties," Chelsea contributed.

"That's a lot of money now," I said. "But how do you know these letters were legitimate? And how the hell did Peter Moon get his hands on them?"

"I was able to find a sample of Wilmington's handwriting on an application for a business permit in nineteen sixty-two. A handwriting expert told me they matched. As for Moon, who knows? It was his business to learn everything he could about the enemy. He hinted that someone inside gave them to him."

"But why give them to you?"

"Who cares? I wasn't about to look a gift horse in the mouth."

I did some quick figuring and realized if this "love-child" actually existed, he or she would now be forty-two years old. There were a lot of people that age on this ship.

"So who's the child?" I asked skeptically. "And where is he?"

"I don't know. I tried to find out, but Dawn Landry's been dead for thirty years; the trail was cold. There were no records of a child, but of course, she was being paid a lot of money to cover it up. Since I couldn't find the kid, I made the mystery about him the theme of my article. 'Where is the love-child now?' That sort of thing. People love that stuff. Everyone hopes *he's* the secret child of a billionaire and any day some lawyer's gonna show up at the door and tell him he's rich, without any help from Ed McMahon."

"I imagine the Wilmingtons weren't terribly pleased with your article."

"To put it mildly. It's the reason I couldn't get a stateroom. But I'm not going to lose any sleep over that. Hey! There's Candy L'Amour," he said, spying the rock star across the room. "What's going on between her and Alexis?"

Candy and Alexis were obviously having a spat. They were glaring at each other like two boxers waiting for the opening bell. As I watched, a waiter approached them and offered a small platter of hors d'oeuvres. Alex was in such a rage he knocked the tray out of the waiter's hands, and Candy shouted something at him as people stopped their conversations to stare.

Goldman was delighted. "Gotta go to work, kids!" he said. He slipped through the crowd, his camera at the ready. Chelsea started to follow him, but I held on to her arm.

"You know," I said, "he's really not a straight arrow."

"I know," she admitted. "But polite guys bore me. Besides, maybe I can reform him."

"Has that ever happened, in all of history?"

She laughed, gave me a show-biz air kiss near my cheek, then traipsed after her journalist stowaway.

I shook my head at the folly of youth. And the folly of every age.

chapter 36

The storm, when it came, had something for everybody—hail, lightning, rain, fog, wind, high seas, and—a few people said later—even snow. Of course, everyone exaggerates about the weather. I'd seen worse, but never while on a ship at the mercy of huge waves, bobbing up and down like a Ping-Pong ball in a washing machine.

It started at dinner when a great wind hit. Then came the lightning, great jagged bolts that lit up the night sky. A moment later, loud booming peals of thunder sounded.

"My goodness!" Gladys Moffet cried after a particularly loud roll of thunder.

"I hope it hits the boat!" Chelsea muttered darkly.

"My dear, what a thing to say!" Grandma said.

"I don't care if we sink!"

Chelsea had been pouting through the first two courses, and I sensed from her manner that the path to true love had hit a few snags. But I had other things to think about. I was wondering how to make contact with the impenetrable Duclerc, who was still sitting at our table, looking as inscrutable and mild-mannered as ever.

I decided on the direct approach.

"Monsieur Duclerc, I'll bet you're sorry now you didn't cross the Atlantic in one of your nice airplanes."

He looked up at me from his soup. *"Comment?"* he said. *"Je ne vous comprends pas."*

"Oh, I bet you *comprends* very well. I think you've been making fools of us, *monsieur."*

Grandma was definitely unhappy with my behavior. "Oh, dear!" she said vaguely. "I always hate a scene."

"Chelsea, how's your French?" I asked.

The girl shrugged. "I studied for four years in high school."

"Good. Will you please tell Monsieur Duclerc that because he's a major financial figure and chairman of the board of Trans European Airlines, I can't believe he doesn't speak English."

"Monsieur Allen a dit que . . . que vous êtes . . . No, that's not right. . . ."

The Frenchman finally took pity on us all. "You will excuse me for being so rude," he said, with only a trace of an accent. "Frankly I have not been in a terribly social mood, and it was convenient to pretend I spoke only French. I'm sorry. I wasn't trying to make fun of you."

"That's perfectly all right, monsieur," Jayne said in her best motherly manner. "There are times I wish *I* could pretend I didn't speak English!"

"Dear, Monsieur Duclerc has been spying on us," I explained to my lovely wife. "He's been listening in on all our conversations. I don't think that's at all right."

"Please, you must allow me to make this up to you," the Frenchman said. "It's true, I have been listening to your most interesting conversations, but it wasn't anything personal. It's Marcus Wilmington I would like to murder."

The little Frenchman smiled with such Old World charm, I was not certain I had heard his last word correctly.

At that moment Christophe, our waiter, approached with a large oval tray piled high with covered plates. Because of the erratic rolling of the ship, our conversation stopped while we watched his progress, apprehensive about the fate of our entrees. With the grace of a ballet dancer, the young man managed to put the tray down on a square wooden serving stand that was permanently fixed to the deck to prevent accidents due to the ship's motion. He then set our plates before us one by one.

"Christophe, you're an acrobat!" Jayne told him.

"Oh, I never spill food on my favorite people!" he replied, as skillful with flattery as he was in juggling hot entrees.

After we were all served, I was ready for some more serious conversation with Mr. Duclerc, but we were faced with a new interruption. Alex Wilmington wandered our way looking like a lost puppy.

"Have you seen Candy?" he asked me.

"Not since the captain's reception," I said.

"*I* know where she is!" Chelsea said angrily, her blue-green eyes blazing. Wilmington had apparently not met Chelsea Eastman. He studied the girl in a speculative way.

"Where?" he asked.

"She went off with someone I *used* to know."

"Damn!"

"You can say that again."

He grabbed a free chair from the next table—with the violent motion of the ship, there were a number of empty seats in the dining room—and ensconced himself between Chelsea and her grandmother.

"This person you used to know . . ."

"Lawrence Goldman! A disgusting journalist!" Chelsea declared hotly. "He was taking photographs of Candy after she stormed away from you. Before I knew it, they'd made a date to go off drinking in one of the lounges. It's what I call fast work!"

"Hell! My mother and Candy had a fight." Alex sighed. "Then somehow I got in the middle of it. And before I knew it, Candy was mad at me. Whenever we argue, she gets even by flirting with every guy she sees."

"That doesn't seem fair," Chelsea sympathized. "After all, you're not responsible for what your mother does."

"That's what I tried to tell her."

"She's probably just insecure," Chelsea said.

"Yeah. Hey, didn't I see you about two weeks ago at the Four Seasons?"

"Couldn't have. I was at school."

"Where do you go?"

"Vassar. I hate it there."

"I went to Princeton," Alex said. "I hated it too. I think you learn all the really important things on your own."

"That's *exactly* what *I* think."

Jayne caught my eye; we smiled. There's an age when consolation for a broken heart can be easily found through a fresh romance. From the way Alex Wilmington and Chelsea Eastman were looking at each other, I suspected Candy L'Amour and Larry Goldman had become instant history.

I left them to their youth and turned my attention back to Duclerc.

"*Monsieur*, what's an airline executive doing on an ocean liner, if you don't mind my asking?"

"Taking a look at the competition, of course."

"And what do you think?"

"*The Atlantis* is a fine ship, but she was too expensive to build. The numbers do not work out, and that is bad business. Marcus Wilmington, he will lose his pants."

"His shirt," I said.

"He will lose them both! And then I will laugh. Let me tell you a story. My brother-in-law was the British industrialist Robert Sutherland. Unfortunately, he wished to own a newspaper in the United States. The poor man earned his money in steel and coal, and he believed to own a newspaper was very . . . er . . . romantic. But Marcus Wilmington wished to own the same newspaper, you understand? They began a bidding war.

The price for this paper, it goes up and up." Duclerc said, using his hands in Gallic fashion.

"Then one day," he continued, "my brother-in-law fell from his New York office building onto the sidewalk." The Frenchman brought his hands down hard upon the table. "And my sister Claudine was made a widow. And her children—my niece and nephew—they grow up without a father. So, no, I will not shed many tears when Marcus Wilmington encounters the justice he deserves."

I looked toward Alex for his reaction, but he and Chelsea were on a separate planet. However; I did see Stewart Hoffman walking toward our table. I wondered if Duclerc knew Hoffman was the policeman who had ruled his brother-in-law's death a suicide. From the way Duclerc was watching Stewart I sensed he did.

Stewart put his mouth to my ear. "We must talk."

"Pull up a chair," I told him.

"No, come with me. Oh, don't look so worried! I have a very public place in mind."

I glanced at the Frenchman as I stood up. He was frowning to himself, and I saw something close to hatred in his eyes.

chapter 37

Stewart Hoffman led the way into the ship's huge, brightly lit, and clamorous kitchen. Long stainless steel counters were manned by sous chefs, cooks, bakers, and kitchen help. It was the peak of the first seating and nerves were frayed.

Hoffman and I stood close to a half-wall separating the food-service areas from the place where dirty dishes were returned, trying to stay out of the way.

"So why have you pulled me away from my dinner, Mr. Hoffman?" I asked.

"I thought we'd play some more make-believe, Steve. I was having such a good time this afternoon."

"Okay."

"Let's pretend I am *not* the bad person who murdered Dicky and Peter Moon, but I am, nevertheless, anxious for you to stop your investigation. My entirely theoretical question is this: How much money would it take for you to forget your game of private eye and just have a good time for the rest of the voyage?"

"You don't have enough, Stu. And neither does anyone else."

"I was afraid you'd say that. There is another—strictly theoretical—alternative. You might have an accident. A man could easily be washed overboard on a night like this."

"If anything happens to me, the police will be all over you."

"Of course. But Agent Schwartz could have an accident as well. It is a *very* stormy night, and they say it'll get worse. . . ."

"Maybe I'm also in contact with the CIA."

He laughed. "You don't mean that clown with the fake Texas accent? What's he calling himself now? Dan Moody? I thought you were smarter than that."

"If he's not CIA, what is he?"

"He's just another hungry carnivore, pardner, looking for his dinner." Hoffman smiled. "Don't you know you're swimming in shark-infested waters?" His smile abruptly vanished. "You don't, do you? That's the problem. I don't think you have a clue as to what this is all about."

He was right, of course. I was only stirring things up, hoping some information would surface.

Meanwhile, Hoffman became bored with playing poker with someone who didn't hold any cards. "Goodbye, Steve. I can't say you don't have nerve."

As he turned to leave, I decided on one last, desperate gamble. I strongly felt that Hoffman could tell me almost everything I wanted to know if I could only keep him talking.

"I have the numbers," I said.

"What numbers?" he asked sarcastically. But he had stopped. And turned back to face me.

I tried to look very knowing. "You know. Dicky had them written down. You were careless, Stu. Or maybe you were in a hurry."

He stepped closer to me. I knew I could lose him with one false step.

"Tell me," he said. "How many digits are there in this number?"

"Four," I replied.

He smiled and turned away. "Goodbye, funnyman."

"But of course one of the digits is a letter."

He turned back again. The game of cat and mouse would have been more fun if I knew what I was doing.

"What do you want exactly?"

"I've already told you that. Information. I want to know who killed Wilmington and Moon, and why."

"And in return?"

"I'll give you the number. That's what you want, isn't it?"

He stared at me with his cold blue eyes. "All right. I have to talk with someone. We'll meet at ten-thirty at The Seven Seas. Is that public enough for you?"

"Well, you know comedians love a large audience."

Stewart Hoffman left me abruptly. I stood alone for a moment, but then an angry cook threw a wet dishcloth at a shouting waiter, who ducked, almost colliding with me. I hurried out, smiling because I had just figured out what the numbers on the matchbook were all about.

chapter 38

"It's a Swiss bank account!" I told Schwartz, with only a small, smug smile. "The way I see it, Dicky was stealing money for himself—a little here, a little there—maybe out of the pension funds he was raiding. He was planning an early retirement as a way to thumb his nose at the old man!"

"At the moment, I don't really give a damn," said the FBI man. He was lying flat on his bed and looking pale as vanilla ice cream—a kind of pistachio-tinged vanilla cream. I had left Jayne and Cass locked safely in the suite upstairs and had come down to B Deck to visit the agent in his cabin. Now was the time to spring the trap.

The Atlantis was rolling and pitching in a sickening manner, and Schwartz was obviously a landlubber.

"Go away!" he moaned. "I just want to die!"

"You've got to pull yourself together. I need you. What do you think about my Swiss bank-account theory?"

"I think it's stupid."

"Why? Dicky knew he'd take the fall should the pension fund theft come to light. The way I see it, he had a padded escape route planned for himself. But Daddy found out about it and told Stewart to knock him off."

"You think he'd order a hit on his own son?"

"Maybe. This is *not* your normal family."

"I'm going to be sick again," Schwartz moaned.

"Just lie on your back and breathe. You can be sick later."

"You're all heart. What *I* want to know is why the hell you didn't tell me about the matchbook yesterday."

"I put the matches in my pocket and forgot about them. How was I to know they were important?"

"With a number written inside?"

"I didn't know about the damned number until a few hours ago."

"God, I can't stand working with amateurs!" Schwartz complained. "Picks up a piece of evidence and *forgets* about it!"

"At least I've come a lot farther in this case than *you've* managed," I told him. "And *I'm* still on my feet."

"Okay, okay. I just wish this ship would stop heaving around."

He was in bad shape, but I was not sympathetic. I needed him to back me up at my next meeting with Hoffman. I picked up the phone.

"What are you doing?" he asked.

"I'm calling the infirmary to get you some dramamine."

"I'm allergic to it."

"Great!" I said, slamming down the phone.

He moaned as he tried to prop himself up on one elbow. "Listen," he said, "cancel your meeting with Hoffman. It's too dangerous. I'll feel better tomorrow, and we'll try again."

I shook my head. "That won't work, Schwartz. If I'm not there tonight, we may lose him."

"Well, this whole thing is crazy anyway," he declared, flopping back miserably onto his bed. "We know nothing for sure. If he's guilty he may try to kill you. Then what? I'm supposed to rush in and save you? This is *not* how I learned to run an investigation."

"He's not going to try to kill me until he has that account number—that's my safety net. I'm only trying to lure him on."

"It's too damned risky." Schwartz groaned. "I want to say, for the record, that I'm against this. You got that?"

"I've got it."

"Good. Now on your way out, don't you dare look in my top dresser drawer! If I see you borrowing what you'll find in there, I'll have to report you to my superiors. I hope that's clear because I'm going to turn over now and get some sleep."

Schwartz rolled over and put his back to me. "Now get the hell out of here," he said.

I opened his top dresser drawer and saw a .38 revolver, of the snub-nosed type.

"The hammer's on an empty chamber," he said with his back still to me. "There are five bullets in it. If you need more, you're dead anyway. I'm not telling you this, you understand."

"What?" I said. To his credit, he chuckled.

I dropped the gun into the right pocket of my dinner jacket. The bulge disturbed my attempt at sartorial perfection, but the dense weight was something of a comfort as I set off down the passageway.

chapter 39

I left the revolver with Cass, knowing I probably would shoot myself in the foot if I tried to use it. As I mentioned, I don't know a thing about sidearms, but having gone through infantry heavy-weapons training, I'm pretty handy with machine guns and mortars. I told Cass to stay in the suite, keep the door locked, and guard Jayne. She was reading in bed, leaning back among the pillows, and wearing a beautiful white nightgown. We both pretended there was no danger because it was easier that way; showing our concern wouldn't have changed anything.

The corridor outside the suite was empty. It seemed later than ten-thirty. I imagined most people were in their cabins because of the weather. The ship creaked and rolled as she made her way over the dark ocean, but her motions were predictable once you got used to them, and I did not find it too difficult to walk.

I used the broad staircase in the center of the ship to descend one deck to The Seven Seas lounge. In the bar, the lights were low and a good jazz trio was performing for a dead crowd. When the piano-player—a veteran named Lou Levy—caught my eye, he segued into "This Could Be the Start of Something Big." I waved a thank you. The rain tapped loudly on the windows, which made the bar feel like an island moving through the mysterious night. I did not see any sign of Stewart Hoffman.

Seating myself in a booth, I ordered a cup of coffee from a white-jacketed waiter.

"Hell of a night," I said to him, despite my aversion to most forms of small talk.

"Oh yes, it's blowing, sir!"

"Do you shut down if the weather gets too rough?"

"We've never closed up yet, sir!" he said with a smile.

I watched him walk to the service bar, then looked at one of the large aquariums full of multicolored fish. The water sloshed from side to side, reminding me so much of the motion of the ship that I had to look away. The trio meanwhile was playing "Come Fly With Me," which struck me as subversive. I spent the next few minutes dictating random ideas into my ever-present minirecorder.

Hoffman did not show up until nearly a quarter to eleven. I was checking my watch when I saw him walk into the bar, though I didn't recognize him at first because he was not dressed in his usual dark suit but wore jeans, tennis shoes, a polo shirt, and a tan windbreaker.

"Get hung up?" I asked as he slipped into the booth.

"Yeah. The weather's kept me busy," he said. "You get a stormy night like this, and people go crazy. I had to keep a married couple from almost killing each other in the Cafe Cabaña and then deal with a real-estate tycoon in the casino. He thought the dealer was cheating him at blackjack."

"And was he being cheated?"

Stewart flashed me a sour look. "The casino is honest. It has to be on a ship like this, or we wouldn't stay in business very long."

"Some other things around here don't seem particularly honest."

"Such as?" Hoffman demanded angrily.

"Oh . . . pension funds."

"Ah! Well, as they say in the restaurant business, that's not my table. I'm just head of security. The casino, at least, has been run right. I insist upon it."

When the waiter came by, Hoffman said he'd have his usual. "I keep my own private bottle of Courvoisier behind the bar. Want to try a shot?"

"I'll stick with coffee."

"C'mon, loosen up. What are you afraid of?"

He flashed his sour grin, and I ended up ordering a beer, just to prove I wasn't frightened. He looked more human tonight in his off-duty wardrobe. I could see he was almost good-looking in a weathered, fortysomething sort of way. Up to now I had only thought of him as a kind of cold killing machine. I wondered how a man got to be as hard as he was. Had he ever been in love? Had anyone ever loved him? I was curious, but he wasn't the sort to invite personal questions—and we had other things to discuss.

"Okay, I want to know the numbers you found by Wilmington's body," he said abruptly when the waiter had left us to get our drinks.

"I'll bet you do."

"Let's make a deal. What do you want?"

"I told you that before, Stu. Information. I want to know why you killed Dicky and Peter Moon."

"Forget them. The world's better off without them."

"Perhaps we mere mortals should leave that sort of judgment to the gods."

"Well, I didn't kill them. But maybe I can help you find out who did, if you're so damned determined to know. I have some pretty good ideas about it. But I want to know about the numbers first."

"We seem to have a standoff," I told him. "The numbers are my security that you won't try to kill me."

He grinned. "You really don't trust me, do you?"

"Not a bit. But it's nothing personal."

"Well, what if I tell you a few tidbits of information up front to establish some good will? Perhaps that'll get us started."

"I'm listening," I said.

"Okay. What if I tell you that the Wilmington family was ready to do just about anything to get enough money together to get *The Atlantis* in the water?"

"I already know that."

"I'm not talking about the pension funds. I'm talking about the cargo."

"The *what?*"

"You heard me. I'm talking about what we're carrying in the hold."

I was about to ask a flood of questions when we both saw Will Sanders walking across the dance floor. Hoffman put a finger to his lips as the attorney noticed us and made a quick left turn to come our way.

"Gentlemen!" he cried in a merry tone. "Having a little nightcap, I see! God, what a storm! How's your wife doing, Steve?"

"She's fine."

"The weather's going to be worse by morning, I'm afraid. It's rotten luck. . . . Listen, I'd join you guys but I've got to meet Gertrude. She's seasick, if you can believe it! This really has turned into a nightmare."

Neither Stewart nor I were sad to see him go.

"What's in the hold?" I asked immediately. "Drugs?"

He shook his head and was about to say something when we heard his name being paged.

"Mr. Stewart Hoffman. Please dial three-zero." The message was repeated by an impersonal female voice.

He swore softly and got up from the table. "Damn, that's trouble. I'll be right back."

He walked to a telephone on the bar. I watched him pick up the receiver and talk in an animated way to someone on the other end. While he was so occupied, our waiter arrived with the drinks—his cognac and my bottle of dark Danish beer. Stewart returned from the phone in time to insist that he pay for my drink. I didn't argue.

"Two brothers from Philadelphia," he said, "were beating each other up in the Atlantis Room. I told the bartender: Let them go at it all they want—just don't serve 'em any more liquor."

"You have to take care of every small disturbance on the ship?"

He grimaced. "With rich folk, there are no *small* disturbances." He held up his cognac and swirled it in the snifter. "*Salut . . ,*" he said, and took a drink.

I only pretended to sip my beer because I wanted to keep my head clear. I sensed he was deliberately showing me a new side of himself, but I didn't know if I could trust the new side any more than the old.

"You were telling me about the cargo," I prodded.

"Was I? You would have made a fair cop, Steve."

I shrugged. "I'm curious."

"Right. I was a good cop once myself. Did you know that?"

"I heard you were."

"Ah! I'll bet you heard the old nasty stories about me! Well, don't believe everything you hear."

"Are you saying you didn't let the old man off?"

"Of course I let the old man off! Because there wasn't a shred of evidence against him. In the American legal system, even billionaires get the benefit of the doubt. The English fellow, on the other hand, was a manic depressive with a history of three previous suicide attempts. Anyway, it wasn't even my decision. The DA told me I'd never build a case—the Wilmington lawyers were too good—and that I should get on with other matters rather than waste the department's time."

"And then the old man offered you a job," I pressed. "Don't tell me there was no connection. I understand he even set you up with a condo in midtown Manhattan."

Stewart sipped his cognac. "But not for anything I did for him in the past. It was because of how he might use me in the future. You see, he thought I was going to be very useful, very loyal—and I was. A lot more than, say, little Dicky boy. And the old man didn't have to pay me nearly as much."

"You never cared much for the Wilmington boys, I gather?"

"Are you kidding? While Dicky and Alex were at their Ivy League colleges, I was learning about life the hard way, in the jungles of Vietnam. If it weren't for family connections, Dicky wouldn't have lasted two weeks in the mailroom at Wilmex, much less as CEO!"

"Let's get back to what you were saying about the cargo," I said.

"Let's get back to the numbers you say you found." He grinned. "I tell you what. You answer one of my questions, and I'll answer one of yours. What do you say?"

"We can give it a try," I said cautiously.

"Good. I'll go first. Where did you find these supposed numbers?"

It didn't seem that this mattered particularly, so I told him. "On a book of matches. Near the body."

"How about that!"

"Now it's my turn, Stu. What kind of illegal cargo is *The Atlantis* carrying to England?"

He smiled. It was the first truly sweet smile I had seen on the man's lips, and it scared me a little. "This is just a guess, since it's something the family tried to sneak past me because they knew I wouldn't go for it, but it's a very educated guess."

"Go ahead," I said.

"We're carrying arms. A shipment of highly classified, brand-new shoulder-launched, surface-to-air missiles, so small and so sophisticated that a single person standing in a meadow can shoot down a jumbo jet flying overhead. Quite a boon to the shipping industry, don't you think? Sell a few of these babies to some people in the Middle East and commercial airline travel could hit a real slump. A disaster or two like the one over Lockerbie and *The Atlantis* might see a brisk increase in business."

I stared at Stewart. "But how can anyone get hold of weapons like that?"

"That's a new question, but I'll give it away for free, just to show I'm not such a bad guy. These new, secret missiles were developed in California for the military by . . . you guessed it, Wilmington Electronics and Aerospace! A special order, off the books, wouldn't be impossible."

For a moment, I could not speak. It was hideous that a shipping company might give surface-to-air missiles to terrorists to discourage air travel. But everything I had learned so far about the ruthless Wilmingtons suggested that such a thing was at least possible.

Stewart coughed and cleared his throat. "Your turn," he said hoarsely. "Tell me two letters."

I did not hesitate. "F and two," I said. "Now where are the missiles, and how are they going to get them through customs into England?"

"That's . . . two questions," he said. He coughed again, so violently that he had trouble speaking.

"I don't care if it is. Answer me."

"If they're on board, they're small . . . easy to carry . . . hardly more than a suitcase. . . ."

"What do you mean *if* they're on board? Aren't you sure?"

He coughed and shook his head. "Think so . . . not sure. . . ."

"Do you want some water?" He was coughing so hard now he seemed unable to breathe. "Do you have asthma? I carry an inhaler if you need one."

He was red in the face, gasping for breath. He reached for his snifter of cognac but knocked it over, sending the glass shattering on the deck. Out of the corner of my eye, I saw the bartender coming our way.

"Stewart!" I said desperately. "Where are the missiles?"

He grinned horribly, trying to speak. His words came out like wind rustling through dead grass. I had to lean forward and put my ear to his mouth to hear him. Even then, I was not certain I understood.

"You . . . tell . . . me," he gasped.

By the time the bartender called the doctor, it was already too late. The man with the cold eyes would not be seeing anything again.

chapter 40

"You poor thing," Jayne said. "Let me put a cold towel on your forehead. How is that?"

"Better," Schwartz responded weakly. "I'm okay as long as I lie here and only look at the ceiling. Thank God *that's* not moving."

It was an illusion, of course, that the ceiling was not moving. Agent Schwartz was simply moving in synch with it as he lay in the grip of seasickness on the couch in our sitting room. He had managed to walk here from his stateroom and then rush into our bathroom. Jayne was nursing him now like Florence Nightingale, wringing out a cold towel and applying it to his forehead.

"Go on, Mr. Allen, please," he managed, gulping in a little air.

"Well, the bartender was terrified," I said. "But he swears he didn't put anything into Hoffman's cognac or my beer. He insists he made the drinks and then left them at the end of the bar for the waiter to pick up."

"Where was the waiter?"

"Across the room taking an order. The bartender claims he then returned to a conversation he was having with two men and a woman at the bar. So our drinks were left unattended for

. . . three or four minutes. Long enough for someone to slip poison into them."

"It seems peculiar," Cass said. "I mean, the guy with the poison had to have everything ready just on the chance that you and Stewart would have a drink and that he might have an opportunity to doctor them up. It seems like an awful lot of coincidences."

"Exactly," moaned the G-man. "But if Hoffman kept his own bottle behind the bar, someone could have doctored it earlier in the day."

"I suggested that to the captain," I said. "He took the bottle, of course, as well as samples of cognac from Hoffman's spilled drink and from my beer. But there's no way to find out if they had been poisoned until the samples can be sent to a forensic lab in London."

"Meanwhile we don't know a damned thing," the agent complained. "Didn't I tell you to cancel that damned meeting. Now look—another fiasco!"

I didn't even bother to answer. It was nearly one A.M., the wind was howling, the rain was lashing the ship as she rolled drunkenly through the heaving seas, and I was brooding. I was sorry to have lost my best suspect, I must admit. Who else could have shot Richard Wilmington and drowned Peter Moon? I had been almost certain Hoffman was the killer. He had had every opportunity. He'd known the ship. He'd even had what I thought were killer's eyes. Of course, it was still possible Hoffman had been a killer, but that he was not the only one aboard.

His death forced me to reexamine everything.

"Uh, God, excuse me," Schwartz said, making another dash for the bathroom.

Cass sang a rousing chorus of his favorite song, "I'm An Old Cowhand from the Rio Grande," so we wouldn't have to listen to our guest's retching, and when Schwartz returned, he arranged himself on the couch, his arms folded on his chest as if he were ready to be laid in his coffin.

After a while I said, "You know, Will Sanders came through the lounge *before* we got our drinks. That guy has always been too slick for my taste. I wonder if he managed to slip something into them."

"Did you see him anywhere near the bar?" Schwartz asked.

"No, but then I wasn't looking. I was talking to Hoffman. . . . And then he was paged, and *he* went to the bar for a moment. It's all hard to fit together."

"Here's an idea," said Jayne. "What if Hoffman was poisoned earlier in the day, and the effects only caught up with him in the bar? Some poisons are quite slow to act, aren't they?"

"That's a good point," Schwartz said, appearing eager to praise his nurse.

"Or he could have been hit with a poison dart from a blowgun," Cass mentioned. "I saw that happen in a movie once."

"Cass, please. This is no time for fiction," I said.

"Well, it *could* have happened." Cass sulked. "Maybe one of those couples with a tropical drink blew a dart at him through a straw. That's exactly what happened in *Revenge of the Voodoo People*. I mean, did you check his body for dart marks?"

"The point's well taken, Mr. Cassidy," Schwartz said, staring fixedly at the ceiling. "We don't have the slightest idea if there was poison in his cognac. The thing is, you can't jump to conclusions. If I remember correctly," he added, looking at me, "you made the very point in your book *Dumbth*."

"You read that?" I asked.

"I did indeed," he replied. "And I liked what you said about the distinction between consistent and conclusive evidence. Anyway, we're not going to have the answer to any of these questions till we get to the forensics lab in England." This was the most talking the FBI man had done since he'd arrived in our stateroom. He now lay back, breathing deeply from the effort.

"Well, what do you suggest we do until then?" I asked. "Nothing?"

"Exactly," he said.

"You must be kidding!"

"Not at all. The killer's not going any place, and we'll arrive at Southampton the day after tomorrow. I'll make certain Scotland Yard seals off the ship, and then we'll have a proper investigation. Until then, we'd only be stumbling around in the dark. Excuse me a moment."

He made a new dash to the head, as they call the bathroom at sea, and Cass, Jayne, and I belted out "I'm an Old Cowhand."

When Schwartz staggered back from the bathroom to fall onto the couch, I was beginning to wish he would reel back to his own quarters and leave us alone.

"So we're agreed, I hope," he said as he settled back into his funeral pose. "We'll just sit tight."

"Although there's a killer on the loose and a lot of ocean between here and Europe," I reminded him.

"Mr. Allen, there's nothing else to be done."

"Well, I'm sure as hell not going to remain locked up in this cabin for the next thirty-six hours. Among other things, I have a show to do tomorrow night."

"You must be joking!" Schwartz said. "You'll have to cancel it, of course."

"Cancel it?" I said, incredulous. "Jayne, tell him."

"Mr. Schwartz, it's a point of honor that the show goes on, no matter what."

"That's right," I agreed. "I'm certainly not going to let some cowardly killer scare me out of performing."

"What about the weather?" he asked.

"Neither rain, nor sleet," I said, launching into an old quotation.

Just then there was a flash of white light and such a crack of thunder that we all cried out. *The Atlantis* had been struck directly by a bolt of lightning! The ship lit up brightly for a split second—and then we were plunged into absolute darkness.

chapter 41

I slept restlessly, disturbed by dark dreams. There was nothing else to do. With the aid of the small pocket flashlight I always carry, we made certain the door to the suite was bolted shut; then the G-man took the couch, Cass an armchair, and Jayne and I made our way through the darkness into the bedroom.

I had a dream that I was riding a bucking bronco in a rodeo, and Cass was cheering me on. I knew we were in Wyoming because I could see the Grand Tetons in the distance as the wild stallion I was riding threw me off. . . .

When I woke in the darkness of my bedroom, it was to bucking; *The Atlantis* was being tossed about on the waves. I reached for the bedside light, hoping to see what time it was, but the switch clicked on without any change to the womb-like darkness. The electricity obviously had not returned.

Jayne stirred next to me. I moved close and put my arm over her waist to reassure her. Somehow I fell asleep again. This time I dreamed that we were bouncing together on a huge blue trampoline.

When I finally woke, the dream had turned into a nightmare.

I opened my eyes to find a dim gray light creeping into our bedroom from the porthole. I tried to close my eyes again, because I was certain from the weakness of the light it must be very early, but the ship dove into the water, then climbed the next mountainous wave. The motion was so violent I feared we would break apart.

Jayne was awake too. "Are you seasick, dear?" she asked.

"Not at all. Merely disgusted."

"I'm certain a ship like this has all the technology needed to handle a storm," she said.

"Naturally," I responded. When I clicked the switch of the bedside light again, we still had no power, which did not seem a very good sign, latest technology or not. Then I peered at my wristwatch, an inexpensive Timex that glows green in the dark if you press a button; it was nearly ten A.M. That did not seem a good sign either, considering the poor quality of the light outside.

"Well," I said cheerfully, "what say we call room service and order up a nice pot of coffee and breakfast for four?"

"Better make that for three," suggested Jayne. "I somehow doubt our visitor is hungry."

"Nah," I told her. "Those FBI guys are tough."

I picked up the bedside phone and dialed 8, the number for room service. As it rang, I told Jayne we'd forget our diet today. "I'm going to get us hot cakes—with actual butter, by God— ham, bacon, fried eggs, maybe some hash browns, and lots of orange juice. We need energy and inspiration."

"That's a good idea, Steve. And order us some little pastries as well. Cass adores those bear-claw things. And you'd better ask for two pots of coffee. . . ."

But the room-service telephone rang and rang. I hung up and tried again; this time I could not even get a dial tone. I stared at the dead phone in dismay. There are few things more disappointing than fantasizing a large and suicidally delicious breakfast—tasting it in anticipation—and then receiving nothing. I tried Operator, then all the other buttons on the phone, but it had become an ominously silent piece of plastic.

"There seems to be a general breakdown of services," I told Jayne.

"Oh, dear."

Cass was stirring in the next room while Bermuda Schwartz continued to snore. It was perhaps a good thing the light was so dim, since that prevented Cass, Jayne, and me from seeing the dismal expression each of us had. To be trapped on an ocean liner in a storm, with no electricity, no breakfast, and a killer on the loose, could not be anyone's idea of a happy vacation.

"Well, they *must* have a backup power supply," I said, determined to be cheerful. "An emergency generator will probably kick in any minute now."

"Why hasn't it kicked in already?" Cass asked gloomily.

I tried the telephone again—this time the one in the sitting room but with the same results.

"I'll tell you what," I said. "Cass and I'll go see how things are and try to find some breakfast."

"Steve, it might be dangerous out there," Jayne worried.

Thinking that a touch of humor might improve our mood, I said, "It might be dangerous in here. For all we know, Mr. Schwartz might just be pretending to be an FBI man. He might even be pretending to be seasick."

Schwartz groaned and fixed me with a maniacal stare. "I've never killed anybody in my life," he said, "although I might make an exception in your case."

Pretending fear, I signaled to Cass and headed for the door.

chapter 42

Just for the hell of it, I put the small revolver in my jacket pocket, and Cass took along the tiny flashlight and his all-purpose Swiss Army knife.

The corridor was so completely black we could not see our hands when held inches in front of our eyes. Nevertheless I told Cass to save the batteries of the tiny light. The hallway was straight, and we could make our way easily enough by feeling along the walls. The motion of the ship was more of a problem than the darkness. We moved cautiously, sometimes holding hands and pressing one palm against opposite walls to stay on our feet.

Halfway down the corridor, a stateroom door opened and an elderly woman peered out. She was lit from behind by the dim light coming from her stateroom porthole.

"Is someone there?" she called nervously.

"Just some passengers from down the hall," I said. "Could you keep your door open a moment, ma'am? The light is very helpful."

"Oh, isn't this awful?" she complained. "Have you seen my room steward? My breakfast is an hour late, and I can't get *any*-one on the telephone!"

I extended heartfelt sympathy about her morning meal and assured her we were checking things out. Meanwhile her open door gave us enough light to make our way more swiftly down the corridor. We ran into a small group of people near the elevator. A young man and three or four older passengers were huddled together, complaining indignantly about the lack of services, the darkness, and the storm. The young man had apparently talked with someone from the crew.

"They're telling everyone to stay in their staterooms until the power comes back on," he explained.

"But what about breakfast?" a woman asked. "My husband is starving."

"They're giving out cold food in the dining room, but it's difficult to get there. Even nonessential crewmen have been told to stay in their quarters. It's just not safe to move around," the young man said.

Two more people appeared from a dark corridor, telling horror stories about their morning, swearing they would never travel by sea again. The storm and lack of electricity had changed *The Atlantis* from a friendly pleasure palace to an alien world. Richard Wilmington had said something about electrical problems on the ship before the voyage, but it was difficult to imagine that a modern vessel like this would not have a readily available emergency power supply. I decided that Cass and I would make a detour to the bridge. It would mean a delay in getting breakfast, but now that we were actually out and about, I wanted to accomplish as much as possible.

"Come on, let's use the outside stairs," I said. "We'll be able to see better."

Pushing open the glass door to the deck, I was greeted by a howling rush of wind and rain. It was hard to tell where the ocean left off and the sky began. A wave broke against the ship and sent salty spray into our faces. Cass and I were soaking wet in seconds. Fortunately, I was wearing a nylon boating jacket with a hood, which I pulled over my head, tightening the string at the collar.

"Let's make a run for it," I shouted. "Hang on to the railing!"

Holding on for dear life to anything we could find that was solid, we made our way up two flights of outdoor stairs. The fury of wind and water was overwhelming. We had to stop often and cling to the rail so that we wouldn't be blown away. Two decks up, we lowered our heads into the gale and the pelting rain and managed to cross the shuffleboard court to another flight of stairs leading to the bridge.

At last we were inside. I closed the door behind us, thankfully shutting out the rain.

"I could use a towel," I said, shaking off the water.

"Holy cow, Steve! I've never seen a storm like this, not even in Wyoming."

We stood in a narrow entryway, dripping water and catching our breaths.

"I'm sorry, this area is closed to the public." The voice came from behind us. I put on my glasses to see a large wet blur, a crew member blocking the stairs to the bridge. I was surprised to see that the blur had a rifle in his hand.

"I want to see Captain Mellon," I told him in what I hoped was an authoritative manner. "I'm on a special assignment, in the employ of the Wilmington family, and I've been up here before. Please tell Captain Mellon that Steve Allen wants just a moment of his time. I'm sure he's busy so I won't keep him long."

The Wilmington name did the trick. The man left, came back a moment later, and gestured for us to follow. With the aid of a powerful flashlight, he guided us to the familiar conference room. In a moment, the captain came striding in. I would hardly have recognized him. His uniform was wet and stained with black grease, and his eyes were hollow from lack of sleep.

"I can give you about two minutes, Mr. Allen," he said. "What do you want?"

"Information. What's happening with the ship?"

"The main generator blew out when we were struck by lightning. We're trying to get it fixed, but a few of the key parts are totally burned."

"What about backup power? Surely you have an emergency generator."

He was silent a moment, and very grim. "There is no backup power," he said, with controlled anger. "The system wasn't finished in time."

"But that's incredible! Aren't there regulations about such things?"

"Yes, sir, there are. But there were . . . financial considerations. I objected strenuously, of course, but it was a million to one that we'd be hit by lightning."

"So you gambled with our lives to save money?" I exclaimed. "Who made that decision?"

"Marcus Wilmington, of course."

"You talked with him personally?"

"No. I got my instructions through Mr. Sanders."

"Not Dicky?"

"No. As a matter of fact, he tried to keep us from sailing until the ship was fitted properly, but he was overruled."

"I'll say he was," I said, remembering for a moment the sight of Wilmington's mangled body.

"I know this all seems abominable to you, Mr. Allen, and I understand. This will certainly be my last voyage as a captain— I'll lose my papers. But if you'll excuse me now, I have to get back to the engine room. It's probably hopeless, but we're still trying to jerry-rig something. Unfortunately the spare parts got left behind."

"How about the engines themselves?"

"Oh, they're still functional. But our computers are down, as well as our radar and navigational equipment. To be blunt, we don't know where we are, and we don't know where we're going."

"Have you radioed for help? Or are those dead as well?"

"Fortunately we had a battery-powered emergency radio on one of the lifeboats. We're sending out an SOS on every frequency. But no one's going to be able to get to us until the weather improves. Now if you'll excuse me . . ."

"Yes, of course. Just one last, fast question. Does the number F267 mean anything to you?"

"Maybe," he said, very much to my surprise. "It could be one of the storage bins down below. They have numbers like that."

"You mean in the cargo hold?"

"No, not that far down. We have a number of spaces available for odd things passengers can't fit into their cabins—statues, pianos, things like that. Most of the spaces are on F Deck."

"Near the indoor swimming pool?"

"Yes."

"Ah!" I exclaimed. I felt like a winning slot machine, bells ringing and lights flashing. Jackpot!

chapter 43

I understood now what Stewart Hoffman had been trying to say to me with his last raspy breath when I had asked where the arms shipment was.

"You . . . tell . . . me!" were his words. At the time I had taken this as an unanswerable riddle, a final shrug of the shoulders. But I saw now that he had meant it literally — that *I* knew where the missiles were because I possessed the cryptic set of numbers on the matchbook.

Meanwhile, life on board was becoming slightly more organized. Crew members with flashlights were standing in some of the darker passageways to guide people along and provide information, and more passengers were moving about now in search of food and news. Some roamed about the ship with dazed expressions. Others already had their orange life vests around their necks, prepared for anything. A number were complaining loudly that they had paid several thousand dollars for the voyage and the ship's going into the storm was outrageous. Emergencies often bring out the best in people, but not always. Crew members told passengers there was no need for panic, but I noticed that the ship's officers were carrying sidearms. There was no longer a pretense that this was an ordinary ocean voyage.

Cass and I made our way to the main dining room. The light

was fairly good here since there were panoramic windows on both the port and starboard sides. A buffet table had been set up in the center of the room, laden with food. There was a little of everything: cold meats, breads, salad greens, and makings, as well as covered containers of eggs, ham, and bacon sitting on small gas burners. Best of all, there was hot coffee. No one was going to starve, at least in the foreseeable future. The dining room had become a gathering place for all those who had the nerve to venture from their cabins. Nearly a third of the tables were full of serious-faced groups who looked grateful for any comfort they might find. Our priorities had changed drastically. Suddenly a ham sandwich or cup of hot coffee seemed more important than the great feasts we had considered our right the night before.

I noticed Alexis Wilmington sitting at a table across the room. He was still in the pink dinner jacket he had worn the previous night, though his bow tie was hanging loose and the jacket looked as if he had taken a shower while wearing it. Despite this, he seemed to be having a grand time. He had a bucket of champagne on one side of him and Chelsea Eastman on the other. Probably neither had slept.

I gestured Cass toward a deserted waiter's station, and huddling with him behind a potted palm, gave him the .38, which he slipped into his pocket. "Go get Jayne," I said. "And Schwartz, too, if he's in any shape to move. They'll probably be happier up here with the hot coffee and food. Anyway, my guess is the killer's going to leave us alone until this storm's over—he's got to be having trouble getting around, too. But be careful. Come right here from the cabin, and don't let Jayne out of your sight."

"What are you going to do? Hit the chow line?"

"I'm going to say good morning to some lovers."

Cass followed my glance across the room toward Alexis, Chelsea, and the bucket of champagne.

"Jeez!" he said. "*That's* a cozy picture! But weren't they each with somebody else last night?"

I could tell that Cass did not approve by the huffy manner in which he walked away. I required more information before coming to a judgment. I got myself a cup of coffee, then wandered toward the new couple. Chelsea looked fresh and bright as a daisy. She was still at an age where she could miss a night of sleep and not be much the worse for wear. Alex, on the other hand, looked every day of his thirty-five years, and a few extra as well. He was disheveled and bleary-eyed.

"Well, good morning," I said.

They stopped looking at each other and turned to me.

"Oh, great. Did my grandmother send you?" Chelsea asked, without any sort of greeting.

"Not at all. I hope she knows where you are, though—she'll be worried."

"Why?" Alex said grandly.

Chelsea however did not appear so carefree at the mention of her grandmother. "Do you think you could do me a big favor, Mr. Allen?"

"And what is that?"

"Sit down!" Alex said. "People make me nervous when they hover over me."

I set my coffee on the table and joined the happy couple.

"Well, it's my grandmother," Chelsea said. "I *did* sort of forget about her last night. Actually, I didn't think of her once. Not until this moment. Do you think you could go see her and sort of pave the way for the prodigal's return?"

"No, Chelsea. This is not my concern."

"Oh, please. You're so good with people," she flattered. "You could say I was watching the sunrise and just forgot about the time."

"There *was* no sunrise this morning."

"Oh," she said, turning briefly to the tempest outside. "I was wondering why it was so dark. Did it rain last night?"

Alex grinned. "She's funny, isn't she? I like girls who make me laugh. That was the problem with Candy. She never made me laugh."

Since I'm not interested in the complexities of playboys' love lives, if love is the proper word, I got quickly to the reason I had come to the table.

"Have you heard that Stewart Hoffman was murdered last night?"

"Yeah. Sanders told me," Alex said moodily, staring out the window. "This is a hell of a cruise, isn't it?"

"At what time did he tell you?" I asked.

"I don't know. Night time. Do you remember when it was, Chelsea?"

"Night time, definitely," she agreed.

"Did he tell you *how* Hoffman died?"

"Sure. Said he was poisoned. Here's to Stu," he said, suddenly raising his glass. "A guy no one cared about. But he was like a brother to me, I swear to God."

"To brotherhood," Chelsea agreed.

And that's when it hit me. The truth, that is. Jolting my brain like the bolt of lightning that had struck the ship.

"My God, he *was* your brother, Alex! Wasn't he?"

"That's what I said, man. The guy was my bro."

"Forget the jive talk, *man*. Hoffman wasn't just your *bro*—he was your half-brother."

He laughed. "Hey, I wouldn't go that far."

"I would. It's the reason your father hired him and gave him the condo in New York. It didn't have anything to do with stopping a police investigation. Stewart was his illegitimate son."

Wilmington turned to Chelsea. "Hey, this guy's pretty good."

"It's true?" Chelsea asked.

"Sure. Stu was the family bastard. Dicky, me, and Stu—we made quite a team."

"Who knew about this?" I asked.

"Just Dad—and Will, of course. And us kids. Oh, and of course Mom knew . . . can't forget old Mom! She hated Stu, you see, because his presence was a constant reminder of Dad's . . . er . . . indiscretion. But there you are—we're a complex family."

"I guess so. And let me tell you something else, Alex, in case it hasn't occurred to you. You're the last brother still alive. So if I were you, I'd grow up. Thirty-five is too old to be acting like a fraternity boy."

With these words of advice, I rose to my feet. I was about to leave, but I don't offer advice often, and I was on a roll.

"And while you're at it, get Chelsea back to her grandmother. There's no reason you should involve this overimaginative young woman in your troubles. Tell her grandma that nothing happened—even if it did, it'll never happen again."

"You're right, Steve," he agreed.

"Alex!" Chelsea cried angrily. "You wouldn't!"

"I have to, honey. Mr. Allen's right. This is a mess you don't want to be hung up in, believe me."

I had intruded enough for one morning, so I left them to work it out. Anyway I had my own problems. Cass was walking my way across the dining room, and I could tell from his expression that there was something far more wrong than the power failure.

"They're not there," he said. "Jayne and Schwartz—they're gone!"

chapter 44

Cass handed me a note written in Jayne's New England finishing-school hand:

> Darling,
> Don't worry about us. We went off with Candy. I think we've found the missiles. You'll never guess where! I'll tell you all about it later.
>
> Me

"She says not to worry," Cass said, trying to reassure me.

"Worry?" I said. "Why should I worry? My wife has just gone off to a secret stash of anti-aircraft missiles meant for God-knows-what terrorist group."

"At least she's got that FBI guy with her."

"A seasick G-man'll be a big help in an emergency. And let's not forget Candy L'Amour, Miss Slut of nineteen ninety-four—which means Jayne's probably also in the company of my least favorite journalist."

"Okay, so we *are* worried."

On the other side of the dining room, I noticed Alexis and Chelsea rise. She was pouting, so I had a feeling he really was taking her back to her grandmother. I walked over to them.

"Tell me Candy's cabin number," I demanded.

"She's in the Arlington Suite. It's on A Deck."

"Oh, swell," Chelsea sulked.

"Honey, we've been all through this. I don't *want* Candy anymore; I told you that."

I charged off with Cass in the direction of A Deck. As we climbed the stairs, the ship gave a mighty lurch, which sent us to our knees. We quickly pulled ourselves up and kept going.

The corridor to the Arlington Suite was dark as a grave, but Cass used the travel flashlight to find the way. I knocked sharply on the door. When there was no answer, Cass got out his Swiss Army knife and prepared for the delicate operation of picking the lock. I told him to give me the revolver and stand aside.

"You think that's a good idea?"

"I think it's a *very* good idea."

I fired. The explosion was loud in the corridor, but the storm was so noisy I doubted the shot could be heard more than a few staterooms away. Candy's door swung open; Cass and I stepped inside. There was no one there. Neither Jayne, Schwartz, Candy, nor Larry Goldman. That established, I began to look at the suite more carefully.

It was even more lovely then the others I'd seen, with a sliding glass door leading to a small private deck. What caught my eye was not the luxury, however, but the destruction. Everything had been torn apart. Clothes had been pulled out of closets and drawers, and strewn across the floor. Tossed makeup boxes and bottles made it a colorful mess. The bed, too, had been stripped; even the toilet articles in the bathroom were scattered about.

"Jeez," Cass said, "someone should teach these young gals to pick up after themselves!"

I wasn't certain he was joking until he grinned at me. But I was not in a joking mood.

"Well, what do we do now?" He sighed.

"I don't know. If I could just *think* a little harder maybe I could figure things out! It's all tied together somehow . . . the murders, the arms shipment, the fact that Stewart Hoffman was Wilmington's son—even old Marcus sending for me the first night. But with Jayne off God knows where I can't think straight!"

"Mrs. Allen's got a good head on her shoulders. For all we know, she has this whole case sewed up."

I was not convinced, but panic wasn't helping matters. I did my best to think clearly. "Cass, the next step—" I stopped talking suddenly because I saw something in the dresser mirror I did not like. A man. And the gun in his hand was pointed our way. He was big, and it was a big gun. The silencer made it look even nastier.

"No need to panic, boys," he said. "Just keep your hands where I can see 'em and step into the next room."

Cass and I had been standing in Candy's bedroom. We did what the man told us and joined him in the sitting room. It was the Texan with the hound-dog face I had met at the captain's cocktail party. Dan Moody. Or whatever his name was.

He was the joker in the pack, and I had forgotten all about him. Apparently at my peril.

chapter 45

The Texan relieved me of the .38, while keeping Cass in the sights of his own pistol.

"Damn!" he said. "You sure made a mess of that door, ol' buddy!"

"Not as big a mess as you made in here."

He glanced around, chuckled. "Sit down, sit down!" he said, jovially. "What are you two fellas doing here anyway?"

"We're fans," I explained. "Just hoping to find a small souvenir of Miss L'Amour in the rubble. How about yourself? A pop star's cabin seems off the usual path for a CIA guy like you."

He chuckled again. "Well, Steverino, I guess I told you a little fib, about working for the CIA."

"I'm disillusioned, Dan—that *is* your name?"

"Why don't you fellas just keep on using that one. A benefit of my job is the chance to go by aliases.

"Which is?"

"Well, you might call me a broker. . . . I break arms, heads, you name it!"

Cass and I did not laugh.

"That was a joke," he mentioned. "Actually, I *sell* arms— that is if I can find 'em to sell, which every now and then becomes a problem."

"You have many buyers?"

"Oh, it's a growing business. Right now I'm specializing in the little guy. I mean, if you were a country like Iraq and you wanted a few fighter planes, you'd have to go to China or some place like that. I couldn't help you. But say you were a bunch of Commie guerrillas in the mountains of Peru—or maybe a nutty religious sect in Idaho—I'd be the guy to see. Machine guns, small artillery, grenades, letter bombs, stuff like that—I'm your man."

"I'll keep that in mind," I told him. "But don't you worry about all the people who get killed with the guns you sell?"

"Hey, I'm a peace-loving guy personally. 'It's a dirty job, but somebody's got to do it.' Unfortunately, as I say, I occasionally encounter a slight snag."

I had a feeling his current "snag" had something to do with why Cass and I were at the wrong end of his gun.

"I hate to think of things not working out for you, Mr. Moody. What's your problem precisely?"

"Well, I've been looking for a certain something that's supposed to be on board. I'm good at finding things usually, but this little item has plumb disappeared."

"Ah! Let me guess. You're seeking a small shipment of shoulder-launched, ground-to-air missiles that will knock a jumbo jet clean out of the sky?"

Dan's face changed. He suddenly had a look you see in a dog's eyes when you bring out a can opener and start to open its dinner.

"Have you seen those babies?" he asked in a worshipful voice. "*I* have. I held one of 'em in my hands once. The whole thing is hardly bigger than a hunting rifle. You just point it at the sky, set the little computer tickin', and POW! it'll blow up whatever's overhead. They won't even see it on their radar screen until it's too late. This little jewel's going to revolutionize terrorism."

"You're the middleman, then, for the Wilmington family?"

"Nope." He smiled. "I'm what you call the odd man out. I

have the misfortune to represent an individual who is no longer alive."

"Dicky Wilmington?"

"No."

"Stewart Hoffman?"

"One more chance, Steve."

"Peter Moon!" I said, astonished.

"You got it."

"But how was Moon involved?"

"He found out about the missiles from Dicky and hired me, knowing I'm an expert on these things. Moon and me, we go back a ways, you see. We started a little civil war together once in Africa, to bankrupt a New Yorker friend of his who had money tied up there . . . but that's a story for another time."

"Dicky *told* Moon the missiles were going to be on board?"

"That's right. It's a scam the lawyer set up—that Sanders fellow. The missiles were brought to New York from California by truck. They were loaded on the ship sometime Friday, and then . . . well, they disappeared."

"How can a shipment of missiles just disappear?"

"That's the twenty-five-million-dollar question, pardner. You see, there're some Irish guys waiting in England for these babies. They put up the first half of the money, twelve point-five million, two months ago. At the moment I figure they're getting a little impatient to see the goods."

"Twenty-five million! That's a lot of money for a small group like the IRA."

"This is going to be more bang for their bucks than anything they've gotten yet."

And it wouldn't be too bad for *The Atlantis* either, I thought grimly.

"But I still don't understand what Moon was up to," Cass said.

Dan chuckled. "Just a sly little takeover move, like Pete always liked to pull. I set up some Middle Eastern buyers—the kinda boys who kill for the greater glory of Mohammed—who're willing to pay even more than the Irish guys. All in all, it was pretty smooth. Dicky was going to tell us where the missiles were, we'd steal 'em, get paid big time, and leave old Marcus in the lurch with some very angry killers from the IRA."

"But something went wrong?" I said. And then it came to me. "Of course! Dicky double-crossed Moon!"

"You got it. After playing ball for months, the creep suddenly refused to tell us where the missiles were stashed. Peter thought he could force it out of him, but Dicky had the misfortune to be killed. *The Atlantis* is a big ship, Steve, and it's like lookin' for a needle in a haystack, as the sayin' goes."

"But Peter is dead now too. . . ."

"Which means *my* head's on the choppin' block. My Muslim friends aren't going to be happy if I walk off this ship with just my underwear in my suitcase, so I'll have to trouble you to tell me where the . . . merchandise is."

"Good God, *I* don't know!"

"Oh, I think you do, pardner. Now, it may take a while—there could even be some pain involved—but you are going to tell me."

Dan laid the gun on his lap and pulled a huge cigar from his breast pocket. Cass had been sitting impassively, listening intently. We exchanged a quick look.

"This is a nonsmoking cabin," I told the Texan.

He chuckled. "It's a nonsmoking world these days, but as long as *I'm* the one holding the cannon, I'll just do what I want."

The Texan lit his cigar, puffed a lazy cloud of smoke, and blew it our way. It was psychological warfare. Cass and I gagged on the heavy fumes; we both hate cigars. I wondered desperately if there was any way to get the gun from Moody. I glanced around and noticed that one of Candy's makeup cases was tipped over on its side on the dressing table to my left; a powder puff and a pile of white face powder had spilled onto the glass tabletop. Could I throw the powder in the Texan's eyes, I wondered, and jump before he shot us? The ship was sluing about like a drunken rocking horse; I wasn't certain if this factor helped him or us. I caught Cass's eye and glanced toward the powder.

"Tell me where the missiles are, Mr. Allen, or I'm going to blow you apart." Moody's eyes narrowed dangerously, his smile was deadly. "Piece by piece."

"Dan, listen, I'd like to help you out, but I'm in the dark about too many things myself. I mean, why bust into Candy's stateroom? Surely you weren't expecting to find the missiles here?"

"You're stalling, but there's no harm in tellin' ya. I was after her husband. I thought he might have left something around."

"Her husband? I think her engagement to Alex is off."

"Not Alex. That writer creep. Goldman."

"Well, I'll be . . ." Cass said.

"Who can account for the tastes of women, huh? They actually got married years ago, before she was famous. They've been separated now for five years at least, but as far as I know, they never actually got a divorce."

"How the hell did you find out about their marriage?"

"Hell's bells, Steverino, information's the name of the game," he said, blowing an odious cloud of smoke.

"Then tell me—how's Goldman involved in this?" I asked.

"He's an investigative reporter. That's reason enough to kill him, even if he hadn't found out about the missiles. But don't worry about him. He'll get his chance in the hot seat. At the moment, it's your turn, pal."

"I really can't help you, Dan."

I had underestimated him. Without warning, the Texan fired his gun in Cass's direction. With the silencer, the weapon made only a muffled pop, but the porthole behind Cass's left ear shattered with a great crash, letting in a howling rush of wind and rain.

"That was your one warning," the Texan said, shouting over

the onslaught of wind. "The next bullet goes into your friend's kneecap."

"Okay, okay," I said quickly. "I found a matchbook next to Dicky's body."

"Yeah? And what was on this matchbook?"

"A number."

"Steve, don't tell him!" Cass interrupted.

"I've got to."

"Goddamned right you do."

"I'm not sure I can remember it. Let's see, it started with an F . . . then a one . . . two . . . Do you remember the last number, Cass?"

"*Three!*" he cried.

We both moved at the same time. Cass and I have spent a lot of time together, some of it in difficult situations, and I had hoped he was hip to what was on my mind. Thankfully, he was. I threw the white face powder toward Moody's eyes while Cass feinted to one side and charged low. The gun popped again. A lamp shattered behind us. But Cass had gotten hold of Moody's gun arm, and I had the other. It was not an elegant fight: Cass punched, and I pounded and kicked. The Texan, big as a side of beef, remained standing with both Cass and me riding on him. I'm not certain how it would have ended if he hadn't been smoking that rotten cigar. Smoking, as everyone knows, is bad for your health. Somehow Moody bit down on the thing, and in the heat of battle partly swallowed the stub.

While he was gagging, I managed to sit on him. Cass quickly ripped the cord from the shattered lamp and used it to tie the Texan's hands. With the help of a hair dryer cord and one from the telephone, cowboy Cass managed to get Moody tied up rodeo-style in record time, the big Texan ending up face down on the floor, hands and legs trussed up behind him as if he were a calf.

"There!" I said. "I guess *that'll* teach you to smoke in a no-smoking area!"

chapter 46

Jayne had not returned to our suite. I looked there first, hoping my fears were unwarranted.

"Why didn't she just stay in the staterooms like I told her?"

"Now, Steve, we don't know what happened, do we?" Cass said, sticking up for Jayne. "And Schwartz went, too, so it must have been important."

I read her note again—I had kept it in my pocket—it was a good thing Moody had not thought to search me. *Went off with Candy,* she had written. *I think we've found the missiles.* Then the tantalizing sentence: *You'll never guess where!*

The fact that Larry was Candy's husband—if it was true—made everything even more unsettled in my mind. I reminded myself that Moody, or whoever he was, was not a reliable witness, even though Candy had gone off with Goldman last night. The relationships on board *The Atlantis* seemed as changing as a kaleidoscope.

I wrote Jayne a note and left it on the dressing table, where she would be sure to see it should she return:

Jayne,
Stay put and lock the door. I'll keep checking back.

Steve

Cass saw how worried I was. "We'll find her," he said encouragingly.

"Right!" A pessimistic attitude would not help matters. I wanted to recheck all the obvious places, so we tried the dining room once again. I say this as if it had become miraculously easier to get from one place to another. It had not. The electricity was still off, the corridors pitch black, and the ocean was so rough that Cass and I found ourselves grabbing anything we could to keep upright and propel ourselves forward. Two people we passed were actually crawling.

The dining room was still the main gathering area. Most of the tables were full—people eating, playing cards, hanging onto their chairs, and sometimes just staring out at the terrifying display of nature. I saw a couple of folks praying, one woman using rosary beads. The large room now looked like a Red Cross relief center, except for the buffet tables piled high with lobster, caviar, and other rich provisions from the ship's stores.

I saw Rusty O'Conner playing gin with her two Beverly Hills friends and hurried over.

"Have you seen Jayne?" I asked.

"I did. She was with Candy L'Amour. When was that, girls?"

One of the "girls" said it was just a few minutes earlier; another thought it had been over an hour.

"Tell Jayne to come and play rumm—Oh my goodness!"

Rusty stopped talking because my windbreaker had fallen open to reveal Moody's automatic pistol stuffed into the waistband of my pants.

"Oh, dear!" she fluttered. "Has Jayne run off with another man? Don't do anything rash, Steve—at least not without telling me first!"

Cass and I left her to her fantasies and separately searched the dining room for Jayne. But we joined up a few minutes later without any luck.

"All I can think to do now is check out the storage locker," I said.

"You think we're going to be able to get down there?"

"We have to."

And we did—though it wasn't easy. E Deck was below the water line, and we stepped into a darkness so dense it swallowed any remaining optimism. Cass had Jayne's miniature flashlight, and I used mine, leading the way. The beams from both were noticeably weaker now, providing only small, ocher-colored circles of light on the step immediately beneath our feet. We moved slowly, hanging on to the banister. The noise was tremendous. At each great swell of the ocean, the hull groaned and creaked and threatened to break apart.

Cass and I shouted at the same time as a small rat scurried into the dim light at our feet, then scampered past us and up the stairs.

"Holy cow, you'd think this ship was too new to have rats!" Cass said.

"I'd say there are a number aboard."

"What the hell!" Cass lost his footing, grabbed out in the darkness, and pulled us both down four or five steps—all the way to F Deck. I knew it was F Deck because the last one had been E; there was no other way to differentiate this particular patch of darkness from the one above our heads. Cass and I sat at the bottom of the stairs, breathing hard.

"Are you hurt?" he asked, pulling himself up.

"No. I banged my elbow a bit, but I'm okay."

There was nothing to do but go on. The flashlights now shone in feeble beams hardly more than two or three feet ahead. I tried to visualize the maze of corridors on F Deck as I had seen them the night I had come down to find Jayne and Peter Moon at the pool.

"Hold onto my jacket, Cass. I don't want us to get separated."

I led the way down the first corridor, running my free hand along the wall. At each door we shined our lights, such as they were, to read such words as PWR ROOM #3 and PA5. I had no idea where most of these doors led, and the few I tried were locked.

We walked a long time. The miracle was, we finally found a door marked PASSENGER STORAGE AREA. This led into a huge room with deck-to-ceiling cubicles on either side. I suppose if you were bringing a marble fountain from an old manor house in England to your estate on Long Island this is where you would put it during your voyage. F267 was halfway down the aisle; the door to it was suspiciously ajar. I took out Moody's gun and Cass brought out Schwartz's revolver. Our flashlights were so weak we wouldn't be able to see what we were shooting at, but the weapons made us feel slightly more courageous as we walked into the dark cubicle. The room was so small that even with our dying light we could see the space contained—absolutely nothing. Except for a sad, broken bundle in one corner.

The bundle was Larry Goldman, journalist stowaway. Someone had stabbed him in the back with an ice pick, which still protruded from the wound.

Cass and I were kneeling by the corpse when something else died as well. My flashlight.

chapter 47

It was like being buried alive, to be this far down in the ship, in the company of a dead man, with only one dim light.

"We've been in worse jams, cowboy," I said, hoping to buck up Cass's spirits.

"Name one."

The lightning-bug glimmer of the remaining flashlight wasn't much help as we felt our way out of the dark hole. The gray light coming in a porthole on D Deck brought a shout of delight. We didn't realize it at the time, but that was the high point of the day.

"Maybe we should check the stateroom for Jayne again," Cass suggested.

"We'll do that later. If she's returned, she'll wait."

I led the way to the top of the ship, to Gertrude Wilmington's luxurious suite near the bridge. The same, armed crew member tried to send us away, but I told him I had a murder to report. I gave him an ominous look, and he stepped aside.

A butler led us into Mrs. Wilmington's quarters. The Picasso was lopsided on the wall and the Ming vases had been put away somewhere. But Gertrude herself, stern and majestic as ever, seemed untroubled by the fact that the only light in the room was the dim grayness that came through the large windows. She was wearing a black cashmere dress and a simple pearl necklace and pearl earrings.

"Good afternoon, gentlemen. To what do I owe the pleasure of this visit?"

It seemed crazy to speak so formally when I could see the bow of the mighty *Atlantis* actually disappear under water spray, but something in Gertrude's manner made us stand up to greet her as if we were visiting her country estate on a summer day.

"There's been another . . . death," I said. Murder seemed too rude a word to utter in her presence.

She froze. Her voice was a strangled whisper. "Not Alexis . . ."

My mind flashed back to her anguish over Dicky's death, and I hastened to assure her. "No, no. A journalist named Larry Goldman. He worked for *Trend* magazine."

"I've never read it."

"Really? Your husband did an interview for them not long ago."

"Oh, yes. If I remember, Will suggested that Marcus needed to improve his public image."

"Sanders carries a lot of weight with Mr. Wilmington?" I said.

"He's Marcus's closest advisor. And since my husband is such a recluse, he has taken over most of the day-to-day decisions."

"Such as selling high-tech weapons to the Irish Republican Army?"

"Whatever are you talking about?"

"I'm talking about small and deadly anti-aircraft missiles Mr. Sanders smuggled on board *The Atlantis*. Are you aware that he's received twelve and a half million dollars as a down payment and he'll get an equal amount when he delivers the missiles?"

"Nonsense."

I was running out of patience. "You're going to hate prison,"

I said. "They won't let you bring your butler, or paintings for the walls."

She bowed her head delicately. "I see," she said finally.

"*Do* you, Mrs. Wilmington? I wonder if you quite understand the evil that has been done to get this ship in the water."

"Evil?" she repeated, looking at me.

"Stealing the retirement money of loyal employees, selling arms to terrorists—yes, these things are evil."

"Someone's been poisoning your mind, Mr. Allen. We have many enemies who would like to destroy us—by rumor if they can't manage any other way. Do you have proof about these so-called missiles?"

"No," I admitted. "But I'll get it easily enough when we reach Southamptom. Will Sanders has led you and your children and your family's empire to ruin. I believe he killed your son, as well as Peter Moon, Stewart Hoffman, and now Larry Goldman."

"Ridiculous! Will's a gentleman."

"What about your husband? Is he a gentleman too?"

Her slight smile was as impenetrable as the Mona Lisa's.

"My husband, Mr. Allen, is *not* a gentleman. He would be quite capable of all the things you've mentioned, and a few other crimes as well, but . . ."

"But what?"

"My husband is . . . dead."

I could only stare at her.

"Marcus has been dead for the past year and a half."

"But that's absurd. I saw—"

"The man you saw was an actor who has been paid—rather well, I should mention—to impersonate my husband."

"But the interview—"

"The journalist, I'm afraid, was treated to the same performance."

"But—"

"If you think about it, I believe you'll understand. My husband died of natural causes at an advanced age . . . but he died at, shall we say, an inconvenient moment. Our creditors, had they known the truth, would have come rushing upon us like a pack of wolves, and *The Atlantis* would still be in dry dock in San Diego. Whatever you may think of Marcus, his name inspired respect. And so a small . . . charade was in order."

My mind boggled as dozens of questions assaulted it, but the butler came into the room before I could ask the first.

"Madame, the first mate is here with an urgent message from the captain," he announced. "It appears possible that the ship may capsize at any time."

Gertrude raised her head high and said in her haughtiest manner, "I'm afraid that's not convenient, Justin. Send the first mate back to the captain with the message that I absolutely forbid it!"

chapter 48

Gertrude Wilmington belonged to another time and place. But even she could keep the real world from her drawing room no longer.

The first mate refused to be sent away. He pushed the butler aside and burst in upon us.

"Mrs. Wilmington, excuse me, but I don't believe you quite understand the seriousness of our situation."

"I understand perfectly well, my good man. You must tell Captain Mellon to buck up and carry on with his duty. It is unthinkable that *The Atlantis* should sink. You may remind the captain how much this vessel cost to build."

The first mate was a crisp-looking man in his late thirties. He looked helplessly at Cass and me, as if seeking support.

"What exactly is the problem?" I asked.

"The rudder has broken. The cable simply snapped," he said. "It means we're starting to drift broadside into thirty-foot swells. We'll be totally at the mercy of the sea. A big enough wave, and we could capsize—or even begin to break apart." He turned back to Mrs. Wilmington. "Frankly, ma'am, I hope they throw you and your husband in prison for criminal negligence."

"I beg your pardon!"

"You heard me. You put all your money into paintings and marble floors and cheated on everything the passengers couldn't see—like the emergency power backup and rudder cable. You'd better pray the lifeboats work!"

"This is utter insolence, young man, and I will not forget it when we reach Southampton."

"Don't worry, ma'am. *If* we reach land, you will have my resignation. And the captain has asked me to inform you that he will be tendering his as well."

"I see," Gertrude Wilmington said icily. "Very well."

"Meanwhile we've managed to make contact with a US naval destroyer that is less than an hour away. If we're lucky she'll reach us in time. The captain wants to gather all passengers in the main dining room—in their life vests. The muster stations outside are too dangerous and wet, but we want to be ready to evacuate."

"Very well," Mrs. Wilmington said once again. "Do what you must. Meanwhile please find Mr. Sanders and send him to me."

"He's at the stern, overseeing a repair attempt on the rudder. They're lowering a pair of divers over the side to see if anything can be done about the problem from below the water line. Frankly it's hopeless, but Mr. Sanders insisted on trying. If you want him, get him yourself, Mrs. Wilmington. I'm too busy trying to save the lives of the passengers. Excuse me, please."

Gertrude sat very still after the first mate left. She seemed to have forgotten that Cass and I were in the room. From her drawing room, I could see that *The Atlantis* was dead in the water, a giant piece of inert metal buffeted by the high seas.

"Come on, Cass—we have to find Jayne," I said.

Mrs. Wilmington appeared surprised at the sound of my voice and turned our way.

"Mr. Allen, perhaps you will do me the favor of locating Mr. Sanders at the stern of the ship. Tell that foolish man I need to see him at once."

"I'm looking for my wife first, Mrs. Wilmington. Once I find her, I'll search for your attorney."

"Yes, of course," she agreed. "One must keep in mind the priorities. I have tried to do that in my own life, you know, for my family. The choices have not always been easy. And then in the end—"

"I'm not certain I understand what you're saying," I told her.

"I'm talking about blind luck, Mr. Allen. This storm, for example. You think I'm a monstrous person for the things I have done. But you see, the rudder cable with the proper strength, the backup emergency generator . . . all those things were going to be installed after the first crossing. Under ordinary circumstances, we might not have needed them for years. The pension funds . . . If our luck had held, we would have been able to replace the money before anyone suspected it was gone. But now, with this storm, we have lost the gamble. Don't you see? That's all it was."

I stared at her angrily. "Next time, Mrs. Wilmington, I suggest you gamble with your own money—and with your own life. Now if you'll excuse us . . ."

She was an unusual woman, Gertrude Wilmington. Proud and dangerous.

"Someone has to take the great chances," she said absently, "or we would be still living in caves."

I gave her a wary look as Cass and I left the room. On the way out the door I heard her say to her butler: "Justin, you may bring my lunch now, even though it is a half-hour before my regular time. It appears we may be required to abandon ship after all."

"As you wish, madame," said the butler with a formal nod.

chapter 49

The ship's great engines were silent. I heard a woman scream as *The Atlantis* was hit broadside by a wave, sending us reeling like a punch-drunk boxer about to go down for the count.

Cass and I passed through the dining room, which was filling up with grim-faced passengers in bright orange life vests. As to be expected in such situations, some were brave, others hysterical. A few seemed more concerned about their luggage than their lives, complaining loudly against the order that they were not to carry any of it into the lifeboats.

I saw Rusty O'Conner sitting at a table, her life vest on and jewelry at her neck, fingers, wrists, and arms weighing her down. She sparkled like a Beverly Hills Christmas tree.

Jayne was not in the dining room, so Cass and I made our way against the lemminglike flow of vests, back to the suite. I found the message I had left for Jayne untouched on the dressing-room table.

"Damn!" I cried. "Where is she?"

Cass shook his head.

"Let's find Sanders then," I said savagely. "If that bastard knows where Jayne is, we'll beat it out of him!"

"You think he's the killer?"

"I don't know what to think, Cass. But we might as well find him. It's better than sitting here doing nothing but going crazy."

And so we set out to find the slick Ivy League attorney, stuffing our guns back into our waistbands. So far the weapons hadn't done us much good except for shooting open Candy's door.

It was now increasingly difficult to walk. We staggered and tripped on our way along the corridor to the stern, then used the outside stairs to make our way down closer to the water line. The stairs at the rear of the ship were protected by overhanging decks, which provided some shelter from the howling wind and rain. Nevertheless, we were drenched by the time we reached the lowest deck, the spot from which passengers often shot skeet in more pleasant weather. And there was no sign of Will Sanders or his repair crew.

"Maybe they gave up!" Cass said, yelling into my ear to make himself heard above the weather.

"Or they're below us!" I shouted back.

Cass and I then did a foolish thing. At least it appeared foolish in hindsight. We leaned over the back rail to see if we could spot any divers by the rudder. It was hard to see much because the deck on which we stood overhung the rudder by several feet.

"I don't think there's anyone down there!" Cass shouted.

"I can't see anyone either."

"That's because you're looking in the wrong place!" a voice said close behind us, almost in my right ear.

I felt a sharp push on my back, and someone pulled the back of my jacket up and forward. For a moment I thought I was going to be able to save myself by grasping the rail. Then there was a second shove, harder than before, and I was falling through the air.

When I hit the cold gray water it took my breath away. It had been a long fall, and it seemed I was under water forever. I came up sputtering, my eyes stinging and the taste of salt in my mouth. Cass was bobbing in the waves alongside me looking more angry than I had ever seen him.

"God damn it! Wait 'til I get my hands on that bastard!" he shouted.

I looked up to the hulking shape of the white ship above us— and couldn't see a thing. My glasses had come off, but I found them in my hand. I suppose I had reached for them unconsciously as I fell. Fortunately my maroon nylon jacket, secured by a drawstring at the waist, ballooned up and provided an extra bit of flotation. I treaded water, put my glasses back on my nose, and peered upward. Even in this terrible situation I had to know. The killer stood at the rail, smiling and waving down at us.

"Well, I'll be damned!" I said.

It was frustrating to know who the killer was and to be unable to do a thing about it. But Cass and I had more immediate problems. As we were treading water, the ghostly shape of *The Atlantis* began to drift slowly away from us.

chapter 50

The last I had seen of Jayne, she had wished Cass and me good luck in our search for breakfast and information. She had then watched us disappear down the dark corridor before wisely locking, bolting, and chaining herself into our staterooms to sit down beside the seasick Mr. Schwartz, who was lying on his back on the sofa and staring mournfully at the ceiling.

"I feel so . . . so impotent!" he confided to Jayne quite unexpectedly. "What good is a seasick cop?"

"There, there . . . You shouldn't put yourself down, Lawrence. Even the strongest people can become seasick."

"Do you think so?"

"Absolutely," Jayne assured him.

"Yeah, but people are counting on me. I've let you all down."

Jayne spent some time nursing his wounded feelings . . . until there was a knock on the door.

Not in the code we had agreed upon . . .

"Yes?" Jayne called cautiously, through the door.

"It's Candy!" The plaintive voice came from outside. "Please, Ms. Meadows, let me in!"

"I can't, dear. Steve's gone, and he left me with instructions not to open up for anyone."

"Jayne, I need help! *Please!*" Candy cried.

Even through the closed door and with the storm raging, Jayne was able to hear Candy's sobs. I should have known, when I left her, that Jack the Ripper himself might have wormed his way into our cabin had he only asked nicely enough, and with a small sob in his voice. Jayne undid the chain, pulled back the bolt, and unlocked the door.

The singer was standing in the doorway holding a small flashlight. She was wearing enormous round sunglasses, which was odd, as she was standing in a pitch black corridor.

"Goodness! Come in," Jayne said. "Whatever is the matter?"

Candy collapsed into her arms and was helped gently to an armchair, at which point the rock star began to weep.

"You poor thing! I wish I had something to give you."

"Like some brandy?" Candy sobbed.

"You know, I *may* be able to help you out!"

Jayne searched through her purse and found a miniature bottle of brandy which she had taken from the airplane a week earlier on a flight from Los Angeles to New York. Candy swallowed the liquor in two gulps, then removed her glasses. There was a swollen purple bruise over her left eye.

"Goodness! Did you fall?"

"It was that—that son-of-a-bitch! He slugged me! And it's not the first time either."

"Which particular 'son-of-a-bitch' are we talking about?" Jayne asked. "There are so many of them around."

"My husband."

"I didn't know you were married."

"Who's *that?*" Candy demanded, noticing Schwartz for the first time as he made an attempt to sit up. He looked at Candy, groaned, and fell onto his back again.

"This is Lawrence Schwartz. He's a lovely man from the FBI."

"No crap?" Candy said, in her usual elegant way. "God, I'm *so* embarrassed."

"Well, husbands *can* be embarrassing," my wife agreed. "Alexis?"

Candy laughed. "God, no! . . . It's Larry."

"The stowaway?"

"I was sixteen, and he was a slick guy who breezed into town one day from New York. I won't tell you how many years back."

"It can't be *that* long ago. Larry doesn't look as if he could be more than twenty-five. And you, dear—you're hardly more than a teenager!"

"Well, thanks. But you're off by about a decade. Anyway, we lived together for a few years, got married when I was eighteen. We weren't exactly Romeo and Juliet after the first few months. And then the rat met an actress he thought was going to be a big star and dumped me for the easy life. Only the joke was on him because her career fizzled, but a couple of years later, mine took off."

"So you lived in New York?"

"Yeah. That was the one good thing he did for me. He took me to the top music clubs, taught me the scene. After he left me, I didn't hear from him again until about two years ago, naturally *after* I was a big success. The bastard wanted me to help him, if you can believe it."

"But he's successful himself, isn't he? As a writer?"

"It wasn't money he was after, it was favors. Information about people. Invitations to parties where there are a lot of celebrities but no press. That sort of thing. It seemed kinda harmless at first, so I went along. Also, he knows a few things about me I wouldn't like to get out."

Jayne looked at Candy for a moment without speaking. "He's been blackmailing you?"

"Sort of. I mean, it's not like he comes out with it directly. He just hints at how we're old, old friends and he's been doing me a tremendous favor keeping some things quiet now that I'm famous—and here he is a journalist whose job it is to expose people."

"He *is* a rat!"

"Yeah. The things I did in the past . . ."

"You don't have to tell me about them, Candy."

"Well, they're not so terrible. They're more embarrassing, really. Like my real age. A juvenile record for shoplifting. Silly stuff like that. And some wild parties I used to go to. Drugs and stuff, you know. But then he shows up again and asks me to pull strings and get him on *The Atlantis*. Ha! I told him to go to hell. To tell the truth, I wasn't surprised when I saw him on board. One thing about Larry, he's got some nerve."

"But why was he so set on coming on *The Atlantis*? Was it only so he could write an article?"

"That's what I thought at first. But there's more to it."

"I see," said Jayne. "Well, perhaps you should tell me."

Candy peered uncomfortably at the seasick Schwartz, who was listening intently but had not said a word.

"I think we have a pretty good idea what you're going to tell us. It's about a shipment of small anti-aircraft missiles, isn't it?" Jayne said.

"My God! How did *you* find out about that?"

Jayne smiled. "It was Steve. Stewart Hoffman told him about the missiles last night before he was killed. But how is Larry involved?"

"I don't know. It's a bitch how he always manages to find out things. Probably Peter told him. . . ."

"Wait a moment. How in the world did Peter Moon know? And why would he tell Larry?"

"I have no clue. I know Larry was blackmailing Peter—for favors, like he was doing with me. Larry's always looking for leverage against people who can be useful to him."

"What did he have on Mr. Moon?"

"It was a small thing, I guess, but embarrassing—like the stuff he had on me. You see, Peter told everyone he graduated from Harvard. He was really proud of it. But Larry found out he didn't even graduate. He was kicked out for cheating on a final."

"So Larry blackmailed Peter into telling him where the missiles were?"

"I guess. All I know for sure is he actually *found* a box in one of the storage lockers and decided he'd better move it. Like I told you, the guy's got a lot of nerve. He was bragging last night that with what he has he's going to be able to retire to a Greek island and write the 'Great American Novel.' The son-of-a-bitch beat me up when I told him I wouldn't help him—and then he went off. God knows where."

"But what kind of help did he want from you?"

"To move the box a second time. He said it wasn't safe where it was, and I was the only one he could trust."

"I thought the box wasn't heavy. Didn't he move it the first time by himself?"

"Yes, but that was before the weather got so bad."

"So where *is* the box?" Jayne asked.

"I know where it was last night. Hey, I bet it's still there! He couldn't move it in this storm. It's outside."

"But *where?*"

"One of the lifeboats. Nine, I think. Yeah, lifeboat number nine."

chapter 51

Bermuda Schwartz made a mighty effort to rise to the occasion. He sat up, gulped some air, and said, "Ladies, I'm going to need your help. We can't let these damned missiles get in the wrong hands. It's a matter of global security!"

Put like that, there was no way Jayne or Candy could refuse. The agent stood, wobbled a moment, made one final charge to the bathroom, and then led the way out the door with the small flashlight Candy had brought. At the last minute, Jayne told everyone to wait while she scribbled the note Cass had found. Of course, she later wished she had left more complete information, but she was in a hurry and also was feeling rather pleased with herself.

Jayne, Candy, and Schwartz had the same problems moving about the dark and tossing ship that Cass and I had, so I won't dwell on each uncertain footstep, each moment when they had to hang on for dear life. It was more difficult for Schwartz to get about due to his delicate stomach, but he straightened himself with grim resolve and led the way along the Promenade Deck beneath the suspended lifeboats, counting the numbers: "Five . . . six . . . seven . . . eight . . . Here it is, number nine."

The agent and his wet helpers looked up uncertainly toward the wooden boat that was suspended by ropes and pulleys a few feet above their heads. The prize was near, yet far away. How to actually get into the boat on such a stormy day, with the deck heaving beneath them, was the problem. Schwartz finally decided to use the winch to lower the lifeboat to their level. Jayne said he looked very heroic, as he squinted against the lashing rain, brought the boat down, then pulled back the canvas top enough so that he could climb inside.

"I don't see a goddamn thing!" he shouted to Jayne and Candy who were waiting on the deck.

"Shoot! Maybe Larry came back and got the stuff," Candy shouted back.

"Give me the flashlight," Schwartz called.

The agent disappeared with the light and crawled about under the canvas. He emerged a few minutes later with a puzzled expression on his face, holding up an olive-green metal box that was perhaps sixteen inches long, a foot wide, and six inches deep. The box was locked, but no matter how you stretched your imagination, there was no way such a small thing could contain an arms shipment for bloodthirsty terrorists.

"*This* can't be it!" he shouted.

"Perhaps it's *part* of it," Jayne suggested. "Isn't there anything else in there?"

"Nothing."

Schwartz handed the metal box carefully to Candy and Jayne, on the deck.

"It's heavy," said Candy. "Maybe the missiles are very compact."

The agent was still standing in the lifeboat, ready to climb out, when he looked over Jayne's right shoulder and said, "Oh-oh!"

"Oh-oh, indeed." The deep voice came from behind Jayne. "I'll take that box, if you please."

Jayne turned and saw a man aiming a small pistol their way. But it wasn't the pistol that surprised her as much as the identity of the man. This was the last person she had expected to see— Captain David Dodsworth-Ellis of the Horse Guards. Jayne insists that no one has ever pointed a gun at her in such a polite and aristocratic way, yet she sensed he would use it if he thought that was necessary.

"You will please hand the box over very gently," he insisted. "And if it's not *too* much of a bother, I will require you to accompany me to the Princess's cabin."

"Or you'll do what?" Schwartz asked, not impressed by Doodie's fine manners.

The Englishman's tone was nonchalant but deadly as he replied. "Or I will bloody blow you away, mate!"

chapter 52

The worst of the storm was over by late afternoon. The winds died, the seas calmed, and the clouds contented themselves with providing a cold steady rain. It was still not weather for a picnic—or a swim—but after all that had occurred no one minded.

The passengers of *The Atlantis* did not have to abandon ship after all, leaving behind their precious furs and Givenchy gowns. A tow rope connected the liner to a navy destroyer, the USS *Phoenix,* several hundred yards ahead. All afternoon, a launch had been passing back and forth between the ships, carrying men and equipment, and by five o'clock in the evening a miracle occurred: there was light! From all over the ship came mighty cheers. The orange life vests were put away, and an hour later the lounges were once again in business—doing a brisk business, as a matter of fact, for people soothed their nerves with martinis and celebratory bottles of wine. By dinner time, it was hard to find many lingering signs of the recent emergency.

Life on *The Atlantis* was not yet completely back to normal, of course. I heard later that rather than two seatings for dinner, there was one buffet for everyone, and it was lavish. I would have liked to have been there. It was the sort of night when strangers shared their harrowing adventures—adventures later transformed into anecdotes that became more dramatic as the days and months passed. Glad to be alive, folks forgot, for a few hours, their petty concerns and breathed sighs of relief.

Jayne said a cheer went up when Kevin Dobbs announced over the intercom that the Steve Allen show would indeed take place in the Grand Ballroom, although with only one presentation at nine o'clock.

"Incredible!" said a young woman. "What a trouper!" said another.

Waiters next passed out white three-by-five cards that said: "Do you have a question for Mr. Allen?" A few blank lines on which to write whatever question came to mind followed.

Perhaps I should explain that I am the only comedian in the business who does not have an act. Consequently, in over fifty years of entertaining I have never done precisely the same show twice. There are certain jokes I have repeated, of course, and certain musical numbers, but because I am unable to resist my brain's tendency toward new thoughts, my performances vary from night to night. And because a good part of my shows consists of responding to questions supplied by my audiences, new subject matter is constantly introduced.

Now, aboard *The Atlantis*, people wrote questions on the cards to be collected and delivered to my dressing room.

Some special invitations had been issued for the night's extravaganza, to such important passengers as Gertrude Wilmington, Will Sanders, Alexis Wilmington, Candy L'Amour, Tracy Devine, Wendy Wilmington, Michel Duclerc, Dan Moody, Captain Mellon, Chelsea Eastman, the first mate, and several others . . . including the illustrious Princess and her two escorts. These personalized invitations were persuasively delivered by naval policemen, men of the shore patrol—brought aboard from the *Phoenix*—who carried sidearms on their leather belts. This was an unusual tactic to get an audience, but then this promised to be an unusual show.

Dinner over, the boisterous crowd elbowed its way into the

Grand Ballroom, filling up every inch of space. A special table had been set up near the stage for the honored guests, a few of whom were escorted to the ballroom by the men of the shore patrol. These navy men also guarded the exits.

Finally, the lights dimmed, and the orchestra struck up my theme song: "This Could Be the Start of Something Big." Never before had that title been so appropriate.

chapter 53

Attired in black tie, I stepped into the white eye of the spotlight. There was a swell of applause. This was an audience wound up to have fun. It would be no problem to get them to laugh. I worried only that they might not tone down when I needed quiet.

"Good evening, ladies, gentlemen . . . and cold-blooded killers," I said. "And unfortunately there really *is* a killer out there tonight."

There was a surge of laughter. I could have said, See Dick throw the ball to Spot, and they would have found it hilarious.

"We have quite a special show tonight," I told them. "Many of you have been kind enough to fill out the cards passed around at dinner, but before I get to your questions, I thought I'd reverse our usual order of things and play some music for you. Since you've probably had enough rocking 'n' rolling for one day"—groans, cheers—"I thought we'd do a little jazz." Hoots, hollers, and much applause.

The orchestra was as good as I expected. I did a medley of tunes I had written myself, as well as Erroll Garner's "Misty" and Jerome Kern's "The Song Is You." The band followed along, without having rehearsed. I sang and played the piano and had a great time for about half an hour. Though there was some serious business to transact, I hate to let an audience down—particularly this one, which had been through so much. So I made it a point to give them what they expected . . . before we got into the unexpected. The musical number that elicited the most hearty response was one I do occasionally when performing at seaside or resort communities, "Mouth-to-Mouth Resuscitation":

> *I was in swimming,*
> *When quick as a wink,*
> *I was caught in the undertow*
> *And I started to sink.*
> *But you,*
> *Wonderful you, were there to save me;*
> *And I'll never forget, my dear,*
> *How you gave me—*
>
> *Mouth-to-mouth resuscitation,*
> *That's what pulled me through.*
> *Mouth-to-mouth resuscitation*
> *Brought me close to you.*
>
> *I opened my eyes*
> *and there you were,*
> *up above me,*
> *Upside down, it is true,*
> *But somehow I knew*
> *You'd love me.*
>
> *Mouth-to-mouth resuscitation,*
> *That's what did the trick.*
> *It was such a strange sensation.*
> *Did it make you sick?*
>
> *There were people standing around,*
> *Looking down at us on the ground.*

Now it's sweeping the nation,
Mouth-to-mouth resuscitation.

At last I rose from the piano bench and stood center stage. I picked the first question at random from the sheaf of cards in my hand. It was personal, which is often the case: " 'Is that really your hair?' . . . This question comes from Barbara Rawlings. Where are you, Barbara?"

A middle-aged woman stood up in the back of the room. I stroked my hair, to the delight of the audience. "Is this really *my* hair?" I repeated. "Well, after two more payments it will be."

The wave of laughter carried us to the next question.

"Mr. O'Brian from Chicago asks, 'Mr. Allen, how much money are you earning for this show?' Every damned dollar, sir. If you think this is easy, you get up here and try it."

I went on in this manner for a few more minutes. Audiences love to participate, and I could have continued for hours. But since I had a special agenda that night, I picked from the pile a question in a handwriting that was familiar. I read: "Dear Steve . . . Tell us, please, who murdered all those men."

There was confused laughter from those indiscriminate enough to laugh at almost anything.

"This difficult question is posed by my wife, Jayne. Where are you, dear?" I stepped to the edge of the stage and peered out into the audience. Jayne was at the large and special table directly in front of me. I spotted her quickly because she was in a red satin dress, looking vivid and glamorous. "Ladies and gentlemen, Miss Jayne Meadows."

Jayne took a bow, to much applause, then motioned to the audience to let me continue.

"I'm afraid I have gotten you here under false pretenses," I said. "But since this has been quite an odd voyage, I was hoping you wouldn't mind an odd show for the final night. Agent Schwartz of the FBI has been nice enough to humor me and has helped arrange this event, along with members of the shore patrol from the USS *Phoenix*—you will notice them stationed at the exits about the room."

"What are we, a captive audience?" Rusty O'Conner called out.

"Precisely," I called back. There was more laughter. "And now, we're going to answer Jayne's most pertinent question: Who is the killer among us?"

Gradually the audience settled down as most of them realized, for the first time, that there had been a series of murders on board *The Atlantis*. I explained that we hadn't wanted to alarm them, but now that we were safely in tow by the USS *Phoenix*, I proposed to solve the mystery once and for all.

"First of all," I said. "I must tell you that our host, Marcus Wilmington, is dead. He died of natural causes a year and a half ago. To understand everything that has happened, you must keep that fact foremost in your mind. For his death came at a most inconvenient time for the Wilmington family, and it set in motion a war of succession among the survivors, as we've seen often in history when kings and emperors have died."

I explained the precarious state of the Wilmington fortune and made it known that the unfinished ship was the family's last chance to save themselves.

"Gertrude Wilmington and the family attorney, Will Sanders, took charge as well as they could," I said. "Their first decision was to hire an actor to impersonate the dead billionaire. This was done to forestall creditors and estate taxes and give the family some time to maneuver. The deception was not difficult since Mr. Wilmington was a recluse and few people knew what he looked like. An interview was arranged with *Trend* magazine, and I, too, was taken to meet the make-believe patriarch—all to make it appear that he was still alive.

"In my case, I was hired as an investigator, supposedly to keep an eye on things and help keep the ship safe from sabotage. This was an unnecessary flourish—and a big mistake. I have a reputation as an entertainer, *not* as a detective, and Mrs. Wilmington and Mr. Sanders were certain I wouldn't get anywhere with my investigation. It was their first mistake, but not their last.

"Now let's talk about Richard Wilmington. . . ."

I continued spelling out the facts. It was a complicated case, and yet at heart fairly simple. The simple part was that the crimes were the work of scavengers eager to get their hands on what remained of the Wilmington fortune. What complicated things was the different personalities involved, and their overlapping schemes to save themselves and secure the prize.

Some things I knew, others I could only surmise. I had actually seen who it was that pushed Cass and me into the ocean, so solving the case was a matter of working backward, making a few conjectures so that the pieces of the puzzle might fit together. I imagined the killer was nervous at the moment, though when I glanced down at the large table on the dance floor I could see only a brazen front.

Just you wait! I said to myself grimly. I was still chilled from my long swim in the Atlantic that afternoon and angry about it. Yet I had not an iota of proof that would hold up in court. Bermuda Schwartz had impressed this fact upon me.

"But I *saw* who shoved Cass and me into the ocean," I had said to him in frustration.

"It doesn't matter. You have to *prove* it," he said.

Which was the reason for this shameless bluff before a captive audience.

chapter 54

To hear me talk, you would have thought I knew everything.

"Richard Wilmington," I said, "was in a bad predicament. His mother, Gertrude, and the family attorney, Will Sanders, held the real power and made the major decisions. But as CEO, Dicky was the first who would go to prison if certain illegalities came to light. This didn't seem fair to the poor fellow, who began to feel sorry for himself. His spirits weren't greatly improved when he discovered that his wife was having an affair with the TV actor, Tracy Devine."

"That's a lie!" Wendy Wilmington shouted from the dance floor. "I'll sue you for that!"

"Please do," I said.

Devine, sitting at her side, cautioned her to be still. He had been holding her hand; now he dropped it. The audience was silent. They had been slightly restless as I described the dark financial situation of the Wilmingtons, but now that we had hit upon sexual intrigue, I had everyone's rapt attention.

"Dicky learned about his wife's affair from Peter Moon, who was in the habit of confiding things when it suited his purposes—and he wanted to upset Dicky. You see, Peter and Dicky had an on-again-off-again deal to take over the Wilmington empire. At first, young Wilmington led Moon on with false information, but when Dicky saw how precarious his own situation was, he began to think maybe it was wiser to throw in his lot with Peter.

"And so he told Moon a juicy secret—that his mother and Will Sanders had set up a shipment of high-tech, ground-to-air missiles to be delivered to unidentified terrorists in England. Fortunately, there *is* no secret arms shipment on *The Atlantis.*"

A few cries of surprise came from the large table.

"Nevertheless, the fact that a number of people *believed* there were caused quite a few things to happen.

"It's my guess that Gertrude Wilmington and Will Sanders *had* investigated the possibility of stealing a few prototypes of the new missile from their weapons manufacturing company in California but that the Pentagon's security measures were simply too tight so the plan was abandoned. Dicky heard about the plan, but not that it had been aborted, so he believed his mother and Sanders had actually pulled it off.

"And so he panicked and told Peter Moon, who told an arms broker presently going by the name of Dan Moody. Moon and Moody set up a deal to sell the missiles to a group of Islamic Fundamentalists. Stewart Hoffman heard about this. And the journalist Larry Goldman did as well, probably from Peter Moon.

"And so the tragicomedy was set in motion. Everybody was scrambling about looking for the missiles, but no one could find them—because they didn't exist. I confirmed by phone with Washington this afternoon that every missile and launcher in the California factory is accounted for.

"Poor Richard, as things progressed, didn't know who to trust. He became increasingly terrified that he would end up in prison or have his throat cut. So he asked to meet me to unburden himself, hoping I might help him cut a deal with the authorities.

"Unfortunately for Dicky, the killer got wind of the meeting. There were other reasons the killer wanted Dicky dead, but we'll get to those later. It wasn't too difficult, when everyone else was occupied at the lifeboat drill, to follow Dicky to the deserted upper deck, take the shotgun, kill him, and set up the scene to suggest suicide. The killer had to move quickly, of course, and in his haste didn't notice that a pack of matches fell out of his pocket.

"But Mr. Moon witnessed the murder—because Dicky's wife Wendy had told him about Dicky's meeting with me."

"*Another* lie!" Wendy Wilmington cried, lurching to her feet.

"Is it? You saw your husband write the note to me because you were sitting at the table with him in the dining room. I have an eyewitness who saw you go to Peter's table afterward and whisper in his ear. Peter was blackmailing you to make you help him, wasn't he? You knew Peter very well, as a matter of fact."

"All right! Yes. I told Peter about the note, but I was only trying to help. I knew Dicky was in trouble. Peter had experience in these matters." Wendy sank back in her chair.

"We'll accept that for now. At the moment I'm simply trying to establish how it was that Peter *knew* of the meeting, why he decided to skip the lifeboat drill and position himself to watch what happened. When the killer fled, Peter ducked out from his hiding place and took the shotgun to his stateroom. This blew the suicide explanation, which suited his purposes. A sensational murder on *The Atlantis* would further destabilize the company he was after, and he'd also blackmail the killer. But because Peter, too, was in a hurry, he didn't notice the seemingly inconsequential matchbook.

"So he took the gun and began to plan his blackmail. Unfortunately for him, he relaxed his guard and allowed himself to be lured to the indoor pool area—where he became a victim himself."

I took a sip of cold orange juice because it was thirsty work to unravel so many mysteries. Glancing at the special group around the large table, I noticed a few people who seemed unwilling to meet my eye, which made me confident that some of my salvoes, at least, had hit the mark. Jayne beamed in an encouraging manner, and Cass flashed me a *V*.

"Now we get to a tragic individual," I continued. "The killer had managed to do away with two victims, but there was one person on board with enough information and resources to figure out exactly what had happened—Stewart Hoffman. The security chief, of course, had the goods on everybody.

"But there was also a special reason to arrange Stewart's death. Stewart, you see, was the illegitimate son of Marcus Wilmington, from a brief liaison with the actress Dawn Landry in the early fifties. As is sometimes the case, the father came to understand that his illegitimate son was more capable than his acknowledged ones. Not only did Stewart stand to inherit a good portion of the estate, but most likely Gertrude and her lawyer friend had promised him a significant sum to help keep the death of the old man concealed a while longer. The killer was greedy and wanted Stewart's share for himself. So one more contender for the Wilmington fortune was taken out of the race.

"We now have had three murders, and with Stewart out of the way, the killings on *The Atlantis* might very well have stopped. Except there was a troublesome journalist from *Trend* magazine on board, and he never gave up on a good story. Larry Goldman had a pretty good idea who the killer was, but he was more interested in discovering the contents of storage locker F267, particularly since he had a suspicion as to what the mysterious shipment actually was. For a journalist, especially one with Goldman's nose for dirt, the contents of this locker were vastly more interesting than any classified weapons.

"Goldman found the storage locker by a combination of luck and hard work. He had come aboard as a stowaway and had been hiding himself in one of the empty rooms on F Deck. It's my guess that he simply happened to observe the owner of the mysterious parcel making a visit to his goods. He was curious enough to investigate further and found a cache beyond his wildest dreams. But he, too, underestimated the killer."

I stopped to inspect my audience—the most quiet one I had ever seen in all my years of entertaining.

"Anybody care to guess who the killer is?" I asked with a smile. "You have nearly enough information."

"It's obvious. Will Sanders, the attorney." This try came from Gladys Moffet.

"Grandmother, don't be ridiculous," Chelsea said. "It's Gertrude!"

"What about Gertrude and Will Sanders working together?" suggested Candy L'Amour.

I smiled at them all. "Well, at one point I thought Gertrude and Will were responsible," I admitted. "But it's been a long day, so let's have no more suspense. The killer, of course, is . . . you, my dear. Candy L'Amour. Or perhaps I should call you by your real name—Bernice Esposito."

Candy laughed good-naturedly to show she could take a joke.

"Honestly, Steve! Be serious!" she said.

"Oh, I am. You were the mastermind, of course, but even a girl as clever as you needed help. Your secret husband was your accomplice."

"What have you been smoking, Steve?" she said, still laughing. "I told Jayne about Larry and me. The marriage was a mistake, but you can't blame a girl for being young and stupid."

"I'm not talking about Larry, Candy. I mean your other *secret* husband, a bigamous situation to be sure, and one that gave you an urgent motive to deal Larry out of the picture."

"Oh, yeah? Well, who is this *other* secret husband?"

"Alexis Wilmington. Who married a dark-haired girl named Bernice Esposito in Niagara Falls, a little over three months ago."

Alex, sitting at the far end of the table, smiled strangely but did not say a word. As for Candy and/or Bernice, she rose half-way to her feet, then sank back in her chair.

"I'd better explain," I told the audience.

chapter 55

"I told you at the start this was a simple case," I said. "I see a few smiles, because many of you probably don't think that is so. Yet it is. Three brothers wanted to inherit their father's kingdom. One of them, urged on by his wicked wife, killed the other two, to increase his share. The story's as old as Cain and Abel. Everything else about the case is window dressing."

Rusty O'Conner, who was taking notes and desperately trying to keep everything straight, raised her hand. "But wouldn't Gertrude be the principal heir?" she asked.

"Actually Marcus—it's quite sad—couldn't stand his wife. He left his entire fortune to his children, with only a small annuity to Gertrude."

Now Mudgie raised her hand.

"Yes, Your Highness?"

"But if old Mr. Wilmington died a year and a half ago, why were the brothers content to wait so long for their inheritance? I should have thought they'd want to get their hands on the money fast," she said.

"Ah, a good question. This is one of the reasons Gertrude and Will kept the old man's death a secret."

"The children didn't know their father was dead?"

"Not Alexis and Richard. They thought their father was alive. Dicky, in fact, was heartbroken that his father had not been willing to see him for so long, though such neglect frankly did not come as a surprise. . . . Isn't that true, Alex?" I directed the question to the table below. "When did you learn that your father had died?"

"The morning after we sailed," he said with a strange smile.

"There you have it," I said to Mudgie. "Of the three brothers, only Stewart knew the truth—and as I said earlier, Gertrude and Will made a deal to keep him quiet. Stewart was smart enough to understand that the estate would be worthless if he tried to pull his money out too soon. Everything depended on the success of *The Atlantis*. But when the maiden voyage was finally underway, Gertrude felt it was time to tell Dicky and Alex the truth, which unfortunately let a monster out of a box— and the killings began."

"Well, I don't know about anyone else," Candy interrupted, brazenly daring to look me in the eye, "but *I* certainly didn't have any reason to kill anyone!"

"Maybe *you* didn't, Candy. But Bernice Esposito from a poor neighborhood on the south side of Chicago did. You're a very cunning girl. It was easy to underestimate you because you put on a dumb-blonde facade, but no one makes it to the big time the way you did without being *very* clever."

"Talk on," she said breezily.

"I will. About two years ago you signed a multimillion dollar recording contract with Wonder Records, the music division of the Wilmington entertainment conglomerate."

"So what?" she said. "Lots of big stars record for Wonder."

"Yes, but few as ambitious as you, Bernice. And you certainly did not drag yourself up by your black-leather bootstraps to reach a dead end at Wonder Records, trapped by an air-tight contract for the next five years." She started to protest, but I cut her off. "Don't bother to deny it. I've spent the last few hours checking details. Two years ago you thought you had signed a fabulous deal, but in the last six months you discovered differently, didn't you? Wonder Records was not willing to spend a penny to promote your latest album—for the very good reason that they no longer *had* a penny. Like every other Wilmex company, all their money had been sucked up into *The Atlantis*. Without promotion, you were facing five years of gradual extinction in the music business. Five years is more than enough time for any rock star to be forgotten by her fans."

"Bullshit!" she shouted, ever the soul of refinement.

"And so you went to Palm Beach to meet Alexis," I continued. "It wasn't a chance meeting at all, as you told Jayne. You'd heard he was a playboy who liked life in the fast lane—which was just your speed. You hoped if you cozied up to him, you could get the Wilmington family to release you from your contract as a personal favor, which, as I said, was a matter of life and death for your career."

"Even if I never sell another record in my life, I have lots of money," she said sullenly.

"Really? I understand the IRS is after you for millions of dollars in back taxes. Still, when you met Alex all your problems appeared to be solved. You liked him well enough, and he suited your plans. You thought if you married into the Wilmington family, you'd never need to worry about money again. But I'm sure it was even more than money, wasn't it? The big house in Palm Beach, the duplex in New York, the butlers, the famous paintings—they were all things you'd dreamed about as a poor kid in Chicago. Sure you had lots of cash to spend as a pop star, but the Wilmingtons represented at least the illusion of something people like you can never hope for—class, respect.

"So imagine your shock, after you and Alex eloped, to discover that the fabulous Wilmington fortune was in danger of disappearing. You'd hitched yourself to a sinking ship."

"Big deal. So Alex and I got married. We only kept it quiet because his mother wouldn't approve and we wanted to break the news slowly. That doesn't mean we did anything wrong."

"I'm afraid it does, Bernice."

"Stop calling me that!" she screamed. When her control

cracked for a moment I thought I had her, but then she caught herself and folded her arms across her breast in a defensive manner. "What is this anyway, a kangaroo court?"

"No, it's just two people talking," I told her. "Now back to your marriage. You're not the sort to accept a bad situation without putting up a fight. You discovered you'd married a charming but weak young man who had no money of his own. Furthermore he belonged to a family on the verge of a spectacular bankruptcy. And on the first morning out from New York, you made an interesting discovery—Marcus Wilmington was dead and all of the old man's money had been left to his sons. If you got rid of Dicky and Stewart, Alex would be the only heir. Even if the family fortune wasn't what it once had been, it would be more than adequate for just you two. And there was still the chance that *The Atlantis* would be a gold mine. So you set about murdering the other heirs with cold-blooded determination. Alex went along with it because he believed it was the only way to keep you."

"This is ridiculous!" she cried. "Anyway, how could I have killed Dicky? I was at the lifeboat drill."

"No, Bernice. Jayne and I left you in our stateroom to sleep. . . . Remember?"

"Oh. I forgot about that. But how the fuck would I know where Dicky was? This is a big ship."

"Because you overheard me giving Jayne the information. You thought you'd get there first and confront him about some interesting news you had heard earlier in the day from Larry, didn't you?"

"That's a lie," she said, but her voice was hardly more than a whisper.

"Larry had discovered storage bin F267, but he didn't know what was in it yet. He asked you to find out. You were interested because you'd heard the rumors about the missiles, and you thought it might be profitable to find out if F267 was where they were hidden. But Dicky didn't know, so you took advantage of the opportunity to sweet-talk the shotgun out of his hands and arrange a very opportune suicide. You didn't realize you had dropped the matches until later. That was bad luck for you, though it didn't occur to me for quite sometime that they belonged not to the victim but the killer."

"You're crazy!" she said, her lips curling into an ugly sneer. "And what about Peter and Larry? You're not trying to pin *those* murders on me, too? At the time Peter was killed, I was doing my show right here in this room, in front of all these people!"

Candy looked around in triumph, obviously feeling she had scored a decisive point.

"I imagine it worked like this," I said. "Peter Moon saw you kill Dicky Wilmington and tried to blackmail you. It was easy enough to make an appointment to meet him in a discreet place such as the indoor pool—an hour or two *before* your show. He thought he could handle you because he didn't know you had an accomplice. But you took Alex with you, and the two of you simply held Peter's head under water until he was dead."

"No!" she said.

"And then, later in the evening, you had Alex lure Jayne to the pool to try to frighten us off the investigation."

"Ha! If we were the killers, we wouldn't want to draw anyone's attention to the body!"

"Why not? You knew it was going to be found eventually. And besides, you were cocky. You couldn't imagine there was any way the murder could be traced to you."

Candy laughed, but it sounded hollow.

"You really are a friggin' nutcase!" she said. "Anyway, how could Alex and I be partners? We weren't getting along, remember? He spent the night with that Eastman broad. And I—"

"That's right. You spent the night with Larry Goldman. You're just digging yourself a hole, Bernice. Your very public fight with Alex at the captain's cocktail party was carefully arranged to draw off any suspicion that you two were partners in crime."

"You're saying I killed Stewart too?"

"No, Alex did that one."

"But how the hell would he be able to poison Stewart's bottle of Courvoisier?"

I smiled. She blushed beet-red, realizing she had betrayed herself. No one had been told Stewart had been poisoned by tainted Courvoisier.

"I'm not saying anything else until I have a lawyer," she said glumly.

"A good idea," I told her. "Meanwhile, for the benefit of our audience, let me finish up the few last details of this sordid story. You were terrified when you saw that Larry had gotten on the ship because you knew he could cause trouble for you about, among other things, your bigamous marriage to Alex. So you decided to kill him, too. At this point you were accustomed to murder, and one more body didn't make a lot of difference.

"When Larry saw you last night, he still didn't know exactly what was in storage bin F267. The ship was dark, and he wanted you to hold the flashlight while he broke in with an ice pick he had stolen from one of the lounges. The ice pick became the perfect way for you to rid yourself of an inconvenient husband and get your hands on some guided missiles at the same time. Once the locker was open, Larry put down the pick—and you came at him with it. He tried to defend himself and you got beaten up a little, but you were quicker and more deadly, and you managed to stab the ice pick into his back. Then you took a look inside the box, realized it had nothing to do with missiles, and decided to hide what you had found in lifeboat number nine."

"Okay," she said, unable to resist the temptation to speak, "if I did that, why would I bring Jayne and an FBI man to the lifeboat?"

"To Larry this box was more valuable than if it had been

filled with diamonds but to you it meant nothing. So you thought you would use it to make yourself seem innocent. A lot of criminals do favors for law enforcement."

"But the box *was* valuable! It had—" Candy stopped, sensing my trap at the last moment. If she admitted knowing the contents of the box, she would be confessing to Larry's murder.

Personally I was willing to leave the contents of the box out of our discussion, but I had one last trick up my sleeve. I held up a pack of matches.

"And finally, Bernice, these are the matches I found by Richard's body with the number F267 written inside . . . in your handwriting. I had an expert examine it, and he tells me it will stand up in court. We've got you, I'm afraid. You and Alex both. Signed, sealed, and delivered."

Candy looked helplessly from me to Alex. For the first time she had a cornered, frightened look on her face.

"Alex!" she cried. "*Say* something, you idiot! They're trying to pin all these murders on us!"

He shrugged and assumed his weak but charming smile. "Hey, babe, the jig's up," he said. "And maybe we deserve what's coming to us. I don't care what we did to Larry—or Peter Moon. They had it coming. But Stewart and Dicky were my brothers! We never should have killed them. You must have had me under some kind of spell."

The color drained out of Bernice Esposito's face. And then, as we all watched, she leaped across the table at Alex, her long red nails clawing at his face.

"I'm going to kill you, you bastard!" she shrieked. But the shore patrol was on her; she kept screaming like the witch she was as they hauled her out. "What do you know about anything! *You* were born with all the money in the world! I had *nothing*, you son of a bitch! Nobody gave me *nothing!* I'm gonna kill you, you rich bastard, for doing this to me!"

And she made other accusations, sprinkling them with four-letter words I will not repeat, before the shore patrol got her out of the Grand Ballroom and we didn't have to listen to her anymore.

"And that," I said, "concludes our show for this evening."

The orchestra, ad-libbing, struck up Irving Berlin's "There's No Business Like Show Business," which, despite my sudden utter exhaustion, made me laugh.

chapter 56

The sun was shining brilliantly in London. Jayne, Cass, and I decided to stop a few days at the Dorchester Hotel to repair our nerves before journeying to visit our friends screenwriter Larry Gelbart and his wife Pat, who have a home in the country. From our sitting room, we could see the trees coming into bloom in Hyde Park. Everything was green, fresh and lovely. And best of all, the floor of our hotel room did not rock.

"Another cup of tea, Gladys?" Jayne offered.

"Well, yes, thank you very much, my dear."

"What about you, Chelsea?"

"No, I'm fine."

Cass and I were drinking coffee so Jayne didn't ask. Chelsea and her grandmother were also staying at the Dorchester, and Jayne had invited them to share with us that most traditional British institution, afternoon tea.

"I think I'll be flying from now on," Gladys remarked.

"You won't try *The Atlantis* again?" Jayne asked with a smile. "I understand Monsieur Duclerc's buying the ship. He'll have it in dry dock for a year, completely refurbish the mechanics, and then run it back and forth between Europe and America."

"Well, I *am* rather glad, for poor old Marcus's sake, that someone cares about *The Atlantis*," Gladys said. "The rest of the Wilmington empire will be broken up now, of course, but that's the way of things. I always thought it was too much money and power for one man anyhow. You can see what trouble it brought. Gertrude and Will Sanders will go to prison, I suppose. A terrible scandal. And Alexis . . . I hate to think of him. He was so beautiful as a little boy."

"Probably *too* beautiful for his own good," Cass said.

"Anyway, justice will be slow," I mentioned. "At the moment, Scotland Yard has Candy, Alex, Gertrude, and Will locked up, but the US is seeking to have them extradited to New York."

"I'm dying of curiosity!" said green-eyed Chelsea, looking prettier than ever. "Mr. Allen, how did you and Cass get out of the ocean?"

"Do you want to tell her?" I asked Cass.

"Not me! I don't even want to *think* about that damned ocean. I thought we were goners for sure."

"So did I," I admitted. "The ship was drifting away from us, but we managed to catch up because the engines were shut off and the rudder was frozen in place. We clung to the rudder and the stern. Still we would have died of hypothermia if the launch from the *Phoenix* hadn't picked us up. The sailors were pretty surprised when they saw us hanging there. They wrapped us in blankets and took us back to the *Phoenix*'s infirmary. When the captain heard my story, he put all his resources at my disposal to bring Candy and Alexis to justice."

"So who pushed you?"

"Alex. I probably wouldn't have recognized him except for his pink dinner jacket."

"But how did he know you'd be at the stern?"

"Chelsea, it's rude to keep bombarding Mr. Allen with your questions," Gladys scolded.

"I don't mind," I said. "I was puzzled about that, too, but fortunately Alex has been telling all in jail. It appears he went to see his mother right after Cass and I left, and Gertrude told him where we might be. Alex was quite apologetic. He said he had nothing against me and Cass personally, he just wanted to get rid of us to conceal his other crimes."

"I still don't understand how you figured everything out," Chelsea said.

"Most of it was guesswork, to tell the truth. I'm sure Scotland Yard or the FBI would have been able to build a case against them if they worked at it long enough, but my strategy was simply to bombard them with enough facts and guesses to finally break them down. Fortunately it worked."

"But you had the matchbook with Candy's handwriting on it, found near Dicky's body. Surely that was substantial evidence."

I smiled. "I'm afraid that was the biggest bluff of all."

"You mean it wasn't her handwriting?"

"I mean, I showed the matchbook to an officer on board the *Phoenix* who knew a little about handwriting; he said it was too washed away to be analyzed."

"Hmm . . . You were taking a pretty big chance there, Mr. Allen. But now you have to tell me about that box everyone was after," Chelsea insisted. "What was in it?"

"Chelsea, now you *are* being rude," her grandmother said.

"Well, I'm curious!"

"Curiosity killed the cat," said grandma with a knowing smile. She was old-fashioned enough to get away with such a cliché.

"And what are *you* going to do with yourself now, Chelsea?" asked Jayne, deliberately changing the subject. "If you don't mind my being a little curious."

"I'm going to finish the year at Vassar. I agreed to do that for Grandma."

"And very wisely, too," said Gladys.

"But then I'm going to transfer to a school in New York. I want to be where the action is. My hope is to get into the Columbia School of Journalism. I want to be— You'll never guess!"

"An investigative reporter!" Jayne cried in horror.

"Well, Larry Goldman turned out to be a sleaze, but I think the career has possibilities. It's halfway between being a writer and a private eye."

"And whenever you're in California, you and your grandmother will have to come and visit us," said Jayne.

"Now we must change for dinner," said Gladys, rising. "Come along, Chelsea. We mustn't be late."

"Wait!" Chelsea said. "Why do I feel there's a conspiracy to keep some vital information hidden?"

Cass chuckled. "She'll make a dandy investigative reporter," he said.

"You can save the compliments," she told him, then turned on me with her no-nonsense look. "*What* was in the box, *why* did you skip over it so blithely during your big speech, and why are you keeping its contents from me?"

Jayne and I looked at each other. I shrugged, and Jayne smiled.

"All right, dear," she said. "But you have to promise me this will remain a secret."

"I promise," Chelsea said. "I can keep a secret."

"That's good, because the contents of that metal box are not any of your business or mine. They're tape-recordings of confidential conversations between the Princess and her psychiatrist, along with her doctor's notes. I understand many private matters are referred to, including her bulimia and the breakup of her marriage."

"No wonder Larry thought he'd stumbled on a gold mine! But why were those records on *The Atlantis?*"

"The Princess was transporting them back to England. You see, she had been seeing an American psychiatrist in London for a number of years—a Dr. David Welsely—but he moved back to the States to head the Bollinger Clinic outside of Tucson. Mudgie saw him a few times there. On this last trip she decided it was safer to bring all her medical records home, where they will eventually be stored in a very safe place. I'm sure you understand the reason we kept this quiet. The Princess deserves some privacy. We all do. You should remember that."

"I will." Chelsea kissed Jayne on the cheek, then Cass and me. "I promise."

When our visitors were gone, Cass, Jayne, and I all said what a nice young lady she was, which was something I had never thought I'd be saying about Chelsea Eastman.

Then we headed out together into the London streets. There was just enough time to get to a travel agent we knew on Curzon Street before he closed—to make arrangements to fly from London, in two weeks time, to China. We wanted to show Cass the village where Jayne had lived as a little girl, and then fly back home to California, over the Pacific Ocean.

As far from the gray Atlantic as we could get.

Amateur sleuths Steve Allen and Jayne Meadows
return this month in

WAKE UP TO MURDER

A Kensington Hardcover

The following is a preview of this delightful new mystery, now
available in hardcover at better bookstores everywhere.

Chapter 1

The earthquake hit at a few minutes past noon. 12:09, to be precise, on a gray, damp Friday in January as I was walking into our kitchen.

"Three point four," I said immediately to Jayne, who was following me "I'd say four point two," she said.

The fact that she was walking behind me had no connection with her having been born in China, one of many cultures in which men are expected to lead the way, nor did it represent a throwing-overboard of her staunch feminist sentiments. She just happened to be walking behind me, probably for the reason that I was walking in front of her. But be that as it may—and I doubt that it was—my wife promptly differed with my assessment, as she has been known to do. "By the way the chandelier swayed over the dining room table I would say it was a four point two," she said, "Maybe even a four point three."

"What's your bet, Cass?" I asked.

"Three point nine," he said with confidence. Jimmy Cassidy is our resident leprechaun, a chauffeur/handyman extraordinaire and longtime friend. Our Man Monday, as he likes to call himself. Years ago he came to Hollywood from a ranch in Wyoming with the ambition to be a cowboy actor in the movies. But his timing was off—Westerns had just gone out of fashion—so he came to work for me instead.

To that point he had made no more progress than getting some sort of an audition reading, through a friend of a friend, for a three-line role in a TV "oater" as the show-biz trade paper *Variety* would put it, only to discover that he had one little problem—he couldn't act.

I realize that there are some major stars of whom the same could be said but they represent the exceptions. It's true, of course, that requirements for acting in Westerns are generally rudimentary but it was still no dice for Cass. When I at one point brought up the question, as gently as possible, and suggested that I would even be glad to arrange a few acting lessons for him at one of the local establishments set up for the purpose of either preying upon or productively instructing would-be thespians he surprised me by the perceptiveness of his response. "No, thanks," he said. "I'd rather learn on the job."

"That works well in lots of trades," I said, "but should it apply to acting?"

"Hey," he said, "It worked pretty well for John Wayne and Clint Eastwood."

Actually, he was right. If you've ever seen either John's or Clint's early movies you'll note that their careers started before they had any knowledge of their craft whatever. But little by little they had truly mastered the trick so that in their later years both men were among the most believable actors in films and deserved their superstar ranking.

Cass helped himself to a cup of instant coffee while the debate about the power of one of mother nature's nastier little surprises continued.

"Let's review the bidding," I said, "and write down our guesses so there will be no doubt later as to who said what." I'm a compulsive note-taker, largely for the reason that I have no confidence at all in the human memory, which has always seemed to me a tragic joke played on us by the process of evolution. "We have a three point four, a four point two, and a three point nine. Anybody want to change his bet?"

"I'll stay," said Cass, ever the cowboy poker player.

"I'll change to four even," Jayne said cagily. This way she would win anything four and above.

"Usual rules?" Cass asked.

"You bet," I said. "Lunch at the Enchanted Broccoli Garden. Winner is treated by the other two."

"*If* the Enchanted Broccoli Garden is still standing," Jayne said.

"Earthquakes never destroy cute health-food restaurants," I assured her. "Particularly when we have a mere three point four on the Richter scale. Hardly enough to stir a martini."

"Let's not bicker, gang," Cass said wisely. "Time to turn on the news and settle this."

I suppose that to people who live outside of California, the fact that Cass, Jayne and I place wagers on the size of earthquakes sounds cavalier. But when you live in Los Angeles, either you develop a sense of humor about these things or you'd better move to Iowa. Between earthquakes, riots, mud slides and fires, life in the Golden State isn't always easy these days.

"I just got an idea," I said, "Come on in to the piano and I'll show you."

We trooped back into the living room to the Steinway standing in the corner near our front door. Two days earlier I had written into a song lyric I was working on a reference to the docks in the Redondo Beach area that had collapsed after being assaulted by the Pacific Ocean in yet another bit of evidence consistent with the theory of the Last Days.

"Aftershocks" I shouted. "That's the rhyme I was looking for." Making a quick pencil notation on the lyric sheet in front of me I played and sang the now completed lyric of the song I had titled "Livin' in L.A." The ungrammatical style is deliberate, given that the category is rock.

> *We got floods,*
> *We got fire,*

We got mud-slides,
With muck and mire.

We got earthquakes
And a million after-shocks.
And, when the tide comes in,
Those old collapsing docks.

We got riots,
People sleepin' on the streets.
We've got drive-by gun-play
And USC defeats,

But hey—
We can be forgiven
'Cause we're livin'—in L.A.
And I think I see
some locusts on the way.

We got talk-shows
Where the guests are freaks.
We got strip-joints
Where you can meet a lotta geeks.
We got cave-ins
And folks who want to close up schools,
And a lot of goofy cults
Takin' money from a lot of fools.

We once had a city
That was really kinda' pretty
And the skies were always blue.
Life was smooth as butter,
Now we're livin' in Calcutta
And that's a kinda dumbo thing to do.

We got poor folks,
Some livin' in their cars.
We got an awful lot of bimbos;
We call 'em movie stars.

But hey—
We can be forgiven
'Cause we're livin'—in L.A.
And I think I see
some locusts on the way.

"I like it," said Cass.

"That's cute, dear," Jayne said.

"Thank you, dear," I said, "and so are you."

As we repaired again to the kitchen Cass used the remote to flick on the television. The good news was that the TV actually came on; you know you're in big trouble when TV stations have been knocked off the air. The screen showed a map of Southern California with an area circled in the desert near Bakersfield.

" . . . initial reports from the seismic center in Pasadena say the shaker was three point two on the Richter scale. The epicenter was in a remote area fifty miles southeast of Bakersfield on a previously unknown faultline. There are no reports of injuries or damage at this point, but . . . "

"I win!" I said cheerfully. "You guys gotta buy me lunch! I think I'll have the lobster and champagne!"

"They don't *have* lobster at the Enchanted Broccoli Garden," Jayne said sourly. "Nor champagne, Steve." My wife actually uses words like *nor*.

"Then I'm going to have the biggest bunch of broccoli in the house, and a giant mango-banana smoothie, and an entire carrot cake for dessert."

Cass could not repress a sigh. I knew he would have preferred a cheeseburger with a pickle and a side of fries for lunch, but the last few years Jayne and I have been working to overhaul his

diet. Now he ate more wisely, but the shadow of regret sometimes clouded his eyes.

"Well, let's get it over with," he said unhappily.

"Last time you said you *liked* the Broccoli Garden," Jayne reminded him.

"Sure," he agreed. "No fat. No sugar. Herbal tea. Swell."

He was about to turn off the TV when something on the
screen got my attention.

"Hold on a second, Cass. I want to see this."

In Los Angeles, an earthquake of three point two on the
Richter scale is nothing. Hardly worth mentioning for us battle-
scarred veterans of paradise. The local station had returned to
its usual programming at this time, News At Noon. What
caught my eye was a young woman Jayne and I used to know,
little Cathy Lawrence, the daughter of our good friend Ed Lawrence. Only she wasn't little Cathy anymore—today the world
knew her as Cat Lawrence. A few months earlier she had
become the highly successful co-anchor of "Good Morning,
U.S.A.," the two-hour network news show broadcast live five
mornings a week from New York. It's always a surprise when a
kid you used to see on a bicycle with bruised knees and pigtails
grows up to become a huge success.

For obvious reasons that sort of thing is more common in the
world's film capitol. Janet Leigh and Tony Curtis's daughter,
Jamie Leigh Curtis, used to come to parties at our house when
she was a teenager since she knew our sons Steve and Brian,
and the same was true of Sally Fields and Cindy Williams.

It's wonderful, of course, but it makes you feel a little old. I
had read recently in *The Hollywood Reporter* that our little Cathy
had just signed a three-year contract with the network, for several million dollars. She could buy a lot of bicycles with that.
The one time I caught her morning show, I was impressed how
cool and beautiful she appeared interviewing former President
Jimmy Carter. Little Cathy Lawrence had become a highly in-

telligent and sophisticated woman. But from News At Noon I learned that today she had had a lousy morning.

"Viewers were shocked this morning to witness a near tragic accident on the set of the highly-rated UBS network news broadcast, 'Good Morning, U.S.A.,' said a newsman. "A klieg light came loose from the studio rafters and crashed onto a desk below, narrowly missing veteran newscaster Peter McDavis and co-anchor Cat Lawrence. . . ."

As the broadcaster continued, Jayne, Cass and I watched a replay of the incident, a shocker. Peter McDavis and Cat were seated behind a desk on the set of a cozy, faux living room, each with a cup of coffee in front of them. Cat was leading into a commercial break, telling the audience about a rock star who was going to appear later in the program. One moment Peter and Cat looked as calm, unruffled and urbane as it's possible to be on live television. And then the next moment it seemed as if the sky fell in on them. A huge metal object crashed thunderously onto the desk with a shattering of glass. Both Cat and Peter screamed and instinctively raised their hands to protect their faces and heads. The camera caught the horror and confusion for hardly more than a second, and then the picture was replaced by a 'stand-by' message as Studio B in New York City went briefly off the air.

A moment later 'Good Morning, U.S.A.' producer Zeke Roth issued a statement that the two co-anchors, Peter McDavis and Cat Lawrence, had miraculously escaped injury. Meanwhile, the network has launched an investigation into how an overhead light managed to break loose from its mounting. Initial reports suggest a bolt holding the klieg light to a metal bar came loose. . . . "

"How awful!" Jayne said, frowning, "Poor Cathy must have been terrified."

As TV veterans ourselves, it was easy to imagine what a nightmare the incident must have been. There is a large part of show business the audience never sees—thick electric cables, heavy lights, cameras, sound booms, and the like, all of which are potentially dangerous. A performer does his job assuming the equipment will not come down on his head. But occasionally—very rarely, considering the technical complexity of films and television—something goes awfully wrong and people are hurt or killed.

Cass turned off the television after we saw a repeat of the incident in slow motion. There was the briefest moment when you could see the look of horror in the eyes of the two co-anchors as the thought flashed like lightning across their minds that they were going to die. Sometimes I wonder if its proper for television to capture and replay endlessly these true-life disasters, the Kennedy killing, the deadly race-car crashes and all the rest.

Jayne Cass and I drove to lunch at the Enchanted Broccoli Garden. But after watching the near encounter with death, none of us had much of an appetite.

It has always, of course, been nonsensical to refer to the more dramatic ravages of nature as *acts of God* now, unless we assume that the almighty is the most purposely vengeful and destruction monster of all history. But there sometimes does seem something almost consciously malign about the connection between natural disasters and the neighborhoods in which they occur. Much of the earthquake damage of the world seems to wreak its most violent destruction in poor neighborhoods. Even the case of the Southern California quakes I don't recall hearing much about serious damage in Beverly Hills or Bel Air. And tornadoes, too, seem to have a way of locating trailer parks which are largely occupied by lower-income folks.

DON'T MISS THESE OTHER
GREAT WHO-DUNITS!

BURIED LIES   (1-57566-033-4, $18.95)
It looks like lawyer-turned-golf pro Kieran Lenahan finally has a shot at the PGA tour, but a week before he is supposed to play at Winged Foot in Westchester County, his pro shop goes up in flames. The fire marshal is calling it arson. When Kieran's caddie falls in front of an oncoming train and his former girl-friend insists he was pushed, can Kieran find a connection between his caddie's death and the fire?

DEAD IN THE DIRT:
AN AMANDA HAZARD MYSTERY(1-57566-046-6, $4.99)
by Connie Feddersen
Amanda arrives too late to talk taxes with her near-destitute client, Wilbur Bloom, who turns up dead in a bullpen sur-rounded by livestock. A search of Bloom's dilapidated farm soon uncovers a wealth of luxuries and a small fortune in an-tiques. It seems the odd duck was living high on the hog. Con-vinced that Bloom's death was no accident, Amanda—with the help of sexy cop Nick Thorn—has to rustle up a suspect, a motive . . . and the dirty little secret Bloom took with him to his grave.

Available wherever paperbacks are sold, or order direct from the Publisher. Send cover price plus 50¢ per copy for mailing and handling to Penguin USA, P.O. Box 999, c/o Dept. 17109, Bergenfield, NJ 07621. Residents of New York and Tennessee must include sales tax. DO NOT SEND CASH.

SINS AND SCANDALS!
GO BEHIND THE SCENES WITH PINNACLE

JULIA: THE UNTOLD STORY OF AMERICA'S
PRETTY WOMAN   (898, $4.99)
by Aileen Joyce
She lit up the screen in STEEL MAGNOLIAS and PRETTY WOMAN.
She's been paired with scores of stunning leading men. And now, here's
an explosive unauthorized biography of Julia Roberts that tells all. Read
about Julia's recent surprise marriage to Lyle Lovitt—Her controversial
two-year disappearance—Her big comeback that has Tinseltown talking—
and much, much more!

SEAN CONNERY: FROM 007 TO
HOLLYWOOD ICON   (742, $4.50)
by Andrew Rule
After nearly thirty years—and countless films—Sean Connery is still one
of the most irresistible and bankable stars in Hollywood. Now, for the first
time, go behind the scenes to meet the man behind the suave 007 myth.
From his beginnings in a Scotland slum to international stardom, take an
intimate look at this most fascinating and exciting superstar.

HOWARD STERN: BIG MOUTH   (796, $4.99)
by Jeff Menell
Brilliant, stupid, sexist, racist, obscene, hilarious—and just plain gross!
Howard Stern is the man you love to hate. Now you can find out the real
story behind morning radio's number one bad boy!

THE "I HATE BRENDA" BOOK   (797, $4.50)
By Michael Carr & Darby
From the editors of the official "I HATE BRENDA" newsletter comes
everything you ever wanted to know about Shannen Doherty. Here's the
dirt on a young woman who seems to be careening through the heady
galaxy of Hollywood, a burning asteroid spinning "out of control!"

THE RICHEST GIRL IN THE WORLD   (792, $4.99)
by Stephanie Mansfield
At the age of thirteen, Doris Duke inherited a $100 million tobacco fortune.
By the time she was thirty, Doris Duke had lavished millions on her lovers
and husbands. An eccentric who thumbed her nose at society, Duke's circle
of friends included Jackie Onassis, Macolm Forbes, Truman Capote, Andy
Warhol and Imelda Marcos. But all the money in the world couldn't buy
the love that she searched for!

*Available wherever paperbacks are sold, or order direct from the
Publisher. Send cover price plus 50¢ per copy for mailing and
handling to Penguin USA, P.O. Box 999, c/o Dept. 17109,
Bergenfield, NJ 07621. Residents of New York and Tennessee
must include sales tax. DO NOT SEND CASH.*